Finch Books by Kacie Ji:

Demigoddess 101

DEMIGODDESS 101

KACIE JI

Demigoddess
ISBN # 978-1-78651-883-5
©Copyright Kacie Ji 2016
Cover Art by Posh Gosh ©Copyright March 2016
Interior text design by Claire Siemaszkiewicz
Finch Books

Published in 2016 by Finch Books Newland House, The Point, Weaver Road, Lincoln, LN6 3QN, United Kingdom.

Finch Books is an imprint of Totally Entwined Group Limited.

DEMIGODDESS
101

Dedication

For Ariana, my biggest fan.

Chapter One
Am I Going Crazy, or Was That a Toga?

I know it sounds ridiculous, but from all the hoopla I've heard about birthdays, I half expect just once to be greeted by a chorus of angels singing me into this new era of my life. You know, something special. Something just for me. But the logical side of me knows that I'll open my eyes and see nothing more than the same old blush pink that has clung to my walls since my 'I'm a pretty pink princess' kick when I was five.

Just like I do every year.

Of course, my logic wins out and I'm greeted by the cheery, if fading, pink. As soon as my eyes become accustomed to the retina-searing combination of wall and jovial brilliance of the morning sunlight, the reality sets in. Having a birthday during final exam season has proved that I'm not destined for anything special. This year I have two final exams on what should be a glorious day. So instead of a day gallivanting in the sun celebrating, I'm stuck slaving over a standardized test that will prove nothing more than my ability to regurgitate facts.

Fun.

With a sigh and a stretch, I get out of bed and stare out at the world. I know what I'm going to see. A couple of oak trees, the street, maybe a glimpse of the sky if the wind is blowing the branches and their accessorizing foliage just right.

This morning I notice a scarf dangling from the second oak. I have to admit I'm a bit confused as I watch it twisting and turning, dancing in an unseen breeze. It's not like I routinely go around decorating my trees with frills. It would be nice in the winter, I suppose — it would give the trees a little life — but I digress.

I stare at it a moment. It's plain, but pretty. Someone out there has to be missing it. Pushing open my window, I stare at it a moment then reach out for the gauzy material only to find that it's caught on a gnarled branch. I pull on it gently, afraid to tear the fine material. After all, it'll be mine if no one comes to claim it. I lean out a little to try to untangle it. The wind plays with me for a few seconds before I finally manage to snag a gossamer edge with my fingers again. I give it a couple of experimental tugs, releasing it in shock when it yanks back.

"What the — ?"

Must be the wind playing with the branches.

I shimmy out farther, determined not to let a stupid scarf outwit me. Reaching out once more, I wind a length of it securely around my wrist so it doesn't get away from me. I wrench again. This time it jerks back violently, and I could swear that I saw a hand do it.

I let go, heart throbbing in my ears. Did I almost just yank someone out of the tree?

"Sorry! Is someone up there?"

The scarf flows upward like a silken waterfall in reverse and disappears into the dense layering of leaves. Well, that answers my question. Then it occurs to my slowly waking brain that there might be someone camping outside my window in my tree. The scarf couldn't belong to a peeping Tom... I don't think. Unless a floaty silk scarf has become an accoutrement for *en vogue* stalkers these days.

So this fashion diva in my tree doesn't seem like so much of a threat. However, there is still the issue of their being stuck in my tree.

"Um, are you okay up there? Can I get you a ladder or something? Someone to shoot you out of my tree, maybe?"

"Ava, dear! Time to get up!" My mother, Tess Goddard.

She's always been loud, which was good since I always had advance warning before she made an appearance—an Advanced Mother Warning System. I bet other kids wish they were so lucky. The sing-song voice comes from the other side of the door a second before my mother sweeps in.

A lot of people have told me that we could almost be sisters—almost. I don't know whether to take offense or not. I mean, to be told that you almost look like a sibling to a woman who's in her mid-forties isn't exactly something a teen girl wants to hear. But it always brings a glow to Mom's face, so I guess it's worth the perceived insult.

Although, when I look at her, I can understand how she could be seen as younger. Her ebony hair is still as glossy, thick and dark as ever. And her stormy gray eyes, so like mine, are vibrant and brimming with life. So looking at her is like looking in a mirror—if it aged you about twenty-five years.

Right now, the aged version of me has dragged me from the window and wrapped her arms around me for a bear hug. The woman may be small, but she's got the grip of an anaconda.

"Happy birthday, Ava darling! Eighteen! It seems like yesterday I was in agony for forty-six hours trying to bring you into the world, and here you are now, a gorgeous young lady."

I go through this every year. The hug and the weepy speech. Though this time she seems weepier than usual. I let her manhandle me for a little while longer. It only seems fair to suffer this for a few minutes annually when she went through nearly two days of agony. Only a few more to go before the debt is wiped clean, by my count.

Finally, she sniffles and relinquishes my person, restlessly smoothing my hair and patting my shoulders and cheeks like she can't get over what she's seeing. "My baby is eighteen. I cannot believe it."

I try my best at a gentle smile. Any wider and she'd think I was mocking her, too small and I would be accused of faking. "If you're going to keep this up, I'm not going to make it to my finals."

"Oh!" She hugs me again, this time releasing me after a second. "I'm being silly, of course. But it's not every day a daughter—but I'm babbling again." She pecks my cheeks and rocks back to smile at me. "Get dressed. You have a big day ahead of you."

"Mom…"

Too late. She's gone. Never mind. It's probably best that I don't tell her. At least not until I find out if there really is someone out there. Let's hope that if there is a person up in my tree that they are a trapped supermodel and not a serial killer. I can't help but giggle at the insane thought. The scarf probably got blown up there on its own and I just imagined everything else.

But just to make sure, I lean out of the window once again to try to see if I can spot a person in it. "Hey! Someone up there?"

No reply and I can't see anyone. The tree's leafy, but not *that* leafy. I'm pretty sure that I'd be able to spot anybody in it. I can't see the scarf anymore either. Damn it! That was a nice scarf.

Shoving disappointment aside, I start on my morning routine. Seeing as it's a nice, warm spring day, I throw on a simple T-shirt with my favorite pair of jeans. I pull my hair back in a ponytail, slip on my black strappy sandals, apply makeup with a light hand and I'm good to go. All this was done in the bathroom, of course. Just a precaution until I find out whether or not there is really someone in my tree.

My bag is heavy with the books and notes I packed the night before. Textbooks I have to return, notes to cram before the test, all the things every girl wants to think about on her birthday.

What does surprise me, though, is the spread my mom has on the kitchen table. We're not especially morning eaters. I might have a piece of toast and some juice, maybe cereal if I'm feeling crazy, but nothing too heavy before noon. What is laid out before me is amazing, seeing as Mom hardly ever cooks. Quite frankly, I'm not even sure she knows how to work the stove.

Belgian waffles complete with cream and fresh fruit piled high is the centerpiece of the meal. A fruit salad, glasses of milk, juice and water are also present, arranged in an artful way — if you can arrange drinks in an artful way, that is. I don't think I've ever seen any meal in this house with this much thought and care put into it.

"This is amazing! Thank you!" I throw my arms around her and give her a big wet one on the cheek. It's the least I can do for all this, even if the thought of eating all that makes me want to get in front of the TV and play *Just Dance* for the next two days. But being the dutiful daughter that I am, I plunk myself onto the chair and dig in.

I manage to get everything down and get up just as I see Mom ready with a second helping. I feel like an overblown blimp as it is. Another mouthful and I'd explode for sure. Or at least burst out of my clothes. Images of me doing my exams in the nude quirk my lips for a second. Um, yeah. Not going to happen.

I wipe my mouth with an intricately folded napkin and get up. "I've got to run! I have some last-minute cramming to do." I peck her cheek again. "Thanks. I'll see you later."

I manage to somehow make it out through the door without keeling over. I'm surprised I can even walk after eating all that. Leaning against the banister, I take a moment to breathe, hoping that it'll settle. It takes more than a few heaving breaths to convince my stomach to retain what it's holding. I lower my head back in an attempt to try to stop reverse peristalsis. That's when I notice the oak tree again.

All gastric-related discomfort is now forgotten as I take a look to see if my Peeping Tom fashionista is still up there.

A furtive glance around me lets me know that I'm all alone. "Hey! You still up there?"

No answer.

"I want you gone by the time I get back, all right? I'll call the cops if I see you again." There. The threat of getting the law involved should be enough to scare them off. I mean, how would they survive in jail if they can't leave their couture at home while stalking?

Proud of myself, I saunter off to academic hell.

* * * *

My school could hardly be described as modern. It was built sometime in the seventies, or it looks like a relic from that era. All brick and small windows, it comes across more like a prison than a school. At least it does to me.

I head to the gym where the exam is to take place, taking a moment to stop at the table where they are collecting textbooks to drop mine off.

Now for the fun part. The small window of time where we try to cram a year's worth of knowledge into our brains and hope it sticks. I realize it's stupid, and yes I have been paying attention and doing my assignments. I know this stuff. It just doesn't hurt to remind myself. Unlike my frantic classmates, I'm relatively calm and flip through my notes, reading at a leisurely pace.

"Ava..."

The agonized moan could only have come from one person. My best friend Beth Coolidge trudges—no, more like stumbles—through the throng of people to fall dramatically against me. She isn't her usual perfect self. In fact, she's more haggard than anyone has any right to be for something as fleeting as an exam.

I drag her off to the side and prop her up against the wall. "Beth, are you wearing stage makeup?" Even as I ask I can see it. She's made herself look a few degrees warmer than death with a healthy pancake-thick layer of sickly pale makeup.

"Do you think they'll take pity on me?" Hope glimmers on her face for a moment before she adopts the pained expression again. "I mean, if they see how determined I am to take this test, even if I'm at death's door, they'll take pity on me, right? Maybe bump up my grade a little?"

I close my eyes, but know she can see them rolling behind my eyelids. If Beth spent half as much time actually doing her work as she does coming up with these plots, she'd be like Einstein, Planck and Bohr all reincarnated in a pretty little overdramatic package. "You're insane, you know that?"

"It might work." She droops against me again when a teacher walks by. "See? She noticed!"

"She thinks you're hungover." I snicker.

"Gee, thanks." She snatches at my notes and starts reading, ignoring my glare. "Like you need to cram," Beth accuses.

"I might. Besides, I don't have a brilliant plan like yours to fall back on."

"Oh, sarcasm. I'm so hurt!" Beth slams her hands over her heart like I've pierced it with my nail file before falling over my shoulder to pore over my notes again.

Despite my protests, I let her have the notes. She needs them more than I do at this point. As a matter of fact, I'm feeling more self-assured than I usually would before a test. I don't ever remember turning into a frazzled mess like some of the people here, but I'm not always so sure of myself either. Call it a flaw.

"Do not doubt your abilities."

What the...? The voice came from behind me, but as far as I know, my back is pressed up against the wall. Even then, I take a cautious look around. No one that I can see could have said it.

Pinching the bridge of my nose, I sigh heavily. Maybe I'm not as together as I thought I was.

Within minutes, the doors to the gym open and we're herded in like mindless, muttering cattle. I realize it's not much of a stretch when I look at the gibbering mass that surges through with me. Beth and I sit somewhere in the middle of the room, sliding into the little desks and pulling out what we need from our bags long before anyone can accuse us of cheating. I roll three perfectly sharpened 2B pencils onto the desk, followed by an eraser, a ruler, two blue pens and a pencil sharpener. No such thing as being too prepared, right?

I hear Beth mumbling something behind me that sounds like a cross between a prayer and a plea. Others are going about their pre-test rituals too. Becky Stevens is banging her head on the desk—none too lightly. Dave Beckett catches my eye and quickly tugs his sleeves down, concealing scrawl in black ink on his forearms. And those are just the ones who caught my eye. Shaking my head, I return my gaze to my desktop. Who knows what the others are up to or what the teachers make of their ragtag band of students?

Mr. Burnson, the head of the English Department— an odd choice to administer the Ancient Civilization exam, if you ask me—has started handing out the tests with the forewarning to leave them face down until everyone gets one. Not like we could do anything with the sealed booklets anyway.

So now I'm drumming the beat to *Jingle Bells* on the desktop for some unknown reason, not that anyone can tell. Nervous energy. What can I say? It does weird things to you.

It's another few minutes before all the tests are handed out. Then, finally, we are allowed to start. The multiple choice questions are easy enough. I start filling in the little bubbles rapidly. There are a few that I stumble on, a handful that really slow me down. I decide to come back to them later rather than let them hinder my progress. The essay questions are just as straightforward. I pick two and expound on them, mixing pure regurgitation, facts and my own flair for words.

With that done, I have roughly an hour to go back and look at the problem questions. Now that I've had a chance to think them over, the answers are obvious. All except for one.

I slowly fill in one bubble only to erase it. I drag my hand back and forth from one bubble to another. Yes, it's one question. But this is my future we're talking about. I want the best possible start, even if the question is vague and pointless and involves something that I don't ever need to know.

"It's that one." A fine-boned hand sneaks over my page and points to the A bubble. "I smote their asses with a vengeance."

"What the hell!"

The arm quickly retreats. I trace the path it took with my eyes until I find myself gazing up at a tall, statuesque woman in the strangest outfit I've ever seen. No wait. It's not that strange. I've seen them before, as a matter of fact, while filling my head up for the subject of this very exam. But it's definitely out of place here in this day and age. Who wears a toga now, except maybe drunk frat guys?

"Ava? Do you have a problem?"

The teachers presiding over the test, not to mention several students, are all staring at me curiously now.

I immediately drop my head back down, mumbling, "Sorry."

I jerk upright again when a thought niggles its way into my consciousness. Doesn't anyone else see this woman? I'm looking around and no one seems to be acknowledging her sudden, and really bizarre, appearance.

"Hurry up and fill in the box. It's not like I have other people to help."

I tilt my head and study her. "I'm not interested in cheating. Go away."

Her stunning gray eyes lock on to mine, her expression shocked. Then, with a muted pop, she disappears. Like, completely. She's nowhere in the room. And I really am searching.

"Ava! Will you please pay attention to your own work."

Mrs. Bernard is peering over my shoulder. I didn't even notice her approaching me.

"Are you all right?"

Well, she isn't known as the teacher with the bleeding heart for nothing. When she finds a cause, there's nothing stopping her until she feels it's been righted. And right now, I'm the subject of her concern. Quick! Before I become the cause of a sit-in or a rally!

I know I'm blushing and seriously fighting the urge to start babbling like an idiot. And I know she probably thinks I'm completely guilty.

I wave her off. "I'm okay."

"Are you sure? You're acting a little strange."

I *feel* a little strange. I'm seeing a person who apparently no one else can see and she's helping me with my exam. But instead of telling her that and risking being carted away in a straitjacket I say, "I'm fine. I think it's the stress."

Luckily for me, Mrs. Bernard realizes that I'm not like that. I have never cheated on a test, nor would I ever consider it. She pats my shoulder and murmurs something that sounds comforting before returning to the head of the room. Whew. No rallies to save the sanity of Ava Goddard will be happening any time soon. I can see her explaining my situation to the other teachers. They all turn my way with concern written all over their faces. They just aren't bothered enough to come over and whisk the test away.

Tired of being here, I fill in the bubble that the mystery person, who I'm assuming was a hallucination, pointed to. I gather my things, get up, drop the test off and walk out without a backward glance. Once on the other side of the door, I heave a sigh of relief. *Done!*

And not a moment too soon. My fragile brain seems to be at its limit. How tragic would it be to lose my mind just as I'm on the cusp of freedom? Snickering to myself, I wander around the near-empty halls to wait for Beth. She likes to take as long as possible revising her answers. I prefer to give my answers and leave before I feel the urge to start changing things.

I'm already getting bored. A quick check of my watch tells me it's only been three and a half minutes since I walked out and I'm already climbing the walls.

Several people trudge from the gym—some look hopeful, others clearly the opposite. The strange thing is they are being trailed by toga-clad figures. A dark-haired woman is patting Becky on the shoulder consolingly. Dave looks like he is getting his already ungainly ego boosted by a blond man who is showing more leg than is really necessary. Becky and Dave don't even notice them there, even though the two weirdos are hanging over them.

My stares are gaining their attention now. Becky gives me a strange glance while Dave grins smugly and makes his way over, clearly mistaking my curiosity for something else.

"Hey, Ava. What did you think about that test? Killer, or what?"

I lift my shoulders in an automatic, nonchalant shrug. "It could have been worse."

He laughs as though he can't believe I'm so calm about the whole thing. "So what are you planning to do after graduation?"

"Maybe travel a little. Then university, I guess. I've been accepted at a few schools. I've decided on the one that gave me a big scholarship…"

Not that Dave seems truly interested in university talk. It seems like he's dying to tell me what he's going to be doing, so I give him an opening. "What about you?"

"Me and some friends are going to backpack around Europe for a couple of months. Isn't that great? You should come with us, if you decide against university."

I mumble something noncommittal as I stare at the beautiful curly-haired man hanging over his shoulder as he whispers something to Dave.

"Invite her along again. She likes you. Don't take no for an answer."

I'm about to take a swing at the guy when Dave takes his advice.

"Think it over. Do you really want to pass up on the chance to travel and party?" He winks. "Let me know if you want in. It's going to be the party of a lifetime!" Dave is distracted from his attempt at recruiting me by shouts down the hall. Several of his friends are out and waiting for him to join them. He pats me on the shoulder and saunters away.

Apparently I was just a way to pass the time. Not that it bothers me. I was barely paying attention to him.

What I *was* interested in was the man hanging over his shoulder. Dave didn't seem to know he was there. How could he not? The guy was breathing all over him. And what kind of self-respecting jock would allow any man wearing a toga anywhere near him, let alone close enough to feel his breath? He seemed to hear him, though he didn't seem to acknowledge it.

Something really strange is going on here.

"Ava, why didn't you tell me about your plan? I told you mine." Beth has finished her exam.

"What are you talking about?" I start walking, knowing that she will follow. I don't particularly want teachers hearing her since I know where this is going.

"You know." She waves at the gym. "That act in there."

"I wasn't acting."

"Puh-leeze! You were acting crazy so they would pity you." She slams her fist into a locker as we pass it. "It was brilliant. I wish I'd thought of it."

"What, and give up this whole Princess of the Damned thing you've got going on?" I poke a finger at her wild nest of hair.

She fluffs her coiffure as if she'd just had it styled. "Mine was brilliant too. Yours was just more subtle. And subtle is good."

"What are you doing now?" I ask as we turn a corner and nearly trip on a student cramming for their next exam.

Beth gives him a scornful look, but keeps talking. "I'm going to go home to recover from my harrowing experience."

"Yeah, all right. Your last final is tomorrow, right?"

There's a glint of envy in her dark eyes. "Yep. At least you're done today."

"It just ruins my birthday, that's all," I snark.

"Oh, I almost forgot!" Beth reaches into her bag and pulls out an envelope. "Stupid tests nearly made me forget." Stuffing it into my hand, she settles back to watch me open it. "Happy birthday!"

I open it to pull out a slip of paper. On it is Beth's loopy writing promising to take me out shopping in celebration.

"Thanks!" Giving her a big hug, I carefully slide the card into my bag. "Nothing like doing something new, eh?" We both dissolve into giggles. We shop together as much as we possibly can. We go out at least once every weekend, even if it's just to window-shop.

"Come on, then!" Despite the makeup, Beth still manages to look cheery.

Well, like a cheery corpse, maybe.

She puts her arm around me and steers me through the building for the last time. It's exhilarating, but also a little disconcerting. How is one supposed to feel when leaving something so familiar? It is like jumping from bunny slippers to Manolos in one fell swoop. Even though leaving school and becoming incredibly successful in everything I do is something I've been anticipating, it's still a little distressing to know that this is probably the last time I'll be looking at the place I've spent most of the past few years wandering around in.

We stop at the top of the steps, listening to the doors bang closed behind us. Beth looks at me and I look at her, both of us smiling.

After a long moment, Beth tugs on my arm. "Come on. Let's celebrate your birthday."

Chapter Two
Goddesses, Jerks and Me, Oh My!

So, here we are, strolling in the slowly waning sunlight, turning the corner to the sparse strip mall. It's our favorite shopping spot—a place we come to as often as our bank accounts allow. Every landmark has been committed to memory. We could probably find out way blindfolded. Navigating traffic would be the hardest bit. But with a little luck and our determination to shop, yeah—we'd make it here just fine.

As we turn the corner, I notice a strange woman kneeling by the rainbow-colored geraniums and marigolds that were planted last weekend. I know this because Beth and I spent an hour—no, an hour and a half, well, maybe a *few* hours—watching the hot gardener put them in while enjoying a refreshing Frappuccino or three.

All thoughts of the man encased in the spanktastic tight denim are lost as we move closer. The woman appears to be talking to herself as she brushes her hands over the bright blooms, seemingly looking for something on the ground under the bright flowers. I tug on the hem of Beth's baby T to steer her closer. Maybe we can help the woman out a little. Call it the innate Girl Scout in me. I have to assist if and when I can.

"What are you doing?" She was about to reach the much-anticipated windows before being rudely redirected by me. For Beth, this is an offense that she'd want me strung up for. And at the moment, she looks like the jury in her head has already condemned me.

I quickly explain. "I think that woman lost something. We should at least try to help her out." I point at her, hoping that her situation appeals to the non-shopping obsessed part of Beth's brain.

Beth screws up her face after searching the area I'm looking at. "What woman?"

"That woman." I wave a hand at the poor woman as she shuffles about on her knees. "She looks like she needs help. Come on. It can't take too long."

Beth sweeps her head from side to side looking over the spot I'm pointing at. "What are you talking about? There's no one there. Has old age scrambled your brain or something? We're wasting good shopping time, Ava. The mall closes in four hours."

I bite back a reminder that she's a month older than I am. A fact that she always seems to forget. My gaze is drawn to the woman in obvious distress before I swivel back to look at my friend. She has to be messing around. "Yeah, and we're wasting it arguing. Fine, I'm going on my own. If I'm not back in three minutes, call nine-one-one."

She shrugs and points. "I'll be at The GAP."

I wave her off and quicken my pace to a merry trot, eager to help the lady.

That's when I hear it.

"Come on, my darlings. Just try to grow. I know it is hard—this place is hardly what I would consider a good home for you. But you must try. Think about how much lovelier this place would be with you in bloom."

Miraculously, the flowers open, revealing their cheerful, bright blooms. Satisfied, the woman pops up to stand face to face with me. Her grin dissolves instantly.

That's a weird reaction. Do I look that scary? I try my friendliest smile. "Sorry. I didn't mean to startle you..."

She's still looking at me as if I'm some weird apparition. Like *I'm* the weird one.

My attention drops to her clothing...

Oh.

She's wearing a toga.

Yep, that proves it. I've lost my mind. Thanks to years of enforced learning, my brain has snapped and I'm hallucinating. Isn't that one of the signs of schizophrenia? But why toga-clad weirdos? Where did that come from? Now I wish I'd taken a psychology class instead of taking that hour off. Obviously that little one-hour break I thought I needed wasn't enough. I might as well have taken that class and pushed myself over the edge. At least then I'd have some clue as to what was going on with my pathetic psyche.

As I stare at her, the woman does the same to me.

She's beautiful. That's the short version of my assessment. Her hair falls in golden-honey waves to the waist of her pale pink toga. She's slender and lithe looking. So much so that I'm pretty sure a stiff wind would knock her over. Her features are dainty. A pert nose, prettily pink lips with a perfect Cupid's bow...

And I realize I'm a little jealous of this figment of my imagination.

Yep, folks. Ava Goddard is going to be on the cover of a magazine — *Psychology Today*. I'll be wearing the latest straitjacket and the headline will read *Girl Jealous of Hallucination, Doctors Consider Shock Therapy*.

The pretty hallucination waves her hand in my face as if she's testing my eyesight. "You can see me?"

"Uh, yeah." I squint my eyes at the petite woman. *What's the deal?* "Why wouldn't I? I thought I could help you look for something. That is, I thought that's what you were doing." I pause my babbling for a moment. "Do you always talk to plants?" *Do I always talk to hallucinations?*

The comment seems to almost give her a coronary. At the very least, it compels her into some sort of conniption that has her bounding from side to side in front of me. "Can you still see me?"

I follow her with my gaze, wondering just what I've gotten myself into. "Yeah, I can see you." I point across the street. "Just like I can see that kid over there picking his nose and that dog over there leaving things his owner should be picking up."

"This has never happened to me before." The woman looks really flustered now.

She's clearly out of her mind, and I've had enough. I'm not wasting another moment of my birthday on her. "I didn't mean to upset you. Just forget I said anything." All I want to do now is to get far away from her before she flips out and goes on a homicidal rampage. Wait. Can hallucinations do that? I don't want to find out.

Edging back toward Beth, I notice that Crazy Blonde, as I have dubbed her seeing as she is my creation, is following me and not being very subtle about it at all. I hear her footsteps behind me as plainly as I hear my own.

This is ridiculous. All I want is to have a nice quiet shopping trip with my friend where we buy lots of stuff that is completely useless but very satisfying to own. Is that too much to ask for? So I turn around to tell her off.

Nothing.

Strange. I could have sworn that I heard her slapping the pavement with those sandals right behind me. I turn around again. This time I spot her trying to blend in with a birch tree.

Does she think I'm stupid? I don't want to get too close to her and choose to shout from where I am. "Look, lady, I'm sorry for bothering you earlier. I'm just going to leave you alone now." Why am I treating her like a real person?

She stamps her feet like a petulant three year old. "You saw me again!"

The woman is looking really aggravated now, and it's starting to scare me a little. "It's not my fault that you can't camouflage yourself. I said I'm sorry. Just leave me alone, okay?"

Crazy Blonde is now pacing back and forth muttering to herself. "Am I losing my powers?"

Whoa. Psycho walking. I definitely don't want to be here. I can imagine her using her *powers* and me ending up on the six o'clock news. "I'm sure whatever abilities you think you have are great and that you're not losing your touch."

Crazy purses her pouty lips and waves her hands in my face once more, eliciting my knee-jerk reaction of slapping them away. Hard.

She doesn't seem perturbed by the force I use. Rather, she's interested in the sensation I've caused in her hands. "This is so strange."

"You're telling me." I watch Crazy run over to Beth, jumping in her face and resuming her crazy arm-waving polka. Amazingly, my best friend continues to stare in awe at the latest khakis hanging in this store. Crazy looks at me again before running around her in manic little circles. Beth still doesn't notice. Well, there you go. Proof that I'm insane. I should go check myself in to some sort of institution right now. Maybe somewhere with a spa. Then it dawns on me. Maybe Beth's playing a prank on me? This is something she would do. She gets one of her actor friends to mess with me, make me think I'm losing it then — *Bam!* Surprise! Everyone laughs. I join in. We shop, have cake and I go to bed secure in the knowledge that I am indeed sane. Fine, I'll play along. I walk over to Beth. Nonchalant is the best way to play this.

I edge closer to her, shoving Crazy aside. "Find anything good?"

"Yes! I have to get that bag in there." She points at a bright orange canvas bag on the dummy.

Crazy Blonde moves directly in her line of sight and there isn't even a flicker on Beth's face. The blonde then taps Beth on the head. There's no sign of anything amiss from my friend. I stifle a scream when her hair turns into green vines that coil off her head and flowers sprout from her ears. Still nothing. Crazy waves her hand and it all disappears.

Crazy Blonde manages to give me a triumphant grin before I turn to stare at my friend. How is she *not* reacting to this? She's right in Beth's face. There is no way Beth can miss her. Maybe my friend's a better actress than I thought.

I've had enough. I just want to shop in peace. I decide to confront her. "This is a joke, right? Some sort of birthday prank? Ha ha, very funny." I make sure the false hilarity is gone from my face when I demand, "Stop it."

Beth manages to tear her focus from the bag and roll her tongue back into her mouth. "Are you all right?"

No! Definitely not! "Oh, yeah, I'm fine. Thanks." What else am I going to say? That I'm seeing crazy people in togas? That's totally insane. Doctors will come after me with butterfly nets.

Beth is giving me a look. The one that she always gives me when she doesn't believe me or when she thinks I've bought something in bad taste. "Are you sure? You look kinda weird. Maybe we should postpone this trip."

My head starts shaking on its own. There is no way I'm letting this ruin my birthday. "I'm fine. Let's just start shopping."

"If you're sure." Beth leads the way. "Let the fun begin!"

I follow her into the store, barging my way in before Crazy.

"She didn't see me!" The insane blonde bounces happily alongside me, grinning like she won the lottery.

"Shut up!" I growl.

Beth's dark curls bounce as she turns to me and, for a second, I fear that she's heard me.

"Did you help that woman find whatever she was searching for?"

My stomach unclenches with my relief that she hasn't noticed me talking to myself. Beth might be a good actress, but I don't think that she could pull something like this off. I stare at her. Not even a flicker of anything out of the ordinary. This is rather unsettling. If this isn't a practical joke then... I shake it off and try to stay in the moment.

"Nah, I couldn't help her find what she's lost." My attention is on the woman next to me. It's obvious that she knows I'm referring to her mind. Or is that *my* mind?

Crazy sucks her teeth but otherwise stays quiet.

That's it. I'm just going to ignore her. Even if she shoves her finger up *my* nose, I'm not going to pay any attention. All I care about is enjoying my birthday and I can't do that while I'm busy watching her.

There's a stand of pretty T-shirts and I immerse myself in it, intent on finding the cutest one. Ah, pink with a little cat motif. Excellent. And what goes best with a pink T? Some new chinos.

I systematically make my way through the store choosing what I want while Beth does the same. I quickly check my watch and I realize that it's taken us close to an hour to go through this one store. If we don't pick up the pace, we'll never get through the others by closing time.

"Beth? Are you done yet? We've gotta get a move on."

"Yeah. Let's get in line." She uses her nose to point at a till over the pile of clothes in her arms. "We'll hit the dress store next. I need a bunch of new dresses for the fabulous undergrad me I'm unveiling this fall." She juggles her load until she has a clear line of sight at me. "What about you? Decided on a look yet?"

Kacie Ji

"I have a specific look in mind. I'm not settling for anything less. Very Abercrombie & Fitch with a bit of Park Avenue Princess mixed in every once in a while."

"I like! I think delicate and cute will suit me best." Beth bounces happily. "I can't wait until we move into our dorm room. I'm so excited! We'll have beanbags and beaded curtains and stuff. Just like we planned."

"You're actually taking plans that we made during an eighth grade sleepover seriously?"

"Of course I am. Plans made over ice cream at midnight are sacred!" She grins and shoves us closer to the till. "We're going to be the two hottest freshmen with the hottest room on campus!"

We giggle and head for the counter.

As usual, everyone has chosen this exact moment in time to pay and the line is winding a serpentine path around the room. If there's anything I hate, it's waiting. I sigh heavily. But what can you do? Taking a fortifying breath, I assume my place at the end of the queue.

"That's not a good idea."

Crazy is back again and looks determined to make me notice her.

Looking straight through her I turn to Beth. "So..."

"Yes. I talked to Noah."

That wasn't where I was going, but hearing about what my crush is up to is more than a satisfactory conversation topic.

I feign only mild interest. "Really? What did he have to say?"

My best friend whaps me with her pile of soon-to-be-newest purchases. "Stop it. I know how much you like him. I think he might be into you, too." She watches me closely for my reaction.

30

I take the bait. How could I not? He might be interested in me, too? I feel like a ticker tape parade is in full swing somewhere behind my belly button. "Really? How do you know?" Crazy is tugging on my arm now, but I shrug her off as subtly as I can.

"Oh, he asked about you. Wondered what you were doing this summer."

I can't stop the grin from spreading on my lips. "Ooooh." The thought of spending time with the dreamy, green-eyed hunk over the holidays turns the ticker tape in my stomach into fireworks. Something tells me this is going to be an interesting few months.

Still, I have to play it cool. "He's probably just being polite."

If there was one thing about the guy that I couldn't fault, it was his manners.

Beth's sharp toe reminds me of where we are and to keep up with the line, which is moving quite quickly considering its length. Crazy is gone now. Perhaps she's taken the hint? I allow a secret smile to curl the corners of my mouth. It looks like my luck is taking a turn for the better.

It takes a few more minutes before I'm at the register dropping my burden before the rather snarky-looking cashier there. I blink innocently and hope she hurries so I can get to the next store.

"Want the hangers?" she growls.

"No thanks."

I try willing her to move faster, but she only seems to slow down. I'm tempted to tell her not to bother folding the clothes and to just shove them into a bag so I can get out of here.

But I bite my tongue and do my best to keep my expression neutral. Frowning causes wrinkles, after all.

She's about to place the last meticulously folded T into the bag when I feel a tug on my arm. Instead of Beth's hand, I see that it's Crazy yet again. I pull my arm out of her grasp and turn to the woman at the till who, if possible, looks even more annoyed than before.

"That'll be one hundred seventy-five, eighty-nine…please." The cashier sighs.

It's a bit more than I expected, but it still leaves me with more than enough to spend in the other stores. I reach into my bag to retrieve my bursting wallet.

It's not there.

Turning to peer into my bag, I realize that I can see my foot. Wailing, I stick my hand through the gaping hole in the bottom. "Oh, my God! All my birthday money!" Not to mention my ID and cell. Panicked, I turn to Beth. "What am I going to do?" Tears start to prick my eyes, and everyone is watching me now. It's so humiliating.

"Don't worry, I'll get it." Beth steps forward and drops her things onto the counter. I hear her begin sweet-talking the woman into adding her things to mine to pay for it all at once. I'll pay her back eventually, though she's got more than enough to pay for everything. Besides being the budding drama star in town, Beth is from a pretty wealthy family. Mom and me never really have to worry about money thanks to her knack with antiques, but compared to the Coolidges' old money, we might as well be paupers.

"I told you not to do it."

The fact that Crazy Blonde's voice is now so familiar irks me. "Do you have my wallet?" I mutter.

She has the grace to look affronted. "Of course not. I just saw Fortuna lurking nearby. Things are bound to get a little…strange with her around." She points through the window at another toga-clad woman outside. The tall, willowy brunette is too busy to notice us, though. She's concentrating on watching people as they pass. One man in particular appears to have caught her interest.

The jerk in question practically barrels a few women over as he enters the store, stomping on a little girl's toy dog. He's shouting obscenities into the cell phone pinned between his chin and shoulder as he barges to the front of the line and shoves poor Beth aside.

"Look. I've got to run. We'll discuss this more later." He swipes his stubby finger over the screen and leans over the counter. "I bought these things last week and they don't fit right." He thrusts the bag at Snarky Cashier.

"I'm sorry, *sir*."

I like how she makes it sound insulting. Like 'sir' is a synonym for dirt.

"But you'll have to go to the end of the line."

"I don't have time to go to the end of the line. I'm double-parked and I have things to do. I doubt you could understand that, only being a cashier and all."

My jaw drops and so does everyone else's. Amid the disgusted awe, I notice that the other toga-clad woman has approached him and easily palms his wallet.

I nearly give myself whiplash as I turn to see if Beth has noticed.

"I know!"

Thank God! She saw it too!

"That guy is a world-class jerk!"

My stomach sinks again. Great, now I'm seeing two of them.

Meanwhile, the new toga chick, whom I dub Crazy Two, since she's obviously got something to do with the other insane woman, is rifling through his wallet, counting the bills as she mutters and glares contemptuously at the man. Whatever is coming can't be good for him.

Crazy Two is now running from the store, and through the window, I see her approaching the tearful little girl cradling her dog. She tugs the dog gently from her hands and tosses him over to a planter with a few lackluster plants in it. She disappears with a flash only to reappear next to the plants and shoves the wallet under the dog.

I watch the proceedings just as gleefully as the two toga-sheathed women are.

The girl's mother looks about to tear the man apart, but is distracted by her daughter's distraught wailing. Noticing the dog has somehow gotten away, she stalks over to retrieve it. When the dog is finally in her hand, she notices the shiny leather that was hidden under the plush.

She looks around to see if anyone nearby could have lost it, I'm assuming, before picking it up and looking inside for identification. The moment she sees who it belongs to, her face lights up. Picking up her daughter, she gives the man still yelling at the teller one last contemptuous glare before walking to the toy store.

"That was awesome." Okay, so my imagination has just manipulated stuff in the real world. Either I'm some sort of psychic with those telewhatsit powers, or these two are real and I'm the only one who can see them. I'm not sure which of those options is better.

Beth glares at me. "What? You thought what he just said was *awesome*?"

Obviously I've missed something as I was watching the scene outside. I just shake my head and wave it off.

"Nothing. I just… Nothing." I'm aware I sound like a complete moron, but the euphoria of the jerk being taken is still fresh so it doesn't bother me too much.

Crazy One is giggling alongside me and waving Crazy Two over. They do a strange little victory dance before they realize I'm watching them.

Crazy One looks at me and it's like a dam breaks inside her. "Wasn't she great? I love it when Fortuna does stuff like that! The idiot pig deserves worse, if you ask me." She sticks her tongue out at the back of the man's head then parts her lips in an enormous, proud grin.

The one called Fortuna scowls at Crazy One. "Who are you talking to?"

A finger is pointed in my direction. "Her."

"Don't be stupid." She waves a hand in my face.

I'm not going through this again. I grab her hand on the second pass and shake it. "Hi."

Startled isn't even the word I would use to describe the wide-eyed, gaped-mouthed astonishment that passes over her face.

"Flora, is this some sort of joke?"

"No! She can see us."

I wave the two women off for the time being. Beth is now getting into an argument with the man at the counter. It's more important to help my best friend than talk to two possible indicators of my impending psychosis.

Annoyed that this is happening on what is a special day for me, I barge in between the two. "Okay, mister. Just get out the receipt and do your thing. I don't have time to waste."

Everyone involved, the man, Snarky and Beth, look at me. The two non-males have a slightly disgusted look on their faces, while the man has smug satisfaction.

It quickly disappears when he realizes that his wallet is gone. His quick, panicked self pat-down yields nothing. "My wallet's gone."

"Aw, too bad." Beth and I shove him aside so that she can pay for our things.

Within minutes we have our bags and are out of the store.

I'm drained.

The feeling hits me when we get outside. It's not that surprising, considering how badly this shopping trip has gone. It's going down as *the* worst in the history of the universe. Maybe an alien somewhere has experienced something comparable, but I doubt it.

"Where to next?" Beth is rabidly weighing our options in stores. "There's a sale over there!"

My head jerks from side to side suddenly. I realize that the two in togas are with me again and Flora, or the one formerly known as Crazy Blonde, is shaking my head for me. It's not like I want to shop any longer anyway. I'm too irritated to enjoy it anymore.

"I just want to call it a day. I'm so tired and that guy just ruined it for me."

Beth purses her carefully glossed lips. "Aw, don't let that jerk ruin your day. There are plenty of other shops to go through."

"Nah, you go ahead. I'm just going to walk off some steam on my way home." Beth looks like she's about to argue, so I tug my bag into her line of sight. "Besides, I don't have any money and I can't ask you to spend more on me."

Beth still looks unconvinced. I'm pretty sure she's plotting ways to get me to continue shopping.

"Are you sure you don't want me to come with you?"

"I'll be fine," I say. I look at the two whispering furiously next to me. It's not like I'm lacking in company. "You enjoy yourself."

Beth rakes her curls out of her face. "Okay, be careful. I'll give you a call later." She gives me a warm hug. "Happy birthday."

"Thanks." I pull out of her embrace and start walking, knowing that the strange women will be right behind me.

The moment we turn the corner the questions start.

"How can you see us?"

"Are you a goddess?

"A demigoddess?"

Stopping, I turn to look at them. "What are you talking about? What I want to know is how I can see you guys when no one else can. You have to be real, otherwise, you couldn't have done what you did with that guy's wallet. Unless I'm some sort of telepath. In which case, I'm wasting my time in this nowhere town. I could be making millions in Vegas or something instead of standing here talking to myself!"

"I can assure you, we are real." Flora is doing her imitation of a hyper rabbit again and is bouncing merrily alongside me.

I can go with that. "Can we start with who you are? How can you two do the things you do? With the flowers and everything?"

The dark-haired woman smiles warmly for the first time. "Fortuna, Goddess of Luck, at your service." She nods at her friend. "That's Flora, Goddess of Spring— and flowers and such."

My jaw slackens. Straitjackets, here I come. "You're kidding me, right?"

Fortuna taps a finger on her chin thoughtfully. "How can we prove...? I know..." She snaps her fingers.

I feel a little stupid, but I look around to see if anything has happened. "I don't see anything."

"A man in Florida just found the varnish for his boat."

Flora is in a fit of giggles while I'm sucking my teeth. "You're messing with me."

Fortuna smiles impishly, twirling a lock of her glossy black hair. "You've already seen what I do."

"You stole a guy's wallet. How is that divine intervention?" I snort.

She rolls her eyes in exasperation. "Fine."

She snaps her fingers, and again I'm looking for something that's changed.

I look at Fortuna, waiting for her to explain this one, but all she does is smirk at me.

There is silence for a few seconds, then I hear it. My cell phone is ringing.

It has to be mine. I'm the only person I know of who has the theme for *Love Story* as a ringtone.

"I thought I lost it!" Heart fluttering excitedly, I reach into my bag and find that the charm on my phone is hooked onto a loose thread inside my bag. That was lucky! I tug it off and take a look at the caller. "I don't recognize the caller."

"Just answer it!" The two so-called goddesses are watching me with anticipation now.

I decide to humor them. Flipping the phone open, I answer. "Hello?"

"Ava? It's Noah."

"Noah?" My voice cracks, to the two women's amusement. I discreetly clear my throat and try again. "Hey, Noah. What's up?"

"I found your wallet and stuff. Just thought I would let you know." There's a slight pause and he coughs. "Anyway, I'm sure you want them back."

"Yeah, it would be nice."

"I'm over at the mall. Wanna meet up?"

My jaw drops. Fortuna and Flora are waving for me to answer him, but all I find myself doing is nodding like a shell-shocked goldfish.

Fortuna rolls her eyes, grabs my phone and somehow my voice is coming out of her face. "I'd love to. See you there in half an hour." She hangs up and slips the phone back into my bag. "So? Do I pass your test?"

Still imitating the fish, I nod again. Thinking over what she said to Noah, I snap out of it. "Half an hour? What are you talking about? He's right around that corner." I point at the one we just rounded. "It'd take less than a minute to get back there."

She taps me on the forehead. "Yes, but this will give you some time to freshen up." She brings her manicured nails thoughtfully to her lips as she critically eyes my clothes. "Wouldn't you like to wear something a little more...special?"

"Good point." Some quick calculations bring a frown to my face. "That doesn't give me enough time to go home and get changed. And I obviously can't get changed right here."

Flora sighs. "You haven't been listening to us, have you?"

She snaps her fingers, and we're standing in my bedroom.

"Right." I'm sure that any other time I would be questioning this, but right now I have more important things to contemplate than breaching the laws of time and space.

"So this Noah is pretty special to you." The Goddess of Luck is wandering around my room, appraising my little knick-knacks as she goes.

My face feels about a million degrees hotter than normal.

The two goddesses share a look. "We'll have to call in the expert." Fortuna turns her gaze to the ceiling. "Venus. Have you got a moment?"

The scent of roses fills the room just before there is a brilliant pink flash of light.

A voluptuous blonde steps out of the light and haughtily tosses her lustrous mane of golden hair. "What is it?"

If there was one word to describe her, it would have to be breathtaking. She looks like every man's perfect woman. My knowledge of mythology isn't the best, but I know the name Venus. The Goddess of Love is here standing right here in front of me.

Fortuna grins at her while continually snapping her fingers. I can't help but think that there is someone out there having the most fabulous lucky streak—or being tremendously cursed. "We think you're the best one to help out this girl."

I turn to the stunning goddess and smile hopefully.

"You can see us."

"Yep." I look at the other two. "I don't have to go through all this song and dance again, do I? You believe me, right?"

She looks down her perfect nose at me. "Well, you *are* talking to me."

Flora cuts in. "Ava is about to meet with someone special to her. We need to make a good impression."

The Goddess of Love has already been inspecting me. Venus tilts my chin with a perfect pink nail. "Quite pretty for a mortal. But could use a little work." She turns me from side to side thoughtfully. "Have you thought about doing your hair a little differently?" She snaps her fingers and my previously long flowing locks are chin length and cut in a way that flatters my face. I swish my head around watching the way the new feathered and angled ends move. They highlight my cheekbones and slim my face. I love it! Makes the job done by the stylist look like a hatchet job. I can definitely get used to this.

"Nice!" I gawk at my reflection and grin inanely. Maybe hanging out with goddesses is a good thing.

Venus isn't looking impressed. "I'm not done yet." She appraises my makeup and starts clicking her tongue. "What is with the young girls of today? Do you not realize that you do not need to cover yourselves with this artificial filth?"

I turn to her, hands protectively and uselessly over my face. "Wha— Wait! What are you doing?"

She snaps her fingers once more and I'm turned to face the mirror again. Gone is the makeup I'd painstakingly applied this morning. Instead, it's replaced by a healthy glow that I've never seen before.

In no time, she has a better and improved me appearing in the mirror, while I just stare at my reflection in an amazed, and grateful, daze.

"Now, what about clothing?" There are several quick snaps and my entire wardrobe takes turns on me in different combinations. Accessories whirl around the room to pair up with the different looks. Venus has got to be augmenting my wardrobe — or I have a lot of stuff in there that I don't know about. For the next few seconds, I'm a living Barbie doll. Goth Barbie. Preppy Barbie. Then a combination of Vamp, Goth, Preppy Barbie. I'm pretty sure I even see Schoolmarm Barbie in there somewhere.

Flora and Fortuna settle on my bed and watch the proceedings with the same fascination as I do, clapping and hooting when Venus settles on a look.

Finally, I find myself wearing a shortish denim skirt, strappy leather sandals and a cute floaty pink blouse that I've never had the chance to wear before. It's a combination that I haven't thought of doing. Separate they are very different, but together they make sense.

I turn my head from side to side, admiring the effect. "You do good work."

"I've had practice." Venus tilts her head as she looks at me. "You are too thin." She snaps her fingers and turns me to look at myself.

My face looks the same so my eyes drift lower, and lower... "Oh my God! I have breasts!"

The delighted shriek I release draws the other two goddesses over, and all four of us are squished within the confines of the mirror frame, although I barely notice them. All I'm seeing at the moment is my new curves. And what curves they are!

Tugging the blouse away, I peer down the neck and grin like an idiot. Then a thought occurs. This isn't the first century BC. Men aren't supposed to objectify women. I don't have to look like what they think I should look like. I'm fine just the way I am. How to tell this to a goddess without offending her?

"Wait a sec. He's probably seen me around the school this morning. He'll think that it's a bit weird that I've sprouted these" — I tug my shirt tight around my ample new torso in emphasis — "since this morning, don't you think?" Venus looks a little miffed and I quickly try to do some damage control. "Not that I don't appreciate this. It's great. In any other situation I'd be bowing at your feet. But…" I give her my best puppy dog look.

"Very well."

There's a warm tingling in my chest and things are back to normal.

"Thanks so much. Is it inappropriate to give you guys a hug?" I don't really give them a chance to reply before I throw my arms around them. "What did I do to deserve this?"

Venus nods understandingly. "We'd love to know that too. However, you have a young gentleman waiting. A lady does not make people wait." She softens her words with a smile as she snaps her fingers.

Chapter Three
Conquering the Space-Time Continuum in Heels

I waver slightly when I blink into existence back at the mall. The instant change in location is too quick for me to adjust, sending me toppling forward against a cool brick wall to steady myself. It's like that feeling you get when you're on the escalator and you're not paying attention at the end. That embarrassing lurch when you realize that you're on solid ground once again. Luckily, there's no one around to witness me trying to come to grips with defying time and space paradoxes in heeled strappy sandals. They're cute, but not the best footwear when one has to kick theoretical physics in the butt.

It takes me a moment to acclimate. Which means that I'm not going to be making an ass out of myself. Literally. I'm wearing a skirt! One wrong move and the whole neighborhood would be seeing things I'd rather not make public. It also means that I'm worried about the reason I'm back here. I run a hand through my hair. I know it's perfect, but I'm so nervous that I have to do something with my hands. Better to mess with that than to screw up something much more difficult to fix. With one last rake and fluff, I force myself to walk slowly around the corner.

My eyes instantly home in on The GAP and sure enough, there he is, leaning against the wall with my stuff clutched in one hand. He looks so cute in his jeans and T-shirt. Normally, I would stand a while longer and absorb what I'm looking at, but I notice him checking his watch. Did I take too long?

My feet take the initiative and start galloping toward him. It's a few steps before I get them under control and slow to a dignified gait. "Hey, Noah."

Is it me or did he just brighten? Yes, I do believe he's smiling, and it's because of me!

"Hey, Ava." He rubs the back of his neck. "How's it going?"

I would love to tell him the truth right now. But I'm pretty sure that he'll think I'm completely crazy. Besides, straitjackets aren't exactly flattering. Can't scare him off, now, can I? "I'm doing good."

"That's great." His neck must really be getting raw now from all that rubbing, but he's still doing it. "Happy birthday. What a day to lose all your stuff, eh?"

"Yeah, it is. I haven't had the best luck until now."

"It was dumb luck that I found your stuff." He fumbles with my wallet. "I kinda tripped on this. I'm sorry. It's a little banged up." He juggles the things from hand to hand before unceremoniously shoving them into my arms. "It was really weird. Like they jumped out in front of me."

"Thanks." To him and Fortuna.

I barely take a glance before dropping them all into my now fixed purse. Like I care if it's been scuffed up a little. I'm actually spending time with Noah! I'm so elated right now I wouldn't care if someone kicked me in the head. Well...maybe a little. For a second or two while I kicked them back. But then I'd be reveling in this moment again.

He coughs, and I stare up at him. Is he blushing? Noah can't even meet my gaze.

"Uh, how about a birthday pizza?"

Oh, my God, yes! "Sure, that sounds great." Did that breezy voice just come from me?

Then it dawns on me. Things are going just a little too good. I try my best to do it stealthily, but I know I look strange with my gaze darting around as I scan for the three goddesses. Could Venus be influencing Noah? Is Fortuna playing around again? It's not funny. They're messing with my happiness.

"Is everything all right?" Noah's observing me with a peculiar expression on his face and I do my best to collect myself.

"Yeah, I'm fine. Just thought I saw something." Then I see a swatch of pink silk drifting around the corner. "Can you hold on a sec? I think I saw someone I need to talk to."

Without giving him a chance to answer, I dash around the corner to confront them. I find Venus, but there is no sign of the other two.

"Venus? Are you doing something to Noah?"

Her nails flash as she drags her fingers through her golden locks. "Why would I do a thing like that?"

"Isn't that what you do?" I peek over my shoulder and notice that Noah is coming up behind me. "Oh, my God!"

He rounds the corner, but doesn't seem like he's heard anything. "Hey, is everything good here?" Dark eyes filled with concern look at me.

How am I going to explain talking to myself to him? My mouth goes dry as I try to think of an explanation.

"Who's your friend? I don't think I've seen her around before."

My what? "Huh?" Oh great, Ava, *real* intelligent.

"Your friend." He extends his hand and reaches around me. "Hi, I'm Noah."

When I finally turn around without any mishap, I see him shaking hands with an incredibly beautiful blonde girl about the same age as us. Golden curls, perfect hair, makeup and skin, and clothes tight enough to show off a perfect figure. I feel jealousy and insecurity tighten my gut. I know she's a goddess, and she can't help but be gorgeous, but couldn't she have helped me out a little?

"Venus. Pleased to meet you." She shakes his hand delicately. "I'm Ava's cousin."

At this point, I feel a King Kong-sized migraine coming on.

His handsome smile grows and he releases her hand. "Ava's cousin, eh? I bet you can tell me some interesting stories about her." He steps over to me and nudges my ribs with his elbow.

Venus gives me a knowing smile and nods. "Oh, I can tell you some stories all right." Her gaze returns to me. "Like I was saying, I'm going to head home. I'll see you later." She gives me a quick hug. "Happy birthday."

"Thanks, Venus," I say. I hope she knows how grateful I am for everything she has done for me today. "I'll see you again soon."

"That's a promise." She waves a delicate hand. "Bye. It was nice meeting you, Noah."

"Likewise."

Venus turns and sashays away.

Noah's eyes stay on her for a moment before he turns back to me again. "She seems nice."

I merely nod, stemming the tiny pangs of jealousy. Who wouldn't stop to watch her? Venus is gorgeous. I just wish he would look at me like that someday. Blah. Time to change the subject before I get so down I forget about this whole thing. "So is pizza still on offer?"

His slightly crooked smile helps dispel the uneasy feeling a little. "Definitely. I'm starving." He hooks his arm loosely around my shoulders and leads me away.

Jealousy's gone! I'm in heaven. Not only am I about to have dinner with Noah, but he's actually touching me of his own volition.

This is the best birthday ever. *Ever!*

* * * *

Dinner is a pleasant haze. The pizza has got to be the best I've ever tasted, while the banana split we're now finishing off is just heavenly. I'm pretty sure it has nothing to do with the quality of the food. At this moment, I could probably eat a slice of the table and think it was ambrosia. And it's all thanks to my company.

But I have to keep calm. How many times have I read in magazines about a girl who acted too desperate and scared the guy away? That's not going to be me. Gotta stay cool. Collected. I slice off a piece of banana with my spoon. "So what are your plans for the summer?"

"After finals, I'm spending the summer at a soccer camp. Then heading off to college, I guess. How about you? What are you planning?"

I shrug nonchalantly. "Nothing much. My mom was saying something about us fixing up the house this summer. So I guess I'm stuck doing that."

Noah chuckles and spoons up some of the soupy looking ice cream from the puddle at the bottom of the dish. "Parents, eh? I'll give you a call when I get back. Maybe I can give you a hand."

I can't stop a massive grin from spreading across my face. "Really? That's so nice of you. Thanks."

"Sure." He leans back and stretches lazily. "I guess I should get you home, huh? Can't keep the birthday girl out too late."

I'm on cloud nine. Seriously. If it wasn't for the ton of pizza I just ate, I'd be floating to the ceiling right now. "It's no big deal. I didn't have anything planned for today. Just shopping with Beth."

Noah smiles mysteriously at me and I can't help but think that there *is* something planned that I don't know about. At any rate, I follow him. While I'm throwing a mini inner celebration of the fact that Noah is spending time with me, I let him lead me out of the place. We start the semi long walk to my house. I only wish it could be longer.

I take back the wish when we're about halfway there. The shoes I'm wearing aren't meant for long treks and my feet are screaming for a reprieve. I'm hoping that one of the goddesses will pop into existence and whisk us to my living room in the blink of an eye. We come to a corner and I'm about to collapse onto the grass and beg for mercy. I almost do it too, but then Noah touches a spot low on my back, sending tingles up my spine as he steers me around the bend. *Walking isn't so bad. I could do this for a few more miles.*

We amble silently, only inches apart. I wish I was brave enough to attempt to tangle my fingers with his. They're right there. I can feel the warmth coming off of them. But I can't do it. What if he rejects me? I decide it's better to wait for another day. I don't want anything to ruin the best birthday I've ever had.

I can't stop myself from sneaking peeks at him as we follow the pavement. My head comes up to just under his chin. Perfect for snuggling. I could just tuck my face up against his chin and... Ahhhhh, perfection. He's whipcord lean from all the sports. Not an ounce of fat that I can see. And I'm really looking. My gaze trails down his arms to his hands, which are perfect. Everything about him from the spiky, untamed hair right down to his ratty shoes is perfect.

I blink hard to get rid of the moony-eyed look that I feel has come over my face. It's a hard fight to not try that nuzzling idea that's insistently nudging at my autonomic neuron response. Or is that automatic Noah response?

Noah smiles at me and I feel every single nerve-ending leap in reply. Firmly beating them into submission, I give him a cool smile in return.

As we approach my house, I notice that there is nothing different about it. No cars line the street outside. The house I call home looks as quiet and dull as ever. Nope, no party waiting for me. My heart sinks, and I realize that I had let myself hope for something I knew would not be.

Tess Goddard, my mom, is constantly working. She deals in antiques, and when she's not chained to a computer researching or searching for her treasures, she's out scouting or wheeling and dealing. I completely understand that she has to work hard to support us, but there are times when I wish she was around more.

Now seems like one of those times that she isn't. Giving myself a mental shrug, I stop at the door of the little house and turn to Noah. He seems to have reverted to awkward guy mode.

"Thanks for walking me home. And thanks for finding my stuff..." I shut up before I start sounding like a jabbering idiot.

He drags his hand through his hair to stop and rub at the back of his adorable head. "Not a problem."

His attention flits to look behind me at the door, and for a second I think he's going to invite himself in, but he's interrupted by a coughing fit.

It's the worst thing I've heard. It sounds like his lungs are partway up his throat. Quickly, I unlock the door and drag him in before he keels over on the lawn. Just what my mom would love to see greet her as she gets home from a long day at work—my dead crush on the lawn.

I lean him up against the counter and fill a glass with water. "Here, drink this."

He gratefully accepts and downs it in one go. I watch his chest rise and fall a few times before his breathing slows to something that looks sort of normal again. "Thanks. I don't know what happened," he rasps. Noah coughs roughly once more and it seems to do the job. "That's better."

I nod. "No problem. I couldn't really leave you out there to die. What would the neighbors think?"

He laughs and it's a wonderful sound. A deep chuckle. A good laugh. Not like a guffaw or a giggle. A nice, manly sound. "Well, thanks for not letting me die."

Noah leans in, and I freeze completely.

But instead of kissing me on the lips, he pecks me on the cheek, leaving it all hot and tingly. "Happy birthday, Ava," he whispers.

When he pulls back, he seems a little embarrassed and looks to be at a loss as to what to do next. Grinning a little goofily, he punches me in the shoulder and turns toward the door, only to quickly whirl around again. "I'll see ya tomorrow."

"Uh, yeah. See ya." I wave at him from the door, watching him amble down the street.

"Did you two have a good time?"

The three goddesses have returned and are standing beside me, all looking young enough to have been taking the tests with me today. It's a little weird to see them and know that even though they appear the same age as me, they have been around for eons.

"Yeah, I had a great time!"

They smile happily at my response. The bubbly euphoria begins to deflate when the doubt starts to niggle at my mind again.

"Did you guys have anything to do with it?" I turn to Venus specifically, who still is as breathtaking as ever, even as a teen.

She, in turn, denies the accusation with a defiant shake of her glorious mane. "We did nothing of the sort. All the ingredients were there. All you two needed was a little push in the right direction." Her smug smile shows how proud of herself she is. "I think you two are adorable together."

"Really?" Her admission is all I need to send me up into the stratosphere again. "We are, aren't we?"

Giggles bubble up my throat. "Come on, I'll show you what I bought. It's all upstairs."

On the way to my room, it dawns on me that they already know what I've purchased. How could they not? They're omnipotent, aren't they? Gods, by definition, know all.

After kicking open the door to my inner sanctum, I move aside to let them in first before entering and closing the door behind me.

"Okay, so it's occurred to me that you already know what I bought, since two of you were there and…well, you're all goddesses." After falling back onto the bed, I lie there for a second before I dump the bag beside me so that everything is laid out.

They were nodding at me even as they were going through my purchases.

It's amazing how normal this feels. It's like we do it all the time. Natural. Fun. All that's missing is pizza and Beth.

Fortuna waves her hand and there is a pizza with the works on the middle of the bed. "I know you've just had one, but we haven't eaten pizza in ages. And sorry about not bringing Beth over, but I have a feeling that the topic of conversation wouldn't be of interest to her."

"I guess you're right. By the way, thanks for the pizza and the thoughtfulness over Beth, but reading my mind kinda creeps me out." Apologetic murmurs come from the group. Guess that's the best I'm going to get from them.

Chewing on my lip keeps me occupied for a few seconds before I decide to ask the one question that's been on my mind since I met the three goddesses. "Why me? How is it I can see you?"

"Well, while you were gone, we discussed this a little." Flora picks the vegetables off her piece and nibbles delicately at it. "We came up with a few theories." She takes a large mouthful and looks over at Fortuna, who is chewing thoughtfully.

"Well, you could be" —she swallowed—"a goddess. But that doesn't seem likely since we'd have known about you. So you could be a demigoddess, but again that's not likely since your ability to see us manifested today. It's not like powers are time released. Then again, you could be a special case…"

Yeah, Fortuna really cleared things up.

"So you must be a descendant of a special sort of seer." Venus was nodding now. "Yes, I remember one in particular…" Venus flicked her eyes over me. "You remind me of her very much."

"So I'm probably the descendant of a special seer. Cool." Definitely very cool. Maybe I'll develop the ability to see into the future or something. I mean, that's what seers do, right? How awesome would that be? It doesn't really make sense, though, because if it was inherited, then how come it appeared now? Time to ask. "But why now? Why would I suddenly be able to see you guys today? Is it because of my birthday?"

Fortuna is now eating the pieces of desiccated vegetable that Flora didn't want and alternating between chewing manically and smiling in dreamy bliss at the taste of it.

"I have a theory on that." Flora turns away from Fortuna's less than delicate display and focuses on me. "I think you might be right because it's a particularly momentous milestone."

Venus snorted. "Well, that was vague."

Flora's head shoots up. "Can you do any better?"

"Perhaps." Venus falls back onto the pillows and flicks her pretty pink nails thoughtfully. "I think that you're right about all this happening because it is Ava's eighteenth birthday." She reaches over and pats my arm. "There's just something about that birthday. It is a magical day."

"Yeah, that's way better than what I said," grumps Flora.

Is it just me or did the plants outside the window just wilt along with Flora's mood? "This is so exciting!"

"Absolutely." Fortuna swallows and, if possible, grins even wider. "Just think of all the things we can show you!"

I'm smiling now. I feel it stretching across my face from ear to ear. Imagine all the things I can see that nobody even thought of. "So why hang out with little ole me? There have to be much more interesting things to do." Like showing me a few new things, maybe?

Flora smiles. "We would never pass up the chance to spend time with someone like you. It doesn't happen often enough. Besides, I think we're overdue for a brief break."

There are emphatic nods from the other two.

So here I am, a newly eighteen-year-old girl hanging out with three goddesses, in the literal sense. What to do first? The possibilities are endless, and I'm positively buzzing with ideas. Now what does a girl ask for from gods?

"Can you get me the latest Prada purse? Oh! And shoes to match!"

Venus rolls her magnificent blues and sighs. "Of course we could."

I fall over on the bed, squealing in a haze of materialistic glee. Oh, my God! The things I could own!

My brain is overloaded with a jumble of designer names. Ferragamo, Chanel, Gucci... Oh! Oh! And Mount Olympus! I want to see where the gods live!

I sit up, ready to list my requests to the goddesses, when I notice that all three of them are shaking their heads at me. "What?"

Fortuna looks a little distracted and snaps her fingers several times in quick succession. Seeing as nothing that I asked for appears in the room, I assume it's safe to think that she's doing her job. With that out of the way, she focuses her attention on me once again.

"We could give you all that you ask for, but it's not how it's done."

"So what do I have to do? Fill out a form or something?" They are goddesses. They should be able to do anything they want. Shouldn't they?

"It's not that easy." Flora looks more serious than I have ever seen her. "You have an extraordinary gift, being able to see us." She flaps her arms as she searches for the words.

Fortuna pushes aside her fellow goddess and attempts an explanation herself. "We can't just give you whatever you want. Call it cosmic equilibrium. To just give you anything you want would throw everything off balance."

Wonderful. "So what you're saying is that I can see and talk to you guys, but that's about it for the perks?" I get nods from all three. "Well, that puts a damper on all this."

"But think of all the things you can experience and learn now."

I see that Fortuna is really working to make me smile again.

"No one has ever had the chances you have now."

"That's not true." The soft voice enters the room quickly, followed by my mom.

I jump up, ready to act normal, when it hits me — she just responded to what Fortuna said. My mother looks completely unfazed and smiles warmly at the goddesses, as if they are old friends coming over to visit. The goddesses in turn look an odd mix of shocked, terrorized and awed.

"Wait," I say, "you can see them?"

"Yes." She nods around the circle. "Fortuna, Venus, Flora." There are titters from around the room as she acknowledges them.

I feel a blush rise in my cheeks. I'm not sure if it's from embarrassment for thinking that for once in my life I'm experiencing something special. Then again, I'm sitting here chatting with three goddesses. How is this *not* special?

"So can you explain how we can see them, Mom?" I want to look her in the face, but at the moment, I'm too unsettled to try. If she had known this day would be coming couldn't she have warned me? Maybe a 'You might be seeing a goddess or two here and there. Don't panic.' Or even, 'Don't worry if you see people walking around in togas, people that no one else can see. You aren't crazy.'

I look up and see her regarding me uneasily.

"I wish I could have warned you. But I wasn't expecting you to just stumble upon all this." She takes a half step forward. "What would you have said if I told you that we have the ability to see past the veil? That we can see and converse with beings that no one believes even exist?"

She has a point there. I'd have thought she was messing with me or that she had finally lost her mind.

"So that's what all that was about this morning." It makes more sense now.

She gives me a big hug. "No, that was because it's your birthday."

"Oh."

Mom has the habit of overcompensating, and the breakfast feast would have made more sense. Then something else flitted into my consciousness. That scarf.

I lever myself up and stalk to the window and throw it open. "Hey! You up there! I know you're still up there!"

"Who are you talking to, honey?" Mom is looking a little concerned now. "Was someone out there this morning?" She clamps her hand down on my shoulder as she tries to drag me back.

Venus puts her hand on my mom's shoulder, making us look like a strange, and extremely short, conga line. "Wait. Do you have a dryad in your tree?" She moves past us and leans out, twisting to look up into the branches. "You! Make yourself known!"

A hand slowly snakes out from the leaves and gives Venus a very offensive gesture.

"Why, you little—"

Fortuna and Flora both keep a restraining hand on the incensed goddess as Flora explains, "Venus and nymphs don't get along."

The spluttering goddess snorts. Looks like they made the understatement of the year. Time to talk about something else.

"So... I can see and talk to goddesses..." Good one, Ava. Not obvious at all.

My mom smiles at me and steers me back toward the bed and sits me down. "I'm sure you're curious about the how and the why of your abilities."

Well, duh! "Yeah, I'm a little curious." And I'm also curious about that weird golden sheen I see shimmering around her. That's never happened before. What the hell is going on here? Something weird, that's for sure.

I settle back to listen to this. I have the feeling that it's going to be one hell of a story.

"Now, ladies, if you will please excuse us. We have some mother-daughter things to discuss."

My jaw drops. I know my mom can be a bit pushy at times, but she just told *goddesses* to leave.

What's even more amazing? They obey.

Chapter Four
Papa Was a...Roman God...

"Jupiter is your father."

Mom's words echo over and over in my head. As in 'I smite thee with thunderbolts', King of the Gods, Jupiter?

Wow.

I'm stunned. For a second, I'm not even sure where I am. Then, gradually, my senses start to realign. I'm aware that I'm sitting. That I can't move. That I am in complete and utter shock.

That story my mom told certainly was a humdinger. I mean, I was expecting it to be good, but wow. I'm still trying to wrap my mind around it.

Okay, so, what I got from the story was that Mom was out one night with some friends. They went to a club, had a few drinks, then in walked this guy. This perfect man. The strange thing is, she can't give me any specifics about him except that he's perfect. Anyway, they chat, have a few more drinks, he and Mom...do stuff that I'd rather not think about and *voilà*, here I am with freaky powers.

I'm having a hard time putting thoughts together. At the moment, they whirl around my head something like this— Mom had sex!

Ew!

My mom had sex with a god!

Ew!

My father is a god!

Wow!

Wow! Just plain wow!

And round and round they go. Chasing around in my head.

And here I thought life couldn't get any stranger.

I'm alone in the room. I remember vaguely that Mom said she's going to leave me with my thoughts for a little while. Something about giving me time to digest the info. I definitely need it.

I also need confirmation. This is just all too fantastic to be believed. Unbelievable. Totally and utterly.

I look up toward the ceiling. "If you guys are around, I really could use someone to talk to right now."

The words are barely out of my mouth before I feel shifting on the bed. The goddesses are back. And they look almost as confused and stunned as I feel.

"I'm guessing you three heard everything."

Nods from all around the bed.

"Is it true?"

Fortuna speaks first. "It must be. We could see the glow on her. It's something that only happens to those…touched by Jupiter. And why else would you be able to see us? Plus, Jupiter is the only one who can hide you and your powers." She stops and appraises me with something that looks like reverent awe. "But why wait until now to let them manifest?"

The other two are nodding, Flora more than Venus. Both are as wide-eyed as Fortuna.

I want their input too, so I ask for it. "What do you two think?"

Flora's green eyes get even bigger and her nodding gets more vigorous. I guess that means she's accepted the story as fact. Venus, on the other hand, is still nodding slowly as she assesses me. Will I pass the Venus test?

"Venus?"

She runs a pink nail over her lips and looks like she's in deep thought. And I mean *deep* thought.

"I don't know. What if it was another god playing around pretending to be Jupiter? It's not unheard of and it would be easy enough to do." She looks me up and down again, raking those amazing blue eyes over me. "The glow on your mother looks convincing, though."

The other two start nodding at that.

"So how do we find out for sure?"

There's a moment of silence before Fortuna jumps up. "Okay. I have a couple of ways of finding out." She waits until she has our undivided attention before she continues. Not like our attention was anywhere else at the moment. Trust Luck to be such a drama queen. "First way is to go to Jupiter and ask him. Which, I'll admit, is easier said than done. We'll probably get fried before we get anywhere near him, but—"

I stop her right there. "Getting fried isn't on the list of things I want to do with my life right now. What's the other option?"

"We can wait to see if Juno tries to kill you. It stands to reason once she finds out, and she will because she always does, that she'll treat you like all the other fruits of her husband's affairs."

How in the world did she say that so calmly? I remember from Ancient Civilization class the stories of Jupiter and his numerous infidelities and his wife Juno's reactions. I shudder. Wonderful.

"Right. Let me get this straight. So either I get fried by my dad, or I get killed in some horrible manner by his wife? Fantastic. Anyone else have any ideas other than crazy Luck Lady?"

"I have an idea."

I look at the beautiful Goddess of Love with pleading eyes. "Please tell me it doesn't have anything to do with me dying."

"Of course it doesn't," she coos. A pair of Bulgari sunglasses materialize on her head. Venus tips them into place as she snaps her fingers.

* * * *

So after doing the little post-space-time-hopping-steppity-step yet again, I find myself standing on the beach staring out at the wide expanse of blue-green sea. In the bright daylight, it looks like a gigantic jewel glittering before me. Is this real? The sun warms my skin. The sand squishes between my toes. The temperate water laps at my ankles. Amazing. I've always wanted to go somewhere like this. It's like a dream come true.

Around us, people are going about talking, drinking, sunning themselves. Not one of them seems to notice our arrival. Where are we? Southern France? Yes, I think so. My smile gets bigger.

Venus looks right at home and finds herself a lounge chair. "I figure, why fret when we can be having fun?"

I like the way this goddess thinks. The rest of us find chairs and arrange ourselves artfully on the loungers while Venus waves her hand at an eager waiter. He hurries away and quickly returns with colorful drinks.

"Couldn't you have just snapped us some drinks?" I ask.

"This is much more fun." Grinning, Venus watches the waiter walk away.

Good point. Well made.

We sit silently soaking up the sun until he comes back and distributes the drinks. The attention he's getting from Venus is embarrassing. Well, for me. He looks like he's died and gone to heaven. He winks at her and saunters away.

"I have to agree with Venus on this one. Fabulous idea." Fortuna sips at a drink, an overly tropical looking one complete with umbrella, stirring stick thing, multiple shades of red and orange...and I'm pretty sure I see a plastic monkey topping off the concoction. She's grinning as if this place was all her own doing.

"Absolutely." I take a nice long sip. "It's going to take some getting used to." I'm sure the smirk on my face gives me away. I'm loving this. "Maybe we should make this a regular thing. Maybe we go skiing in the Alps tomorrow?"

Flora splashes me with a wicked smile "Don't get too used to this. It won't happen often."

I'm not going to push it. Like Venus says, I want to enjoy this while I can. I could just lie here like this forever—I really could. Who wouldn't want to just lounge in the sun all day while watching beautiful people stroll by? Then again, not everyone is like me. And unfortunately, I may have an enraged goddess ready to unleash unspeakable horrors upon me.

Time to change the subject. I lift my glass to take another sip, inadvertently blinding myself when the sun glints off it. There's something…in the sunlight… Before I think about it, I open my eyes to get a better look, but immediately regret it. I close my eyes to try to ease the pain, and that's when I notice a silhouette burned into my eyes. In the middle of the sun, I clearly see the form of a man on a chariot.

Just as I go to open my eyes, I feel the sensation of very warm hands closing over my ankles. It actually feels quite nice until they start sliding upward.

I let out a little shriek and kick my legs, a heartbeat away from jumping up and doing the heebie-jeebie dance.

"Ava? What's the matter?"

I'm getting strange looks, and not only from the goddesses.

My heart's slowing now that the phantom hands are gone. I think in the future I'll be using an umbrella on the beach. "Um, are the stories about Apollo's… womanizing true?"

The three of them nod, all looking like they are remembering something pleasant. I don't even want to know.

"Did he just try something on you?" Venus looks equal parts amused and put out.

I shake my head. I'm not going to let some letch of a god ruin my vacation. "Let's just enjoy our time here."

"Absolutely," agrees Venus. We turn to see her lapping up the attention from several men as they make their way past.

Fortuna rolls her eyes, as if she is contemplating throwing her drink over the Goddess of Love. Instead, her expression turns thoughtful and she snaps her fingers. Two men walk into palm trees as they gawk at Venus. Another falls into the pool. Looking particularly pleased with herself, Fortuna settles back and resumes sipping from the umbrella decked drink.

"You never let me have any fun." Venus is pouting now, gaining even more attention. "I should get going. I have a million things to do." She stretches languorously, eliciting even more reaction. I can almost hear the choking gasps from the men within the vicinity. She gets out of her seat slowly. Venus knows that all eyes are on her and she milks it for all it's worth. Finally, she winks at me. "I'll see you again soon." With a flash, she's gone.

I take a quick glance around, wondering if anyone noticed her quick getaway. Surely, with everyone gawking at her, someone must have seen it. But there is nothing. Not even a glimmer of confusion or fright.

Flora hops over a little wave, giggling like a little girl. "Don't worry. No one has noticed a thing. Just a little trick we can do."

"Like a sort of god cloaking device, eh?" I giggle to myself at their looks of confusion. "Never mind. As long as no one sees and comes asking questions or bearing pitchforks, I don't care." I let myself relax completely. Thanks to my surroundings, I'm able to let go of my worries and just live in the moment. It feels wonderful.

"It's nice to see that you've finally relaxed." Fortuna opens one eye and looks at me.

"What are you talking about? I wasn't that stressed to begin with."

"I meant that after learning about…all this…you got a little wound up."

"Wouldn't you?" I flip onto my side to face her, fully aware of some admiring glances I'm getting. I could definitely get used to this. "But now that I've seen the perks, I can say very truthfully that I'm okay with it."

"It's not going to be all fun and games, Ava. As the daughter of Jupiter, things are bound to get a little sticky for you."

Why does she have to get so foreboding all of a sudden? It is not what I want or need to be hearing right now. "I don't want to think about that. Can't you just let me have a little fun before I get so bogged down with horrible things happening to me that I can't enjoy myself?"

Fortuna shrugs. "If that's what you want." She takes another mouthful of her drink and smiles. It's a little forced, but at least she's making an effort. "So, what would you like to do now? Are you bored with this scene yet?" She appraises the scene with jaded eyes. Almost as an afterthought, she starts snapping her fingers. In the aftermath, there are a slew of people suddenly very happy or very sad.

Nuzzling the fluffy towel on my chair, I shrug. "I don't know." What should we do next? Where could we go? I have to make the most of this opportunity if it's not going to happen often. The possibilities are buzzing happily in my brain. The Great Wall? Eiffel Tower? Excitement bubbles through my system. Then another thought enters my devious little mind. "Can we... Can we see what other people are doing?"

Flora is fiddling with a pretty flower, coaxing a dozen more to bloom. "Why do I get the feeling that a certain boy is about to become part of our day?"

"Stop it, Flora." Fortuna frowns at her. "You know what infatuation is like. You want to be with them all the time. And if you can't, then you want to know what they are up to."

"Borderline stalking, if you ask me," grumps Flora.

Fortuna gives me a look that says 'ignore her', so I do.

The weird thing is, I would have expected it to be the other way around. Fortuna should be the one against me stalk—I mean, wanting to be near Noah while Flora, Goddess of Things You Give to People You Love, should be on my side. Go figure.

"Can you do it? Can we see what he's doing?" She's got my full interest now. What would Noah be up to? I'd bet it was something utterly cute.

"Let's take it one step further. I'll take us to him." Fortuna has her hand up and ready to snap, but stops to look at Flora first, waiting. "Come on, Flora, this will be fun! Come on!" The brunette sighs and rolls her eyes in acquiescence.

The beach winks out of existence, and instead of white sands and glittering water, I'm greeted with a neat lawn and gray siding. I'm assuming, yet again, that we are on Noah's lawn since he was the last thing we were talking about. Peeking in through the window I see that I'm right. Noah's in there gathering his things for soccer practice. Oooh, maybe I'll get to see him play. I'm tingling from the thought alone. What am I going to be like if I get to see him on the field?

"Can he see me?" It wouldn't be great for my reputation to be caught peeping. Both goddesses are shaking their heads at me. Good, because I want to see more. I know I'm acting like a stalker, and if Beth was here with me right now she would be railing at me for being so obvious. But there's nothing obvious about being invisible, now, is there? So no worries there, then.

Noah is digging around under the bed looking for something. After a minute he retrieves a cleat...and a crusty looking sock, which he summarily tosses over his shoulder. Gross. It takes him a few minutes, but he soon gathers all his gear and shoves it into a duffel bag. I bounce from foot to foot, getting excited thinking about soccer practice. A couple of hours watching guys running and getting sweaty—sounds like time well spent to me.

My pleasant reverie is interrupted when Noah tugs his shirt off. Eyes wide, I press my face up against the window. *Come to Mama!* A hand covers my eyes and drags me back. "Hey! Wait a sec!"

I tear at the hands. When I finally get them off, I see Fortuna shaking her head at me briefly before I'm snuggling up with the cold glass again. Unfortunately, Noah has already swapped T-shirts. Not an ab left in sight.

"Damn it, Fortuna! You made me miss it!"

I hear her mumble something, but I'm happily watching Noah again, letting my eyes trail over his very fine form from the top of his head right down to his feet. That's when I notice a silver strand trailing from his foot. It gleams and shimmers even though there's no direct light on the room.

I tug at the nearest goddess' sleeve. "What's that?"

Flora suddenly gets interested as well and the two shove me out of the way while they get a look. Whatever it is they see, it must be pretty fascinating. They turn to stare at each other and start a furious, but near silent, debate. There's a quick glance at me, wild gesticulation and more arguing. I don't think that they want to tell me what's going on. I'm not giving them the choice not to.

Stepping forward, I cram myself in between them. "What's wrong?" The thread trails behind him, disappearing through the wall. "What's that thread thing attached to him? Where does it go? What does it do?"

Fortuna is glaring at Flora and vice versa. Neither appears like they care to explain.

"Fine." I turn around and start walking toward Noah's front door.

"What are you doing?" The two goddesses latch on to my arms and drag me back.

"I'm finding out what that is. If you're not going to tell me, I'll just have to figure it out myself." Brave words, but I'm worried. It has to be something bad if they refuse to talk about it. "Is there something wrong with Noah? Is something going to happen to him?" My chest tightens uncomfortably.

The hands that are clenched around my arms loosen immediately. Instead of biting into my flesh they become gentle, almost like a caress.

"Those..." Fortuna is fighting to find the words. "Those strands are... They lead to... They... It's Morta."

The name is familiar. I know she's a goddess and she's linked to two others...the Parcae. The Fates. The goddesses attributed with giving and taking life. I quickly wrack my brain for any info I have on them. The three Fates were supposed to be the ones who created the thread of a person's life, Nona spun it, Decima measured it, then Morta cut it when it was time for them to die. My jaw drops. Morta. If I recall correctly, she chooses how the mortal dies when she cuts the thread. And she's about to cut Noah's.

My stomach is now somewhere in my shoes as I stare at the goddesses. Their bleak faces tell me that I have come to the correct conclusion.

"You have to stop her! What's Noah done to deserve this?" Frantic, I break away from them and run to the door. I hear them say something about it being his time, but I'm not listening.

I dash up the stairs and into the house before they can say another word. Noah's mom is in the living room, dusting one of the many little knick-knacks decorating the place. For a moment, I just stand there waiting for her to scream and kick me out of her house for barging in uninvited. But there is nothing. No reaction at all. She continues attacking the dust like she's scourging the delicate porcelain cats of evil. She's petite and pretty, but that's about all I have time to observe as I run past. If she notices me, she doesn't make it obvious, which I'm sure she would if she was a normal human being. What kind of person would calmly clean while some maniacal girl comes charging into the house? I'm taking the fact that she's not screaming and calling the police as a good sign and I plow ahead. I hurry, though, giving her a wide berth. Don't want to antagonize her, do I? In the hall I pause to count doors to figure out which one he's behind. It takes a split second for me to go for Door Number Three.

Noah jumps back when I kick the door open. Guess he was just on his way out.

"Ava?"

I hear his voice somewhere in the background. It also occurs somewhere in the back of my mind that he sees me. But my entire being is focused on the silver thread at his ankle. It glimmers for a moment, then steadily grows brighter as I watch. I pounce on it, gripping it in my hands. I have no idea what I'm doing, but I've got to try. I know that pleading won't help. Morta has a job to do and my sniveling won't stop her. Instead, I find myself praying, beseeching her mentally, maybe even aloud, I don't really know at this point. All I know is that I will do anything as long as she doesn't take his life.

Flora and Fortuna are on my arms again, trying to pull me away from the thread, but my hands have convulsed around it. I couldn't let go if I wanted to. My fingers start to go numb, cold. They tingle, like the life is slowly being drained out of them. Still, I cling to it.

The tingling intensifies. I close my eyes against the searing ache. I hear Noah calling me now, his voice joining the other two. It comes to me through a haze, like I'm hearing it from far away or through cotton a mile thick. I find myself vaguely wondering how he knew I was there. My consciousness narrows until all I know is the pain in my hands as it razors up my arms. Just as I reach the limit of my pain threshold, it stops.

That's when I open my eyes and am greeted with the blackest, deepest, scariest eyes I have ever seen in my entire life.

"Ava Goddard."

I have never heard my name said in such a terrifying way. Morta's voice is cold, hollow and raspy. Then again, what did I expect? We are talking about the Goddess of Death here.

I fall back onto my butt, too scared to even register the throbbing that results from the movement. I'm too focused on the figure before me to care about anything else. Well, almost. I stand up and wipe the stones off me. That's when I notice we're in some sort of cave. I'm assuming it's a cave. It's dark and dank and everything is echoing, so I'm thinking it's safe to assume we're in a cave.

Her eyes are still on mine when I finally gather the courage to look at her again, and they become the center of my universe for a moment. There is so much to be found in them that I'm mesmerized.

"You have interrupted my task." Her hollow voice holds no malice. She is simply stating a fact. The way it echoes in this place just adds to the creepiness of this whole situation.

I manage to turn away. The woman before me is old. More than old. She is hunched and frail, more so than any other elderly person I have ever seen. A strong puff of wind would knock her over. I expected the hands still clutching Noah's thread to be gnarled, arthritic looking. Instead, while they are not young, they are strong and dexterous as she winds the thread around her fingers as if it was no more important than a strand of wool.

It reminds me why I'm here. "Please don't cut that."

Her eyebrow rises slowly. Just one. You know that skin that forms over custard? Ever push it? Well, that's what it looks like. I'm so fascinated by the fluid formation of ridges I almost miss her question.

"Why ever not?" Her face furrows even more. This time I'm more confused than interested.

Is the Goddess of Death giving me a cheeky grin? My expression must be priceless because she creases up, laughing. It is several moments before she sobers, her eyes boring once again into mine.

"He is important to you, Daughter of Jupiter. But why? You have only known him a short time. Nothing serious." Her eyes flicker back and forth as she takes in my eyes one at a time.

My jaw slackens momentarily when she addresses me as 'daughter of Jupiter'. I recover quickly. As least, I hope I do. Of course she knows. She's probably got my thread around here somewhere. The thought brings forth a shudder. *Better think of something else.* I focus on her question. I can't explain it. From the moment I saw Noah, I knew he was special. At least, to me he was. Since then, the little time we spent together were treasured moments. "I don't know. He just is." Juvenile, I know, but there is no other way of explaining it. Besides, she's the goddess. If anything, she should be filling *me* in.

Her eyes narrow as if she is searching the depths of my mind for a more suitable answer. "You feel you have found your mate."

She nods as if she has confirmed her suspicions. I'm not so sure that's a good thing.

"So certain for one so young."

Is that hope bobbing in my chest? I can feel it lift my heart a little. "So you won't kill him?"

"I never said that." She lifts her hand to my chin and uses a rough finger to tip my face until we are staring at each other once again. "I cannot put aside his fate because of a whim."

So she was asking why he was special, eh? I can start listing things right here and now, starting with how cute he is and how the world is short of cute. But, for some reason, I know that's not the type of thing she is looking for. I'm pretty sure 'I just know' won't impress either. I'm wracking my brain for examples and reasons when it occurs to me that he saw me. Just before I was transported here he yelled my name.

I'm feeling all bubbly inside. Not only could Noah see me while the goddesses had me cloaked, but he cared enough to try to get to me even though he had no idea what was going on. For all Noah knew, he could have been killed and yet he tried to help me. There's a pinch on my chin and I realize that Morta is impatiently waiting for an answer.

"I will make it easier for you. I will take another for now."

Oh, thank God! My knees have lost their ability to hold me up and I fall back against the cold wall. "Thank you, Morta." I stop talking. I can't believe I just addressed her using her name. Is that okay? Did I just commit a deadly cosmic *faux pas*? I get the sinking sensation that she's going to kill me in Noah's stead. The way she is looking at me doesn't make me feel any better. A shiver skitters its way up my spine at the way her cold eyes regard my rigid form.

"I'm sorry — I —"

She stops my bumbling excuse with the twitch of her hand. "Enough. I will give you the chance to choose between two." Morta waves at the wall and two heartbreakingly familiar images appear. "Choose. Noah Hanson or Tess Goddard."

Everything falls away until all I hear is my heart thudding in my ears and all I see is a blur. I can't believe she's doing this. I can't breathe and I can barely see, but my eyes flick back and forth between the two images as

I try to make up my mind. How can I decide between the potential love of my life and my own mother? I feel myself stepping backward. I know it's stupid, but I need to distance myself from the images. I keep going until I hit something solid, rough. That's when my knees give out. Sliding down the wall, I prepare for the inevitable thud when I reach the floor. How do I decide?

"I think I'm going to throw up." I don't care that I've voiced it aloud. It's going to happen and I figure giving her a warning is better than not giving her the chance of avoiding me regurgitating all over her sandals.

"Choose."

By the time I reach the floor, I'm reduced to a trembling mess. Morta watches, as calm and craggy as ever. How dare she look so serene when I am agonizing over a problem that she created in the first place? The truth is I'd rather die than hurt either one of them. I would give up my life for theirs.

My brain ceases its panicked whirring.

Choking back bile, I force myself to stand up and literally stare death in the face.

"You have made your choice." There's a strange twinkle in her eyes. She already knows what I'm going to say.

"I have."

I take a deep breath and stare straight in her eyes.

"Cut *my* thread."

Chapter Five
My Morta...lity

"Very well."

Morta steps closer. With each step, a little less breath enters my lungs. My heart feels like it's going to explode. It's beating so fast, so hard. She gets close enough that I can feel her breath, scent the dank musky smell of her.

I'm shivering, and my muscles are all threatening to go on hiatus and leave me a quivering mess on the floor, but I'm still standing. Still staring Morta down.

Flora and Fortuna choose this moment to appear. And apparently they heard everything.

"Ava!" They step in front of me. As if that would help anything. The two look as though they are trying to act like a shield. "What do you want with Ava?" Even from behind I can see them shifting nervously. Looks like I'm not the only one who's twitchy around Morta.

Morta is beaming. Her twisted teeth are proudly on display as she pushes her way past Fortuna and Flora. The moment she touches them, they disappear.

I can't stop myself from backing up, pressing against the wall even more. Having Morta coming at you is scary enough without thinking of what we were just talking about. What was I thinking? She just looks too happy. Does she enjoy her work that much? The last thing I want to see is most definitely not Morta gleefully bearing down on me.

"Please, can I see my mom and Noah before you do it?" The tremble in my voice is irksome, but who can blame me? I'd like to see someone in my position smile. Hell, I'd give anything to swap places with someone right here and now just to see how they'd cope.

Instead, I stare straight ahead, knowing that she's going to ignore my request. Morta's tiny form hobbles closer. It takes me a moment to take in just what is happening. The Goddess of Death is smiling at me. Not in a scary way or a frightening way, but in a friendly way. Or at least as friendly as that face can get. She lurches forward and I close my eyes, ready for whatever comes next.

I expect blackness, maybe even pearly white gates. Instead, I get two withered, sticklike arms closing around my waist. I'm still breathing, thinking. I'm not dead.

"What are you doing?" The arms around me tighten.

"You, my dear, are quite the girl, aren't you?"

"What's going on? Why am I not dead?"

"You think I would kill the Daughter of Jupiter on the day she finds out who she is?" She snickers. "I just wanted to see what kind of cloth you were cut from."

The pain clustered in my chest eases a little. Couldn't she have asked me what kind of movies I like? You can tell a lot about a person by their choice of movies. Or hobbies. Hobbies are a good judge of a person too. No need to go scaring me to death, which would be the complete opposite of her objective anyway. I want to point this out to her, but I'm still trying to convince my lungs to take in air again.

For some reason, Mom's voice nagging about manners pops into my head. "Um, thanks for not killing me." That's polite, right? If not, she'll just have to excuse me. I'm not sure what the etiquette is for dealing with this type of situation.

"Not at all, my dear." She putters around for a moment, just walking back and forth mumbling to herself. Then she stops. "Can I get you some tea, dear? Some cocoa, maybe?" She ushers me into another room. This one looks like something that would belong to someone's grandmother. Chintz and doilies. Everywhere. What was it about women over a certain age and the need for this sort of stuff? I suppose since Morta has lived for countless millennia it makes sense that this place looks like a shrine to all things floral and lacy.

But I'm glad I'm not in that cold cavern anymore. This place is warm, homey even. It's nice. It smells of roses, cookies and cinnamon.

"Please, sit!"

I'm pushed unceremoniously into a very chintzy Queen Anne chair and a tiny bone china cup is placed in my hands. I look up and there's Morta, except she's not so scary looking anymore. In fact, she looks about as scary as my grandmother. She's even wearing a cardigan! Her formerly grotty, stringy hair is now swept up into a tidy silvery bun. A bun, a cardigan and pearls. Wow.

So what now? Here I am sitting in Morta's very nice living room trying to make small talk with someone who has power over my life. Can you say uncomfortable?

"You have a very nice home." Lame! But hey, it might get me some points.

"Thank you, my dear." She sits across from me after depositing a plate of homemade looking cookies on the doily covered coffee table. She looks at me with a curiously knowing smile on her face. "This isn't what you expected."

I shift about uncomfortably. "Well, no."

Morta laughs. It's a still a bit rough, but no longer terrifying. "All that is just an act. I prefer working from home now."

That's when I notice the basket of knitting next to her chair. At least, at first glance it looks like knitting. The balls of *yarn* are actually glistening threads like the one that had been attached to Noah's foot. They sparkle and shine in all sorts of hues. I wonder if the color means anything. She picks up a ball and uncoils a length. I see now that the threads are a lot shorter than they appear. The *balls* seem to be more like spheres holding the threads inside, like an ultra-fancy Christmas tree ornament. The moment the thread comes free from the ball, they both evaporate.

That was the end of someone's life.

It's a weird feeling to know that you just witnessed someone die. I'm glad I'm not the one doing the job. If it was left to me, this room would be filled with the little balls, and not just because I think they look cool.

Morta picks up another and does the same, then another, as if she is doing nothing more than unwinding balls of yarn.

I do my best to ignore it and sip at my tea. Mmm, nice. I pick up a cookie, quickly giving it the once-over. It looks like your traditional chocolate chip, and a good one at that. Taking a small bite, I quickly chew and swallow. It's good too. So far two for two. My confidence is returning.

"So why did you feel that you had to scare me half to death?" Another sip and bite. "I mean, why couldn't you have talked to me like this?" At least I wouldn't have nearly had a heart attack if I had been faced with a kindly cookie-wielding grandma.

"It's all about testing your character, my dear."

"Why?"

"Let's just say I was curious." Another thread is pulled. "It's been a long time since we've encountered a new child of Jupiter." Another thread. "That we know of, anyway. How did you keep it a secret for so long?"

"I have no idea. I didn't know anything until today." Or was it yesterday? I have totally lost all sense of time. Oh well, it doesn't matter. She didn't ask what day it happened, now, did she? "When I woke up, I started seeing these weird-looking people doing even weirder things. I thought I was going crazy because of stress or something."

Morta chuckles as she works. "I can imagine that was quite a shock. I find it rather strange."

"So do Venus, Fortuna and Flora."

"How did you manage to befriend those three?"

I finish off the cookie with one bite and wash it down with the rest of the tea. "We met when I was out spending my birthday money. I guess we just clicked."

"You must have more than just clicked for all three of them to want to spend time together with you. "

I'm a little insulted that she thinks there is more to it than them just liking me, but I brush it off. What am I going to do? Argue with the Goddess Who Could End

Me with A Flick of Her Wrist after I've eaten her cookie? And it was a really good cookie too. If I rub her the wrong way I may never get another one. Then again, if I irritate her, cookies will be the last thing on my mind.

So I shrug.

We sit silently for a moment. I'm looking around. She's doing her thread thing. There is so much I want to know, but I don't want to risk offending or annoying her. Do I just ask my questions? Do I wait until she wants to talk? Maybe I can manipulate the conversation so that she asks the right questions.

"Or you can just ask me."

Or that.

I smile sheepishly. Of course she knows what I'm thinking. She's a goddess. I wonder if I'm going to get any other abilities or if this is it. I can see gods and goddesses... Woo! Yes. Feel that enthusiasm. Why couldn't I have super strength or super beauty or something? You know, something useful.

"You have a charmed life and still you complain."

Morta seems to have no trouble reading my mind. And no compunction against it either. Well, to be fair, I would probably be the same. Why have a power and not use it, right?

"Give it time. You've only had one day. You never know what you will be able to do. The abilities Jupiter gifts his children with are often varied and unpredictable. You may receive more or you may have to learn to enjoy what you already have. Just be happy you have any at all."

Well, that's true. "Don't get me wrong. Seeing...all this is great. All the things I'll see and learn. The people I'll meet. It's incredible. I think it still needs to sink in." I like to think I'm quite eloquent. It's got to be pretty incredible to have me speaking in choppy sentences.

"It will soon be time for you to return home." Another thread is pulled. "Is there anything you wish to ask me before you go?"

"Is there anything I can't ask?" I'm hoping for a no-holds-barred question and answer session.

She smiles warmly. "There is nothing you can't ask."

"Yeah, but will you answer?"

Her smile grows wider. She knows I'm no fool. "I will tell you this. Your life is about to become much more interesting, but do not take your old one for granted."

"Okay, thanks." That's it? She's not going to allude to my future? Will I be a success in life? What do I end up doing? Do Noah and I end up married? *Speaking of Noah...* "Can I ask you one last question?"

Morta nods curtly. She's losing patience so I ask quickly, "How come Noah saw me? I thought I was invisible. So did the other three."

"Now that is a good question."

Morta's dark eyes narrow as she thinks it over. Shaking her head, she drops a ball back in the basket and stands.

I immediately get to my feet and go on the defensive. "What? What are you doing?"

"We have to ask him what exactly it was he saw."

She claps her hands. Noah, Flora and Fortuna appear.

"Ava!" He dashes over and pulls me into his arms. I don't think I've been in more emotional turmoil in my entire life. One second I'm sure I'm going to die, then I'm sad, angry, scared. On the flipside, I'm now relieved, thankful, elated and nervous. Put that all together and you get one very queasy girl.

"Noah." It comes out in a weak, relieved sigh as my knees give out. He follows me down and sits with me on the floor.

"God, Ava. I saw it all," he murmurs against my hair. "Why? How could you do that for me?" His voice sounds so tortured, so worried.

A small smile tickles my lips. He cares. Right at this very moment I struggle for words. How can I tell him that I care for him? On the other hand, if he can't tell from my recent actions that I'd rather have Morta take my life than his, then I don't think there is any way of telling him. "I-I had to. I couldn't—let her—you know…" Great. Now, of all times I have to get tongue-tied.

Noah doesn't seem to notice. He just holds me tighter. After a few seconds, he loosens his grip, but doesn't let go entirely. Pressing his forehead against mine, he peers into my eyes, his voice a husky whisper like he's trying to control his emotions. "You shouldn't have done that. Not for me."

He moves his face closer, and my breath hitches. Oh, my God! He's going to kiss me!

"Ahem."

We jump back, remembering that we aren't alone. Venus is with us now, bringing the grand total of goddesses watching us to four. They all have unadulterated grins on their faces, which makes my face heat up even more. Noah doesn't look so composed either. I try to pull back a little, but he doesn't seem to want to let go. Instead, he winds his arm around my waist and gazes inquisitively at the women surrounding us.

"So you guys are goddesses." It's not a question. He takes them in slowly one by one. "How is this possible?"

I'm a little fazed by this. Noah's handsome face is as calm as ever. There isn't a flicker of anything out of the ordinary in his dark blue eyes. How is he taking this so well? I suppose it helps that he wasn't seeing weird things all day long and trying to figure them out himself.

Morta's glee is barely leashed. She's almost buzzing with something that looks akin to happiness. Flora and Fortuna are looking to Venus who, in turn, is gazing at us fondly.

"Ava is the daughter of a god."

Like that explains *anything*.

Noah absorbs this and seems to take it in stride. "Sure. I'll go with that. But that doesn't explain why I can see you." I feel his entire body tense an instant before he pulls away from me a little. "You're not going to tell us we're related, are you?"

My stomach tightens as I recoil from him. *Ew! Ick! Don't say it! Please don't say it!* The idea mortifies me. That is, until I see the grins and hear the chuckles from the circle of goddesses.

"No. I am glad to inform you that you are not blood relatives."

Morta winks at me, though I barely notice because my attention has gone back to Noah.

She takes his hand and pulls him up. "How long have you been able to see past the veil, boy?"

Noah hasn't let go of my hand and he's pulling me up to stand next to him. You know those paper doll chains that you cut out? Well, we're a live version of that. At least, that's how I feel.

"I noticed weird things going on this morning."

He shrugs an adorable shoulder. Wait, can shoulders be adorable? I don't care, it's adorable to me.

"I pushed it out of my mind so I could focus on my exams. I haven't seen anything weird since."

"But you talked to me this evening," Venus chimes in. "Didn't you notice anything strange?"

"I haven't seen you before."

I get the feeling from his expression that he would most definitely remember Venus if he had seen her.

Goddess Venus disappears in a flash of hot pink light and Teen Venus is back. Noah's eyes widen when he recognizes her.

"You're Ava's cousin." His eyes narrow. "Are you really her cousin?"

"No." She smiled beautifully. "I'm sorry I had to deceive you, but it was the only way at the time. Obviously, it was a wasted effort."

I'm not sure Noah's even paying attention to her. He's got this grin on his face like Christmas and his birthday have rolled together and come early for him. "So I can see you guys, huh? What else can I do?"

I can almost feel Morta rolling her eyes. There's nothing I can say now. I wait for Morta's reaction.

"What is with kids these days? Is anything enough for you?" She stares directly at Noah. "Be thankful you have this one gift. Until I know more about you, I am unable to say whether or not you will have any more abilities."

There is a sharp clap of dry hands and I am left alone with Morta once again.

"What did you do that for?" I finally get time with Noah and I can't even enjoy it.

Her smile is waning and she's beginning to look like the sour old woman from before. "I need your undivided attention. Unfortunately, that boy is a distraction to you."

Very true, but I'm not going to admit to it. I'd rather pay attention to Noah instead of doing a lot of things. You know—class, dishes, talking to goddesses. Can I help it if I find him utterly fascinating? "What's so important that we have to talk in private?"

"I have been looking for someone like you for a very long time, Ava."

"Someone like me? What's so special about me?"

She looks a little too interested in me at the moment. There's a manic look in her eyes that's very unnerving. It starts off a chain reaction. The look creates a weird sensation in my stomach that triggers my brain, which starts up my mouth.

"Well, I know I'm different. I can see you guys. But is that really so weird?" My lips cease to flap when she holds up her hand to silence me.

"Stop."

She rubs the deep crease between her eyebrows. Can goddesses get headaches? I'm pretty sure she's got one now. Oh, my God! I've given Morta a headache!

She rolls her eyes. Of course, she knows what I'm thinking. "I won't kill you, you silly girl. At least not for something as trivial as giving me a headache." The wicked grin she throws my way would have had me quailing again if she hadn't said she wouldn't kill me. But she did say she wouldn't kill me for something trivial... So if I do something that she considers not trivial... Time to stop thinking before I end up making a bigger fool of myself.

My thoughts swell on the fact that I have the ability to give a goddess a headache. I wonder if it's natural or one of my special abilities? Talk about a talent. Look at me! I can give you a headache, so don't mess with me!

Morta hobbles around me like a wounded wolf appraising its last meal. "Yes, you are quite the mortal. I do not remember the last time anyone has offered themselves in place of another."

"So, just because I'd give up my life for my mom or my crush it makes me special? I'm sure plenty of people would do the same."

"You would be surprised at how few have," Morta says with such finality that any thought of a retaliating remark leaves my head.

"So… What does that mean?" A horrid thought goes through my mind. "You're not going to sacrifice me, are you? I know I'm a virgin and all, but you're not going to, right? Even if I am a special one?"

Thankfully, the idea seems to disagree with Morta as her nose wrinkles even more, a clear indication. "No, no. You are a tough one. That is a valuable trait. A trait that I have been looking for."

"Why? Why have you been looking for that?" My chest is throbbing almost as much as my head now. "If you don't tell me soon you'll have to start searching for someone else with those qualities, because I'm going to have a heart attack right here and now."

"Don't be silly. You are as fit as any human I have ever seen." She gives me a crafty little smile. "You think I would not know when your time is up?"

Well, duh! Look at who I'm talking to. "Sorry. I start to get overdramatic when I get anxious. Will you please tell me what this is all about before I work myself up into a frenzy?"

Morta's smile dims a little. "I need your help."

"Me? Aren't you all-powerful and all that? What would you need me for?"

"I am not the one who needs you. Mors is the one who needs help."

Mors? It takes me a second to figure out who she's talking about. I remember a small entry in a textbook about him being the personification of death. It was a tiny blurb. It's amazing I remember it at all. "Why does he need my help?"

"Mors...is complicated. He has been doing his duty for so long now that I think he has become disillusioned with it."

Disillusioned? It never occurred to me that a god could become bored with their work just like a normal shift worker could. Then again, a shift worker didn't have to do the same thing for a millennium or two. "I just thought you did what you did. You know... Just did it." How's that for a compelling argument? Morta is looking at me like I've completely lost my mind. She might even be reconsidering the idea that I'm the special someone she's been seeking. I'm not exactly sure if that's a good thing or not so I stay silent. What would she do if she figured out I wasn't of any use to her? Keeping my mouth shut, I keep a close eye on her and try not to flinch whenever Morta's face twitches.

"He is different. His job is different. His job is to be with a person as their life ebbs away. As you can imagine, it gets somewhat depressing."

No kidding. That has to be the worst job description in the universe.

"So you're telling me this because..." I swear my eyes bulge out of my head when I reach my conclusion. "You want me to take over his job, don't you? I can't do it. I'm telling you now that I can't do it. I get all weepy and queasy when I watch sad movies. What makes you think I can deal with the real thing?" My voice is getting higher and squeakier with every word. I've reached what I'm pretty sure they call hysterics now. "Please don't make me do it. Please!"

Morta is now rolling her eyes for the fourth — or is it the fifth? — time in our short acquaintance. I have a knack for exasperating the goddess in charge of ending lives. This can't be good a good thing.

"Calm down, you silly girl. I'm not asking you to take his place."

Jelly-knees time again. I pour myself into one of her overly floral chairs, taking deep breaths, all the while hoping that I don't pass out. Fainting right now would totally negate the whole 'you're a tough mortal' opinion she's got of me at the moment. Not good. *Must breathe. Keep breathing.*

"I can see that no matter what I say, you're going to take it the wrong way and go off the deep end." She twiddles her fingers at me and the room shifts. All the floral and doily mayhem melts away until I'm surrounded by bright pink. I'm back in my room. "I will contact you again soon." Her disembodied voice echoes ominously before disappearing completely.

Okay, so now I've annoyed Morta so completely she can't even stand to be in the same room with me. This can't be a good thing. And now I'm left wondering what she has planned. What could the Goddess of Death have in store for me? Images of gore and babies crying flit through my mind. It can't be that bad, right? She wouldn't do that to me would she? I mean, she said I was special. She wouldn't give someone special a job like that, right?

I'm going to give myself a headache if I keep this up. Best push it aside and not worry. At least not until she creeps into my life again.

I flop onto my bed and reflect on the turn my life has taken. Incredible. It's just soooo amazing. Now I'm squealing and kicking my pillows all over the room. How fabulous is this?

"Don't get too excited. I know I wouldn't be if I found out I was Jupiter's daughter."

Well, well, well. It looks like my fashionista, tree-dwelling stalker has decided to make an appearance.

I notice the scarf first. It drifts into the room as though it has a life of its own. It curls around the sill as a lithe figure drops into view and sits in my window. Like moonlight personified, she's slender and pale, with silvery skin, hair and eyes. She looks as substantial as mist. I could swear that if the sun shone straight in the window right now she'd evaporate. But no, the sun behaves itself and she smiles a little, cocking her head to the side as she inspects me as thoroughly as I am inspecting her.

"So you are the latest addition to Jupiter's family, eh?" Her gaze sweeps over me again.

"Apparently. What's it to you? And why are you in my tree?"

"Ooohh, attitude. Don't get all uppity yet, small fry. And it is *my* tree."

No wonder Venus doesn't like dryads. If they're all as warm and friendly as this one, it'd be a miracle if anyone did.

"I don't really want to get into a debate with you right now, okay? I've had a lot thrown at me today and I don't think that I can take any more."

She shrugs and leans back, gripping a branch with one hand. Her smile is devilish. "I just wanted to get a peek before Juno comes for you. Some excitement at last." She swings herself up into *her* tree and all is silent again.

Juno… She can't be as bad as she sounds, right? I do my best to convince myself of that.

Chapter Six
How Tess Met Jupiter

It's two a.m., and I'm online surfing the net for any information I can find about Jupiter and the rest of the gods, especially my apparently psychotic stepmother. According to my many searches, Jupiter had well over a hundred offspring by about as many mothers. Nice. You'd think that the King of the Gods would have a little more self-restraint.

Wide awake and a little too nervous to sleep, I keep up with the searching and reading. Thank goodness for Google. The more I read, the more I'm intrigued by the exploits of these figures. We looked into the stories a little in my Ancient Civilization class, but it was just a quick gloss over everything. If this was more of a part of the syllabus, I'm sure more people would be interested in the class. This stuff is better than the soap operas you get on TV. I mean, you've got it all. Love and loss, betrayal, adventures, monsters. Amazing stuff. It does get me wondering, though, about their more recent exploits. It's too bad none of them are documented. I get the feeling that it would be just as fascinating, if not more so.

Now I'm on to reading about Juno's revenge tactics. Sounds almost like a computer game, only it would be much bloodier. It seems that being married to such a persistent womanizer has given her a flare for the dramatic.

I flick through a very frightening list of stories and can't stop myself from shuddering. They just get worse and worse the further along I read. One woman wasn't allowed to give birth! How evil is that? Some of the stories seem to work out in the end, but it doesn't take away from the scariness of the initial torment. Who knows if she's learned a new trick or two in the few thousand years since she's done anything like that? She could have TV or watched the *Saw* movies... You know what? I'm a little freaked out. Who wouldn't be with someone like her after them?

I'm up and pacing now, mumbling to myself. I really don't want to be tortured. I mean, it's not my fault I'm here. I didn't ask to be born. She can do anything to me. *Anything.* She could turn me into a rock. Or throw me into the middle of the sea. Or turn me into a plant of some sort—and while having a pretty flower named after me doesn't sound so bad, it would suck to be a plant. I throw myself onto the bed and wail into my pillow, "I don't want to be a plant!"

* * * *

At about four a.m., I notice my message indicator is flashing. I roll off the bed and back into my chair.

Beth: My Life Is Now Beginning: What are you doing up?

Beth: My Life Is Now Beginning: Hello? Are you there?

Beth: My Life Is Now Beginning: Don't tell me that you partied so hard you passed out.

Beth: My Life Is Now Beginning: If you don't answer me soon, I'm coming over.

Beth: My Life Is Now Beginning: Answer me! I don't want to have to trek over to yours.

Beth: My Life Is Now Beginning: Helloooooooooooo

What am I doing up? What is *she* doing up?

Ava: What the hell are you doing up? It's four a.m.

No answer. So in the past, what, ten seconds she's fallen asleep on me? So I try again.

Ava: Beeeettthhhhhh. Wake up! I'm here!

There's nothing for a few seconds before I see a reply.

Beth: My Life Is Now Beginning: I'm here! I'm here!

Beth: My Life Is Now Beginning: I was just chatting to this guy.

Beth: My Life Is Now Beginning: He's soooo funny!

Ava: Shouldn't you be sleeping? Don't you have a final tomorrow?

Beth: My Life Is Now Beginning: Yes, but I'll be fine. I have a plan.

Ava: Oh God, not another one.

Beth: My Life Is Now Beginning: Yes and it's even better than the last one!

Ava: I shudder to think. Guess what happened to me today!

Beth: My Life Is Now Beginning: Oh, I heard all about your pizza date. I'm miffed that you didn't tell me about it right away.

Ava: Sorry, but that wasn't the only thing. You won't believe what else!

At the same moment that I hit the enter key, several things occur. First, the screen goes blank. Not the Blue Screen of Death that is the bane of every computer user. Just black. Then there was a flash like a bolt of lightning inside the computer tower and the monitor at the same time, leaving my computer a smoking mess.

"Hey!"

"And it begins." The dryad's head drops in from the top of the window. Her hair is almost long enough to brush the bottom sill.

"Go away." I tap at the tower with my finger, hoping that some, until now unbeknown, power will burst forth and fix it. Nope, nada. There is no hope for this thing.

The dryad isn't taking my hint and stays there, hanging upside down, smiling her mocking little smile. "You should have known that they wouldn't let you tell anyone. Stupid girl."

I've had it. I'm not going to take this from her. "I swear, if you don't get out of my face right now I'm going to burn down your tree and flush the ashes." But not before I punch her. I must be pretty scary because she pales even more and shoots back into her tree.

Kicking at my destroyed computer, I stomp over to the window and slam it shut. I doubt it'll do any good, but it makes me feel better.

Now what am I going to do? Besides talking to Beth, I wanted to do more research about my *extended* family. Now that's been taken away from me I don't know what to do with myself. I'm exhausted. Who wouldn't be after the kind of day I've had? But I'm not sleepy. Does that make any sense?

Despite my lack of fatigue, I flop onto my bed. With all the newfound information and all the possibilities they bring, I'm pretty sure I'm going to be up for a few days at least trying to process it all. I close my tired eyes for a moment to try to ease the ache. I snuggle closer to my pillows. They really are comfortable. Hugging another pillow, I realize that sleep comes a lot more easily than I thought it would.

* * * *

When I wake up, I'm not sure if I want to open my eyes. What's going to greet me this morning, I wonder? The goddesses? Maybe. Perhaps a monster waiting to tear me limb from limb? Unlikely, but possible. Might as well bite the bullet and just get it over with.

Cautiously, I open one eye then the other. Nope, nothing out of the ordinary so far. Everything seems to be the same. At least I think it does. I glance at my desk, ready to mourn the loss of my computer.

It's gone.

In its place is a new, very sleek computer.

I slide from the bed and dash over to it to run my hands over its glossy splendor in awe. It's beautiful. But who do I have to thank for it? I'll worry about that later.

Right now I'm going to fire up this bad boy. The computer boots up and I swear the start-up tune blaring from the huge speakers sounds like a choir of angels hailing me. I'm loving it already. The huge monitor practically engulfs me as I stare in wonder. It seems that this computer has everything I had on mine pre-implosion—plus, I see a camera and microphone. All the icons are the same. Even the wallpaper on the desktop is. Only this looks much better. I didn't lose anything, thank goodness! Just to make sure, I start clicking randomly. That's when I notice a strange little icon in the bottom corner. It blends in so well with the wallpaper that I almost missed it. It's definitely not something I had before.

The little lightning bolt seems harmless enough. I right-click on it to see if any useful information about it comes up. Nothing does. There's no name, no link, nothing.

Weird.

I leave it alone for the time being and concentrate on checking out the other icons. It doesn't take me long to try them all out. Even the games don't keep me occupied for long. I find my cursor hovering over the little image again. There's no harm in clicking, right? Hopefully whoever gave me this computer will be able—not to mention willing—to fix any damage I manage to do to it. Hopefully.

Holding my breath, I double-click.

Nothing happens. I'm not sure if I'm relieved or disappointed at the anticlimax. At least if there was some sort of activity, even if it was negative, it would have been something. Sighing, I lean back in my chair. I guess I should turn off the machine and see if I can catch Beth before her exam and talk her out of yet another brilliant plan. I check the time on the computer and see that I have enough for a shower and some breakfast.

As I get up, I notice a strange little tune coming from the computer. A quick check reveals that whatever I clicked on did do something. It seems that whatever it is just takes a while to initiate. A window pops up on the right side of my screen, stretching from top to bottom. Next a list of names appears along with corresponding avatars. It looks like the typical chat-slash-messenger program until I get a look at the names.

Apollo
Bacchus
Ceres
Diana
Fortuna

Even though the list goes on for quite a while, I stop when I see the Goddess of Luck's name and double-click. Her face immediately appears.

"Ava! Your computer's been upgraded! That was quick!"

"So you didn't have anything to do with it?"

The goddess shakes her dark mane of hair. "Nothing whatsoever."

"So what is this thing?" It's pretty obvious now, but I'm hoping that she'll take things a bit further and explain in more detail.

"It's basically an instant messaging system so that we can keep in contact easily. It was Mercury's brainchild. He's been working on perfecting it over the past little while. I think he just got sick of constantly running messages for us. No one ever thought that he was technically proficient enough to pull something like this off." She shrugs. "Who knew, eh?"

"So you have a computer too?" The thought of divine entities sitting at computers chatting to one another tickles something in my gut and I fight back a giggle.

"No, it doesn't work quite like that. I suspect that you have yours on your computer because you don't have the ability to communicate the same way we do. All we have to do is think of who we want to talk to and we can. It's mortals we can't directly communicate with. And he's got all his other duties as well." She snorts. "I bet Mercury is planning on lounging around somewhere and getting fat."

A fat Roman god? Now that would be something worth seeing. But I keep myself thinking about the present. "So I can contact anyone through this? This is great!" I scroll through, and sure enough all the names I know are listed and then some. There is one, however, that I don't see—Jupiter. "How come Jupiter isn't on the list?"

Fortuna shrugs. "You'll see him from time to time, I'm sure. He's busy and all that."

It makes sense, I guess. He must have a lot to do being who he is. "Soooo, what's up?" She's doing her job, duh!

"The usual. I was actually thinking of visiting you later. Would that be all right?"

"Of course! I have to go meet up with Beth in a bit, but you can do your thing and turn into a teen and join us if you want."

"Sounds like fun! I'll see you later then!" She gives me a grin and the window closes. This thing is so cool.

I rush through my morning routine and dash downstairs to grab something quick to eat. Mom's puttering in the kitchen again, making yet another breakfast, though nothing as elaborate as the one yesterday. This is more of a 'sorry I didn't tell you the truth' type breakfast where yesterday's was more like 'OMG, it's my daughter's birthday!' coupled with guilt and maybe a little trepidation at what I might encounter. At least, that's what I think. There's only one way to find out for sure. I have to ask her.

After sitting, I start eating, glancing every once in a while at Mom, who's eating quietly. Now I know something's wrong. The only time she's this quiet is when she's worried about something. I can understand where she's coming from. She must have been dreading the day I discover everything for a long time now. Maybe even as far back as when she found out she was going to have me. Still, she should be well prepared for this conversation. I mean, if I had been planning what I was going to say right from the beginning. I'm pretty sure I'd have it down cold.

I nibble at my toast to give her time to start a conversation. When it becomes apparent that she's not going to, I sip my juice and push my plate away.

How do you start a conversation like this? Do I just come out and ask? Do I hedge around the topic and hope that she jumps in? Considering how long it's taken her to tell me, I decide not to wait for her. It might take a couple of decades before I learn anything.

"So… Jupiter is my dad?"

I know I've been saying it over and over in my head for the past ten or twelve hours, but it still hasn't sunk in. I mean, saying it is one thing, but believing it is quite another. I know I can see Fortuna and the others and interact with them, but I don't think I can really believe the rest of it until I either talk to the god himself or my mom fleshes it out in full, *Technicolor* detail. Well, maybe not that full. But until I hear more than 'Your father is Jupiter', it's not going to fully register.

"I thought you said my father died in a car accident."

Mom clears her throat, takes a sip of her juice, and clears her throat again. "Yes. I know it was horrible of me to lie, but I didn't think you would understand. I know you must have questions about everything. It must be really confusing for you. I hate that it was all dumped on you at once."

By this point she's shredded the toast on her plate. I feel a stab of sympathy for her. This must be such a tough topic for her to broach. So I sit quietly, patiently waiting for her to continue. It takes her a little bit but once the words are out, they start to flow.

"Like I told you last night, I met your father in a club. It was my last year at university. We kept running into each other. He was so handsome that he was the object of many women's attention, but he seemed to gravitate toward me. I can tell you it was a huge boost for my ego." She smiles wistfully.

Mom isn't exactly ugly, so I'm not entirely sure why her ego needed boosting, but I keep quiet, not wanting to throw her off.

"As the night wore on, we kept meeting. At the bar. On the dance floor. It was obvious it was more than just chance that this was happening. I know now that it was all his doing, though at the time I wasn't sure if it was him or me or a combination of both making it happen. By the time the club closed we had grown close enough to exchange smiles. On the way home, my friend and I ran into a little trouble. Some guys decided to follow us."

"You walked home in the middle of the night?" This information goes against everything I know about post-clubbing etiquette. Never walk home after drinking comes in third to never driving under the influence and never leaving your drinks unattended. "That wasn't so smart."

She gives me a rueful look. "I know. And if I ever hear of you doing the same..." Her eyes narrow evilly. "Anyway, back to my story. The guys approached us and weren't going away. Your father swooped in just as things were getting hairy and saved us."

I feel like she's just described a scene out of a romance novel. "You know how clichéd that sounds, right, Mom?"

"Oh, I know. But who doesn't want to be saved by a knight in shining armor?"

I grimace but refrain from spouting feminist doctrine. "He wasn't actually wearing armor, was he?"

"Oh, heavens no!" She titters. My mother is actually giggling like a schoolgirl. "*Armani*. Very well cut Armani. Well, he walked us both home, dropping off Clara first and then me. The walk home is a moment that's imprinted itself in my mind. We hit it off right away. We talked about everything. He was so worldly, so intelligent, so handsome."

"So, what did he look like?" I know she fielded this question yesterday, but I'm trying again in case she's willing to tell me more.

"I told you yesterday, I have an image in my mind of his appearance. But other than that, I only have faint impressions besides that he was handsome."

"Didn't you find that a bit...weird?" I know I do. How can you get that close to someone and not even know for sure what he looks like? "Never mind. What do you *think* he looked like?"

"Tall, dark, handsome..." Mom would have been a good candidate to write for Harlequin. "European, which of course makes sense now." She grins goofily.

I fight to keep my eyes from rolling. "So when did you find out who he really was? How did you react?"

"He told me a few months into the relationship."

Oh, thank goodness! The last time we talked I got the impression it was little more than a one-night stand.

"He explained who he was and his situation."

"And you believed him right off the bat?"

She throws me a scathing glance. "Of course not! Who would believe such an insane story? It wasn't until he actually showed me that I believed him."

"What did he do?" I'm leaning forward, openly interested.

"Took me all over the world, did some crazy things with his powers. Enough to get me to believe him."

"You guys sounded happy. Why did he leave?"

"His life, his..."

"Wife?"

From the quirk of her eyebrows I'm guessing she didn't think I knew as much about the situation as I did. And she was a bit embarrassed.

"Yes, his wife. He left because he wanted to protect us. If she found out about you the consequences would be dire. He made sure that we would never want for anything and that I could see everything that was going on around us just in case."

Well, that explained how she was able to see the goddesses as well. It made sense. She would be able to see anything coming at us and be able to react. It still hurt that he knew about me and never once came to see me.

"I know what you're thinking. He did. When you were born, he was there. He was the first to cradle you. The first to give you a kiss. Then he was gone. I know it isn't much, but the fact that he showed up at all means a lot. Haven't you always felt secure? Have you ever worried about anything? Wanted for anything?"

It was true. I've never thought about it much, but now that I do there hasn't been anything that I couldn't get or achieve if I set my mind to it. Even though Mom took care of me on her own, I've never seen her struggle for anything. I've always had everything I needed and most of what I wanted.

The room is reeling.

"That's because of him, isn't it?"

Mom nods.

I can't believe it. I really have had a charmed life. I feel cheated. I mean, I've had everything, but I feel like it's all worthless because it's been handed to me. Am I even as smart as I think I am? What if all my life someone has been giving me the answers like at the exam? Everything I ever thought about myself is under question.

I feel suffocated. I need to get out of here. "Thanks, Mom." I get up and run outside before she can say anything else. I can't listen to any more. I can't breathe.

"Guess you've heard the story. Can't take it, eh?" The now annoyingly familiar voice came once again from the tree.

"Go away." My head is reeling. I need to hide somewhere away from all this. But where can you go to hide from divine beings?

"Just saying. You look a little piqued." There's a moment's silence. "You should know that Juno will stop at nothing if she knows of your existence."

"Yeah? Why don't you go and tell her then?" Stupid, I know, but I'm so angry I can't hold it back.

She drops out of the tree to stand in front of me. "I might. I might not." Her smile is challenging. "What's it to you?"

"You will do nothing." The voice is deep, hypnotic, and one I've never heard before.

Between us appears a tall figure swathed entirely in black. His back is to me, but from the look on the dryad's face he must be a terrifying sight. Her eyes are wide as she clamps her mouth shut and scrambles back up her tree.

The figure turns around, and I realize that the sea of black that I thought was clothing is actually a pair of wings. Gorgeous black wings as glossy as a raven's. His attire is what is expected of a Roman god — he's loosely clothed in a toga, albeit a black one. One that looks like it could be whipped off by a strong breeze. Like the statues of gods I've seen, he is the perfect male specimen. I can barely stop staring at that perfect skin. His hair is thick and sleek and his face belongs on billboards. If I wasn't so scared I think I'd be attracted to him

"Um, hi?" Stupid. Stupid. But it's all I can think of when I look at him. There's something about his eyes that just sucks me in. Their intensity, how deep and bottomless they are, makes me forget about everything else.

"I sense you are confused. Allow me to introduce myself." He bows deeply, his right hand over his heart. "I am Mors."

My eyes bulge out of my head and I feel the blood draining from it faster than soda being sucked out of a bottle by a kid. That conversation with Morta…

"How… How can I help you?" Oh God, he's come for me. I want to say something, do anything to try to gain his favor. Only I can't move and the only thing coming out of my mouth is a choked gurgle.

Mors doesn't look phased by my reaction. As a matter of fact, I think he expected it. He barely manages a shrug. "Good manners would have you invite me inside."

Nodding, still slack-jawed, I step back and motion him toward the door. I dash in after him and head him off before he reaches the kitchen. Can you imagine Mom's face if she sees him? I herd him upstairs to my room, sit him down on my bed and aim him at my TV. "Please make yourself at home." I turn on the TV and force a smile in his general direction. "Can I get you something to eat? Drink? I'm going to get something for myself so…"

"Whatever you are having. I have not indulged in mortal food in a very long time. I am interested in seeing how it has changed."

"Right." I whirl around on my heel and fly down the stairs.

Mom is waiting in the kitchen, obviously wondering what I'm up to.

"I thought you left." She sounds miffed and seems a little hurt as she slices up a freshly baked loaf of bread.

"I changed my mind. I just want to take some food and lock myself in my room for a while."

"Fine. Do you want me to make you anything?" She keeps slicing without missing a beat.

My head is already in the fridge. "No, thanks. I'll just grab a bit of everything." I figure if the food is good, then he'll have to be nice to me. Food is the way to a man's heart, right? Does that work the same for gods? I'm praying that it does.

What would he like to eat? The guy is dead scary, pardon the pun, not giving me much to go on. There's Black Forest cake, so I grab a large slice of that. Nab a little for me as well. Coke. Can't go wrong with that. So I grab a couple of cans. I suddenly have an epiphany and decide to have a little selection of cold cuts and cheese and whatever else I can find that would look appetizing on a plate together. I know I have to make it good because it might be my last meal.

"Got enough there?" I finally notice Mom peering over my shoulder at my creation. "Planning on locking yourself in your room for a week?"

I shrug and heft everything in one go. "I'm not sure what I want." I hope she accepts my explanation, but I don't look back as I run out again.

Don't want to keep Death waiting, now, do I?

Somehow, I manage to make it up the stairs and to my room without mishap. Kicking open my door, I walk in food first.

I don't dare meet his gaze for fear that I've displeased him and busy myself with placing the offering in an artful way on the bed next to him. "I've brought up a selection of things. I wasn't sure what you'd like." With everything on the bed I have no choice but to check to see if what I've brought is good enough. I take a quick glance at him through my lashes first. He seems to be appraising everything. He doesn't appear offended.

I release a pent-up breath only to feel my chest constrict again when I notice he's not going for anything.

"Um, the cake is nice. It's one of my favorites. I think I could live on that alone."

He nods absently. "I am sure it is wonderful. But I was thinking about a program I caught on that box." He motions at the TV. "It was about a group of youths...much like myself..."

I'm staring at the TV now. What in the world is he talking about? Unfortunately, there is a commercial playing. The annoyingly catchy jingle is going to be stuck in my head for the next few hours at least, I know it is. Already there's a segment of song that's repeating in my mind, making me curse Mors internally. Sighing, I turn around to ask for an explanation. What I see explains it all.

Mors, while still breathtakingly handsome, now looks only a few years older than me. But that isn't the shocking thing. His hair is now longish and straight, hanging over his right eye in a thick black spike. He's toga is gone and in its place is a black T-shirt with the sleeves sheared off and 'The Clash' emblazoned across the front. His long legs are encased in skinny black jeans and I'm pretty sure I see an earring or two flashing in his ears. And one in his perfect eyebrow.

Oh, my God! I turned Mors into an emo!

Chapter Seven
Me and My *Cousins*

Okay, I'm trying not to stare, but it's really hard not to. I mean, *really* hard. Seeing him this way isn't so scary, and even with the hair covering half of his face, he's hot. Normally, I'm not into the whole emo thing. I'm not against it per se, but why dress all dark and dreary when you don't have to? Where's the sense in that?

"Why do you presume that I am here to take you away?" He's moved on to the Coke now and twists the can this way and that, trying to figure out what it is.

Well, duh! I pick up mine and demonstrate how to open it. "You are Death, aren't you? Isn't that your job?"

He follows suit and takes a tentative sip. "Yes." The taste must agree with him, because he takes a healthy swig.

Does he really not see where I'm going with this? "So, if you're here..."

"I was curious. Morta speaks highly of you and I wanted to see you for myself."

"So you're not going to...you know?"

"No." He finishes off his can and reaches for mine.

I wait for him to get a couple of good glugs in before pressing for an answer. I'm feeling a little braver now. I guess finding out you're not about to die does that to a person.

"So what are you doing here then?" My stomach has settled enough so that I'm eyeing the food on the plate. He can't possibly eat that all, right? Judging from the way he inhaled the cake and the Coke, though I'm going with the assumption that he can and will. I don't care. I reach for a cracker and some cheese. "Do you mind?"

He shakes his head. "As I was saying, I was curious. I wanted to spend some time with the girl who turned her nose up at death."

"I didn't turn my nose up at it—you..." I watch him more closely to see if I can read him. Turns out I can't. "So... I'm guessing you know who I am?"

"Yes."

Then why the hell are we having this conversation? I'm on the verge of either strangling this guy or just running out into the street and screaming in frustration. Somehow I don't think either option will go over well with him. So I bottle it and shove a slice of baloney in my mouth, using the time it takes me to chew to calm down a little. It's working, so I repeat the motion. Hopefully he's going to leave soon, because if he doesn't and this continues, I'm going to end up the size of a heifer.

"Why are you so nervous? You have met several other deities from what I gather and have faced Morta without this fuss. What is the matter?"

Where do I begin? "Well, first of all, you're Death. The whole idea terrifies me and here you are, the one who makes it happen. In my room. A room that has never before seen a male — let alone had one in it, lounging on my bed eating and watching TV. A fact that would probably have Mom in fits. I'm stressed out by who — *what* I am, something I have to hide because Juno is more than likely going to come after me. I have a dryad in my tree who is driving me crazy and I've only interacted with her twice. And to top it all off, I'm supposed to be figuring out what to do with the rest of my life. And that's *if* I have a rest of a life to figure out. So excuse me if I'm a little frazzled!"

It felt good to let that out. But, of course, I begin to think about to whom I just unleashed it all. Mors is watching me with his black eyes, no emotion showing in them or on his face. I repeat to myself what parents are always telling their kids — telling the truth is good. Telling the truth is good!

"That is a lot to consider."

Well, yeah, it is. It's enough to have me going into meltdown.

"I would like to spend time with you and I would like to help…with at least some of your troubles. I will stay with you."

Wha… *What*? "Um, Mors. That's very kind of you to offer, but I don't think you staying with me will help matters. It might complicate things more for me." Might? Damn straight it will. How am I going to explain it to Mom? What about Noah? What's he going to think when he sees Mors hanging around me all the time? And Beth? I don't even want to think about that.

"Nonsense. It makes perfect sense." He climbs off the bed and surveys my room like he's about to do some serious redecorating. "It would be easy to rearrange things in here to accommodate me."

Has this guy got no sense of propriety? "You can't stay here. My mom will freak out. And I have no intention of letting you invade my space." I run around the room pointing at the various pieces of feminine paraphernalia scattered around the room. "This is a girl's room." I swing around with my arms extended, hoping he's looking at the things I'm trying to draw his attention to. "I don't want you messing with the mojo in here."

"Mojo… Why would I mess with such a thing?"

He's eyeing the nest of stuffed animals on my bed as if he's wondering why I would be worried he would mess with them. I can't be bothered to correct him.

"The point is, you can't live here."

"I tire of arguing with you." He gets up and shrugs, his grungy shirt shifting nicely along with the body underneath it. "I will visit again soon." He bows formally. "Thank you for the food. It was adequate." And with that he disappears in a blast of lightning and smoke.

I sag with relief and start falling onto the bed long before I realize that I'm about to dive headfirst into a plate of deli meat. Too late.

"I knew you were hungry, but I didn't know it was that much."

I sit back, peeling off a cold slice of ham from over my eyes, to find myself face to face with Mom and Beth.

"Beth came to visit." Mom pulls me up and gives me a narrow-eyed glance. "I thought I'd come up to see if you needed anything else." From the way she's eyeing the room I'm sure she knows someone else was up here. She's checking to see if they are still around and if not, if they left any traces.

Luckily, she says nothing. Beth, on the other hand, is about to burst. I give Mom a look hoping that she'll get the message. She does.

"Dinner will be ready soon. I'll call you when it's done. Do you like chicken Caesar salad, Beth?"

"Love it!" Beth gives Mom a huge grin and closes the door. The grin instantly evaporates the moment the door is closed securely. "Where were you today? You said you were going to meet me after my last exam."

"Sorry, I lost track of time." I really did! How did I spend the entire day in here arguing with Mors? Were we really in here for that long? It makes me wonder if he played with time a little.

"What's the matter? The only time you stuff your face is when you're upset. What's going on?"

"I'm not exactly stuffing my face." That's the truth, at least. With Mors around I didn't get the chance.

"Okay, so you were rolling around in your food. That's not better, you know."

There's no good way of getting around it, so I'm moving on, hoping that Beth will just go with it. "I'm sorry I didn't meet you. What do you want to do now?"

Beth picks up some bits of stray meat from my bedcovers and flicks them onto the plate. "Well, considering that your mom's almost done with making dinner, I think we should eat it. Once we're done with that, we can figure out what to do."

"Good plan." That's all I can think of saying. Seriously. My mind's a complete blank.

"Are you okay?" She puts the plate on the floor and sits down next to me. "Is this about your date last night? Did it end badly?"

The date? *The date!* It felt like I went on it eons ago. "Oh, it went great."

"Sure doesn't sound like it. And what happened last night? You got disconnected before you could tell me what happened. How come you never came back online?"

"My computer went all weird." I realize my mistake and purposely keep myself from turning to the machine in question, hoping she won't see the awesomeness that is my new computer. If she does, the questions will be never-ending.

She twiddles her fingers, flicking away my words. "Never mind all that. I want to know more about your date with Noah."

"It was amazing!" Then it occurs to me that Beth wasn't around when it all happened. "Wait a sec. How did you know?"

"I wandered around looking for you after you supposedly left. I felt guilty for leaving you alone on your birthday." She wiggles her eyebrows suggestively, "But then I found you and realized that I shouldn't have worried. You guys looked like you were enjoying that pizza." Beth bumps me with her shoulder. "Soooo… I want details. How did it happen? Was it planned? Were you just trying to get rid of me? What did you do after the pizza?"

Just focus on the stuff involving Noah, I remind myself. "Well, you know how I lost my stuff? My cell was dangling from a thread on my bag and he called me to tell me that he found the rest and wanted to meet so he could give it back. So we did, and he did."

"Yeah, but when I saw you, you were in a new outfit *and* had a new haircut."

Crap. "I quickly got my hair cut at that new place on the corner, then took a cab home, had it wait, changed, then got back in the cab and took it back out again." That's all I have to explain, right? That has got to be all of it.

She grins. "Well, you were so cute. You have to let me borrow that outfit sometime. I bet you blew his mind." Beth grabs on to my arm. "Soooo? What did you guys talk about? Did you hit it off? Are there more pizzas in your future?"

* * * *

It takes until Mom calls us to dinner for me to finish answering Beth's questions. Even then, I'm sure she had more and only stopped because we were interrupted. Dinner is quick and painless, though Mom keeps studying me strangely. Beth seems oblivious an only appears to care about hoovering her food so that we can get out of there so she can interrogate me more.

Finally, we escape from Mom and head back upstairs to formulate a game plan.

"So what do you want to do?"

That's strange. Beth is usually the one with the plan. What's going on? I narrow my eyes at her. "What are you up to?"

The expression that comes over her face is way too angelic. I get the feeling that instead of the halo that just blinked into existence over her head it should be two horns sprouting from her forehead.

"I was thinking we could go and find Noah."

"What? Why?"

"I want to see what you two are like together."

"Are you serious? You watched us last night."

"For about five seconds. I'm not a voyeur, you know."

I don't understand why she wants to see us together. What would watching us accomplish? What is she hoping to see? Besides, I'm a little too off my game right now to even attempt spending time with Noah. I was hoping to sit and talk to him about what happened last night. That was a conversation I didn't care to share with anyone. I don't think he'd want to talk about it in front of others either. Time to think of something to distract her.

I hear a knocking at the door downstairs, Mom's surprised voice greeting someone and some quiet murmuring.

"Ava! You have another visitor! I'm sending her up!"

"Thanks!"

Beth gives me a questioning glance. Like I know who's here. I'm not psychic...yet... I don't think.

We wait in absolute silence for the few seconds it takes for whoever it is to make it up the stairs, as if we would be able to divine who it is from their footsteps alone.

"Ava?" The voice drifts through the door just as it swings open. "It's me." Teen Fortuna steps into the room.

"Hey..." What do I call her? The name Fortuna sounds a bit weird. But then again, there are plenty of weird names out there. What about the poor kids who are blessed not only with celebrity parents, but also with their choice in unique nomenclature? Those poor schmucks are named after fruit and deities... Hell, if they can, then why can't she? "Fortuna! How's it going?"

"Great!" Apparently Fortuna favors leather. Like last night, she was poured into another tightly stitched, shiny outfit. This time it's motorcycle chic—black leather jacket and pants. She's foreboding even with the sunny smile on her face.

She turns to Beth, who gets up and extends her hand. "Hi, I'm Beth Coolidge."

"Fortuna."

They shake hands.

"Hippie parents?"

"Something like that."

Beth grins. "So how do you know Ava?"

I've been trying to think of a cover story since the moment Fortuna walked into the room.

"I'm her cousin."

Well, I guess that's that. Another cousin. At this rate I'm going to end up with dozens of cousins that I can't explain, all with hippie parents. Fantastic. Pointless getting all bent out of shape right now, though Beth seems to accept it. I'll freak out when torrents of my *cousins* show up.

"So what are you two up to?" Fortuna eyes the plate of meat I'd forgotten about curiously before sitting on the bed next to me.

"I'm trying to talk Ava into meeting up with her boyfriend." Beth turns to me. "With Fortuna here, I won't be a third wheel. It's perfect. We'll make it a little outing. How about the amusement park?"

Fortuna's eyes light up. "Fun!"

Great, now I've got two of them. I shudder to think what kind of stuff Fortuna can get up to at an amusement park. But then again, with her on our side we could probably win all the games and get on all the rides in record time. It's very promising.

"It does sound like fun," I hear myself saying.

"That's settled then!" Beth is up and bounding around the room. "Call Noah! I'm going to raid your closet for some proper fun park attire."

That's nothing new. "Help yourself." I pick up the house phone and look at it. "How am I going to call him? I don't know his number."

Fortuna gives me a wry smile and looks at my bag. "He called you yesterday, remember? His number is on your phone."

"Oh, yeah. Thanks!" I grab my bag up from the floor and dig through it.

"How did you know, Fortuna?" Beth's voice is muffled from the depths of my closet. She's gone deep inside. We'll probably have to get a spelunking team together to find her now.

"Ava told me last night."

I roll my eyes at the Goddess of Luck as she shrugs and mouths, "It's the best I could come up with."

"She told you?" Beth's head peeks out from inside the closet and she eyes me semi seriously. "And you couldn't take five minutes to tell your best friend?"

I give Fortuna a 'Now you've done it' look then turn to Beth. "It would have taken more than five minutes, and you know it."

"Yeah, that's true. And your computer went all mental on you, blah blah blah." Beth plunges back into my cavernous closet. Her voice muffled, Beth adds, "Besides, you've told me now, so it doesn't matter."

Thankfully, the matter is dropped and I manage to relax a little. I give Fortuna a warning glance, willing her to keep quiet and to take my lead. She nods. It's a good thing that one of us is psychic.

A loud chime rings and I look at the leather-clad goddess next to me. What the hell was that?

She jerks her head toward the computer. "*Someone* is trying to communicate with you."

The way she says someone leads me to the only conclusion that makes sense. A god is trying to talk to me and Beth is here.

Fortuna waves me toward the computer and saunters toward the closet. "Hey, Beth. Need some help? Ava's closet is like the abyss. You could be lost in there for days." She winks at me and plunges in.

At this moment, there is no one in the world I love more than Fortuna. I run to the computer and turn on the screen. There's a blinking box with no one in it. There's no way of telling who's there without actually seeing them. So I hazard a conversation.

"Hello?" I don't dare say it too loud. Otherwise, Beth, who has the ears of a bat, will hear and come running, full of more questions.

"Ava?" Flora appears from the bottom of the computer screen and grins, her nose smudged with dirt or something. She sees me and waves. "Hiya. I was wondering if you want to do something. I finished with Spring here and have nothing to do."

"Fortuna and I are going to go to a theme park with my friend, Beth—"

"Great! I'll join you!" The window disappears and Flora is standing next to my desk. "I can't wait!"

"Shhh!" I clamp my hand over her mouth. "My friend's here—"

"Who's that?" I'm not sure if Beth is asking me or Fortuna, but I can hear someone trying to get out of the closet.

"Beth, wait! I think I found the perfect pair of jeans to go with that top you love!" Fortuna is doing her best to keep her distracted, but Beth's like a pit bull. Once she's got her teeth into something, there isn't much that's going to dissuade her.

Too late. Beth's out and staring at Flora, who luckily heard her coming and switched to teen mode. "Your room's like grand central station today, Ava." She smiles and extends her hand. "Hi, I'm Beth. Ava's friend from school."

"I'm Flora."

Don't say it. Don't say it!

"Ava's cousin."

Beth shakes her hand while she smirks. "You guys' family really has a thing for unique names, eh?"

Flora turns to me with a questioning expression on her face as Fortuna steps out.

As comprehension dawns on Flora, I nod. "You remember Cousin Fortuna, don't you, Flora?"

"Of course!" She gives Fortuna a quick hug. "It's been quite a while."

"Yet it only seems like yesterday," Fortuna replies sardonically.

We haven't even left yet and I'm already ready to collapse. I've never lied to Beth ever. *Ever.* Even if I wanted to, she could see right through me. It's amazing I've gotten this far without her jumping all over me. How am I going to keep this up for an entire outing?

Flora is running around my room taking another look at everything while Beth is still rummaging through my closet. What is she hoping to find in there? The Hope Diamond? The secret gateway to Shangri-La, perhaps?

Fortuna pulls me aside. "Are you okay? You seem a little tense."

"Wouldn't you be if you had to hide the biggest thing that has ever happened to you from your best friend? I don't know if I can do this. I'm already frazzled. I don't think I've ever been this messed up in my entire life."

She gives me a questioning peek.

"Mors was here earlier. He was already working at my nerves before Beth showed up. Now I have to pretend that you two are not only my cousins, but regular girls as well. I'm not good at hiding things and I'm not good at lying and I'm certainly not good with dealing with too many surprises all at once."

Somewhere in the middle of my speech, Fortuna hugs me. I'm not sure when, but by the time I'm done and practically sobbing on her shoulder, she's got her arms around me. It feels nice. Like she's absorbed into herself all the negative energy I'm emanating.

"Would you like me to send Beth away? Just until you get to grips with everything? I can make it so that she doesn't even miss you."

"You would do that?"

"Easily."

I think it over. It doesn't seem fair, but if Fortuna can make it so that Beth doesn't even realize we've had time apart it would give me time to work out a story and get used to everything. I think that's what the problem is. Everything is just too new and weird and wonderful. Once I've settled down, it should be much easier to deal with her *and* everything else that is going on.

I find myself nodding. "Please. But only for a little while. I feel guilty for doing this."

"Don't. Beth will be fine."

She snaps her fingers and I no longer hear any noises coming from the closet.

"What did you do with her?"

"Nothing really. She'll go about her daily routine and act normally only without the memory of you for a little while. When you are ready I'll return everything. She won't realize anything is amiss."

I find myself breathing a little easier. "Thank you." I inhale deeply and shake out my arms, willing the tension to leave me. It helps a little but I still feel like I'm wound up tighter than the bun on Morta's head.

"Not a problem. So are you still up for some fun at the amusement park? I'd bet you could use it."

I nod. "It sounds like fun. And I really could use some fun right about now."

"No problem."

We both look over at Flora and I notice that she's got my cell phone. She gives me a little smile and sets it down. Her 'I haven't done anything' look doesn't fool either one of us.

I bite. "What did you do?"

Flora seems to be considering several different stories in her head. Her eyes are shifting from side to side as though she's playing out the different scenarios in her mind. Finally she shrugs and says, "Noah will meet us there after soccer. Practice will be ending soon."

At least one of us has initiative.

Chapter Eight

So Two Goddesses, a Demigoddess and a Boy Walk
into an Amusement Park...

I can't remember the last time I went to the amusement park. No, wait. That's a lie. I remember the last time I was there very vividly. I'd just managed to block out the whole experience.

I was six years old, and after having spent a day waiting in lines that hadn't seemed to move, my cotton candy had been knocked to the ground by some big kid goofing off. It had taken all my persuasive abilities to get that thing—the hours of pleading, pouting and eyelash-batting that went into getting Mom to buy me one, it had been exhausting... Finally, near the end of our day, she had bought me the biggest, fluffiest mass of spun sugar I had ever seen. I had just taken the first amazing bite and was letting the sweet goodness melt on my tongue, when out of nowhere this teen ran into me. In slow motion, I watched my pink sugar cloud sail through the air and land in a suspicious puddle, only to dissolve into nothingness right before my eyes.

The crying. Oh, how I cried. I don't think I've ever been more upset before, or since. By the time Mom managed to get me another one, all they had was blue and they weren't making any more since the park was going to close. I had eaten it grudgingly. It just wasn't as good as the pink one. Mom had also managed to get me on one of those rides where you sit in various flying animals and it whips you up and down to simulate a real aerobatic experience.

Unfortunately, all the crying and the vigorous shaking coupled with a belly full of sugar hadn't been the best combination. The moment Mom lifted me out of the sparkly lavender elephant I had been sitting in, I relinquished the tenuous hold I had on my stomach — all over Mom.

So, yeah. Never went back.

We walk past the very ride that it happened on and I can't help but cringe. The two goddesses with me smile sympathetically.

"Come on. We're going to have some fun." Flora threads her arm through mine and leads the way through the crowd.

The sights and sounds are all the same. The smell of hot dogs and onions mingles with the scent of grease from the enormous machines. The sounds of laughter, screams and the squeals of the machines aren't unpleasant. I think that today is going to be exactly what I need. I'm already relaxing…a little. As long as nothing goes heinously wrong and I don't throw up on anyone, I'll be good.

We wander along, looking at the rides and games. Fortuna is snapping up a storm as we go, leaving a mix of happy and disappointed people in our wake.

At about her millionth click, she sighs. "That's it. It's my turn to have a little fun."

It's this moment that I know we're in for something entertaining.

Fortuna leads the way to the rows of booths, ignoring the shouts and entreaties of all but one booth operator. The Ring a Bottle. The three of us line up and Fortuna hands the man some money.

"Thanks, darlin'. All you gotta do is throw a ring around the tops of one of those bottles. The gold ones are worth the most an'll get you one of them." He points at the gigantic, wildly colored animals hanging from the roof of the booth. "You've got five chances." He proudly displays five dingy green plastic rings.

"Yeah, yeah, yeah. Give me the rings." Fortuna's on a mission. She smiles at us and makes a feeble throw that ricochets off the bottles closest to us.

"Too bad, darlin'. Try throwin' a little harder."

How's that for genius advice? Fortuna screws up her face like she's concentrating really hard on this next throw. She sends it too far, earning another tut of disappointment from the carny.

"I think I've figured this out now," she says to the man. Fortuna deftly flicks the ring and it lands right over the gold bottle. "I did it!" She sounds fake even to me.

The man looks surprised, but nods. "Good shot! Two more, darlin'."

Flora shakes her head. "Hey, you said if she gets a ring on the gold bottle she gets a prize."

"Yes..." His eyes narrow. He knows where this is going.

"Well, give her one." Despite her innate cuteness, Flora is pretty scary right about now. The scowl on her face shows she means business.

They are playing with the man. They could have easily clicked their fingers and gotten him to do what they wanted. Hell, we didn't even have to be here to win prizes. It dawns on me that this is what they do for fun. Act human. I can't stop the smirk from spreading over my lips. It *is* fun. At least, it is for me. The booth guy doesn't look like he's enjoying himself so much.

He patiently asks which crazy stuffed animal thing Fortuna wants and gets it for her. She sets her new blue unicorn next to her and settles in for another toss. He's pretty confident that it's the only one he'll be losing to us.

He thought wrong. Fortuna quickly dispenses with the other two rings, winning another two animals, a pink and green panda for Flora and a purple and fluorescent green spotted snake for me. He chucks them at us and shoos us away.

We smile, thank him politely and walk away. He should be happy. At least with us displaying these the way we are, people will know that the games really are winnable and will go and play.

Fortuna is beaming. "That was fun! What should we do now?"

I point at the guy at the dart game. "How about we go and harass him for a while?"

The Goddess of Luck is way ahead of me. Poor Dart Guy.

It takes us a few hours, but we make our way through all the games, giving a lot of our winnings away to whomever happens to look like they could use a pick-me-up. The smiles on the kids' faces make me feel all warm and fuzzy inside.

Meanwhile, Fortuna is having a ball. She's doing her job and all the while she's tormenting the cheating game booth workers. Apparently there were a few honest ones who she had mercy on, but the rest were several toys lighter by the time she was done with them.

Now Flora is in charge and is leading us through the crowds toward the entry arches. Just as we get there, I see Noah walking in.

"Hey!" He seems relieved to see us. "Thank God. I wasn't sure how I was going to find you in all this." His brown-eyed gaze sweeps over all the activity going on around us. His lopsided grin grows. "You guys have been having a lucky day."

All our eyes turn to Fortuna, who ignores us. "Let's try out the rides! Now that there are four of us we can sit in pairs." She grabs Flora's arm. Obviously, she intends to be paired up with her and leave me with Noah. She's so thoughtful. A pair of drunken butterflies start somersaulting in my stomach. I know it's partially because I finally get to spend some time with him but I also want to talk to him about what happened last night. Now that I've got the chance I don't know how to start. This isn't the best place to be talking about that sort of thing anyway. What if someone overhears? So no talking about the secret god stuff. But what about that almost kiss? I know I'm still thinking about it. I wonder if he is. I glance over to see if I can figure out what he's thinking and find him watching me.

He grins as he eyes the huge rollercoasters. "So what'll it be first?"

I haven't eaten anything since dinner and it should be well digested by now. There's no reason I shouldn't get on one. It's only a million years old. Well, maybe not a million. Besides, what do I have to be worried about? I'm hanging out with two full-fledged goddesses. They'll be able to protect me if anything goes wrong.

Right?

We seem to be gravitating toward a hideously twisted coaster. The people in line for it look excited. The people getting off are looking green and wobbly. This is going to be great!

The line winds around what seems like half the park and we get on the end of it and settle in for a long wait.

"We've got quite a wait ahead of us, eh?" Noah leans up against the railing, settling in for a wait.

"I wouldn't get too comfy. With these two around, things tend to go their way." As I say it, Fortuna's up to something already. I can almost see the divine wheels in her head, whirring with a plan. She peeks up and down the line. Is she counting people? Flora disappears for a second then reappears to whisper something in Fortuna's ear.

Noah and I trade looks. His questioning, mine amused. I wonder what they are going to do this time. There are innumerable possibilities. With their powers *anything* is possible. I can't believe I'm all excited about the prospect of watching these two wreaking havoc with mortals. Maybe it's my malicious divine side coming out? Who knows? Whatever it is, I'm indulging it.

Fortuna is rubbing her hands together gleefully as she prepares herself. Flora grins at us and gives us a thumbs up. That also seems to be the go-ahead signal for Fortuna. She clicks her fingers.

And we wait.

Everything seems normal. Everything feels normal. Did Fortuna make a miss-click? Is that even possible? I hold my breath. Something's going to happen soon, I can feel it. And it's going to be big. Don't ask me how I know. I just do.

That's when I hear it. A helicopter. I know it has something to do with the two goddesses, and I turn to them. Why would they need a helicopter? They're definitely awaiting something. The anticipation is killing me. The sound gets louder and louder until we see it overhead. It's one of those twin engine helicopters used for heavy lifting. The copter looks like it's in trouble. The large crate it's carrying seems to be weighing it down really badly, which, of course, is strange, considering that's what it's made to do. One of the rotors suddenly splutters to a halt and the helicopter tips dangerously. The load is too much for the one remaining rotor and it starts to spiral downward. It disappears from sight and lands somewhere in the vicinity of the parking lot.

Screams go up from the crowd and people start heading toward the exits, presumably to get a glimpse of what's going on.

Fortuna clicks her fingers.

A radio somewhere turns on, loud.

"Breaking news. Just one hour ago a large gold shipment went missing." There's a shuffling noise and the voice continues. "Apparently it was stolen by robbers and is being transported by a large helicopter headed in the direction of the amusement park…"

That's all I can hear since people start to move and talk. Calmly at first, then turning into a human tsunami as people surge out of the lines and out of the park.

Pretty soon the entire line is gone. I think even the ride operators ran off in the hopes of grabbing some gold.

The four of us stand dumbly for a moment, just staring at one another.

Flora's jaw is loose. "I didn't think it would actually work."

"Of course it did. I've been around mortals long enough to know that greed gets them every time." Fortuna smiles approvingly at Noah. "I'm glad you had enough sense to stay behind."

He smirks and shrugs.

Fortuna leads the way up the now empty channels used to corral patrons of the park like cattle. We run up the path to find that everything truly is deserted. Luckily, people got off the ride before the operator took off. Otherwise that could have been a real mess.

Fortuna waves us into the cars of the coaster and gets in next to Flora. She clicks her fingers and we're off. The ride is even better with no one but us on it. We take turns choosing rides and eventually make our way through the entire park, from one ride to the next, terrifying or not, until my legs are wobbling from all the adrenaline coursing through my system.

I pour myself onto a bench and put up a hand. "I give. I can't take any more." I laugh.

"Me either." Noah looks tired, but happy. He's had a good time. And who wouldn't have after having had the full run of a park like this? Especially since I think the goddesses did something to the time so that we were able to fit everything in before it got too late. "Time to call it a night?"

I nod in agreement as I check out the quiet park. It's dark now and, with the lights on, it looks like a glittering wonderland. It's on the second sweep of the park that I notice a ride I hadn't seen before.

"What about that ride, you guys?" I point at the giant metal monstrosity. Somehow this feat of engineering has eluded us up until now.

The rails could have been picked up and mashed between the hands of a giant before being thrown back to the earth. It looks truly terrifying and I can't wait to get on it.

We climb into the first two cars, Noah and me in the front and Flora and Fortuna right behind us.

We immediately begin our slow ascent up the steep incline. The anticipation mounts. I can't wait for the thrill of being pushed and pulled and thrown by gravity. The feeling of being out of control is such a rush. A complete release. However, the moment we reach the zenith, all that excitement dies away. Instead of being on a thrilling ride, I'm staring into a gaping abyss. I can see something moving in the darkness, glittering in the depths.

"Stop! Stop the ride!" I manage to choke out the words, but there is no one there to hear me. The car I was riding in is gone. I'm dangling from the rocky edges of a cliff, clinging to the stone by my nails. The rock crumbles away, cutting into my fingers, shredding the skin as I scramble to keep from plummeting to my doom. The fear is constricting my chest so I can't breathe. Tears and sweat burn my eyes until all I see is a blur of black. I struggle to keep hold, but my strength gives out. I'm falling into the dark.

I'm screaming. Pleading with anyone who'll listen. If they'll only stop this. I'll do anything. Anything!

Then the darkness fades. It disappears completely in the blink of an eye, and I'm left staring up at three very concerned faces. Panting for breath, I try to sit up, but the vertigo leaves me reeling. I examine each face. Is this real? Are they really there? Are we safe?

"Ava? Are you all right?"

The blood pounding in my ears makes it hard to hear. Noah's voice reaches me though it's muffled like it's coming through miles of cotton. His face is pinched and white. I think I might have scared him a little. That's probably a huge understatement, but whatever. I realize he's holding my hand in his. Besides him clutching it a bit too tight, it actually feels kind of nice. It would feel even nicer with blood flowing, but for the moment I just ignore the death grip.

"Yeah, I'm fine. I don't know what happened." I really don't. For a moment there it felt like I was losing my mind. I look at my hands, expecting to see my fingers shredded and bloody. There isn't even a scratch. "I saw..."

"What did you see?"

Fortuna is very serious right now. I don't think I've ever seen her like this. A glance at Flora and I come to the same conclusion. They're both so grim it's beginning to frighten me.

I struggle to sit up. It's a little hard to do when you're practically pinned down by three people, especially when two of them are goddesses. I keep pushing at them until they finally relent and let me sit up. How did we get back in my room? I snort internally. I just about died and I'm worried about how I got back to my room? Yeah, that makes perfect sense.

I'm a bit shaky still, but other than that I think everything else is back to normal. I can see and hear again, and my chest is free for me to take some deep breaths before I relate what I saw.

"I was hanging by my hands on the edge of a cliff. There was a black chasm below me and I could tell there was something in it waiting for me. It was scary. No, terrifying. I don't think I've ever been so frightened in my life." It sounds so stupid now when I say it aloud. Their faces are impassive. Do they believe me or do they think I've just had sensory overload thanks to riding too many intimidating rides? "It sounds stupid, I know…"

"No, it doesn't." Flora has taken my other hand now and is stroking it lightly, soothingly. "It does seem strange, though, that none of us saw what you did. It must have been specifically targeted at you."

She doesn't say it but I know what she's getting at. Someone is trying to frighten me. Most probably Juno. Who else would want to freak me out? "Do you think someone is testing me? Seeing what'll make me break?"

Fortuna inclines her head slightly. "It could be. Or it could be a practical joke. There are several mischievous gods who enjoy this sort of thing. They seem to think sending people to insane asylums is good fun." Her eyes narrow. "I can think of one in particular."

She and Flora glance at each other and say the same name at the same time. "Loki."

Another name I remember from class. "Wait a second. Loki isn't from the Roman pantheon."

Noah is thinking, and hard. The concentration shows on his face. "Doesn't it go to say that if Roman gods exist that others can too?"

He's right. I've gotten so fixated on the Roman gods that I didn't consider that others could be wandering around. Ones that I can't see. That's a disturbing thought. It was different when I couldn't see any of them doing their thing around me. But the idea that there are some gods out there interfering with my life without my knowledge really irks me. Call me paranoid, but if there is someone out there messing with me I want to know about it. Okay, so paranoid isn't the word for it. More like control freak. I'm pretty sure that most people would side with me on this point, though. If there was a choice between knowing and not knowing, I'm pretty sure a lot of people would want to know.

"So, Loki? He's a Norse god, right?"

"Some might consider him a god, but I think of him as a pain in the ass." Fortuna's appearance is pensive. "Though this doesn't seem like his usual thing. He likes to play tricks on gods, not meddle with people's minds."

Flora nods in agreement. "He really is a pain. I remember this one time he thought it would be funny to reverse the seasons on me. You know how long it took me to sort things out?" She scowls at the memory.

Yeah, this guy sounds like a royal pain, but would he be messing with my mind just for some amusement? It doesn't seem like his usual MO.

"Could it have been Juno?" I whisper. I know it's stupid. She could probably read my thoughts if she wanted to. Whispering isn't going to help me any, but hey, if there's a chance that it might keep her from finding me, I'm going to do it. Slim as it is.

"There is that possibility. But again, it doesn't seem like something she'd do." Fortuna shrugs. "If she was going to get you, she wouldn't waste time with games. It would be more like *bam*!" She slams her fist into her other hand. "You're dead."

Now there's a happy thought. "So what you're basically saying is that if she wants me taken out, there's nothing I can do about it? No warning. Nothing?"

"I'm sure there'll be warning signs. You should have a split second to react."

"Sure, I'll just use my superhuman power to move faster than light, shall I?"

Noah's being very quiet throughout all of this. After his emotional spew after I saved his life, I'd have thought that he would have more to say about this whole 'I'm probably going to get killed by a vengeful goddess' thing. But apparently it's listening time. For a soccer jock, he has some good listening and reasoning skills. I'm not saying that he's athletic, therefore he must be stupid. It just reminds me that I don't know him all that well. Yet here he is, privy to my biggest secret and the first boy — Mors doesn't count, because I didn't want him there — in my room. There's something I'm going to enjoy explaining to Mom if she decides to come barging in here. Let's hope the fact that Flora and Fortuna are around as well will help keep her from running him off.

"Are you two hungry?" Flora seems to have a real thing for my stuff. My fake flowers especially. She keeps fiddling with them. I'm sure they are a crime against nature in her eyes. But if she likes to play with them, then I'll let her. At the moment, she seems very interested in changing the subject.

Since I have no objections about talking about something rather than my impending doom, I nod as I push the window open. Need to get some air in here.

"I know I'm starving." The voice drifting down from my tree gets my hackles up without my even having to see its owner.

"No one asked you." I start to close the window again. Who needs air, right? Carbon dioxide is good for the brain. All those textbooks are wrong. Doctors? Pfft. What do they know, eh?

Unfortunately for me, she's already slipped her way in through the crack and comes to stand in the middle of the room.

The two goddesses are eyeing her distastefully while Noah is just staring. The dryad smiles defiantly until she sees Noah's blatant interest and realizes her mistake.

"He can see me?" She twiddles her twig-like fingers at him. "*He* can see me?" She says he like it's synonymous with 'that piece of slime'. She studies him for a moment and a broad grin spreads over her face. Guess she no longer considers him to be slime. As a matter of fact she's looking a little *too* interested.

"Get out!" I step in her line of sight, blocking her view of Noah.

"Yes, do get out." Venus has appeared and is now standing next to me now, glaring contemptibly at the tree spirit. "No one wants you here. Least of all him." She stares at Noah meaningfully before returning her cold blue eyes to her. "There's a spirit stuck in a mud puddle not too far from here I think you would be perfect for. I hear he's not too fussy and likes dryads. I can help you out if you like — "

The dryad doesn't listen to any more. Hissing at us, she dives out of the window and into the trunk of the tree. I slam it shut the rest of the way behind her.

I can't stop laughing. The expression on her face was priceless. I hope she chokes on tree bark. I'm pretty sure none of us are going to miss her. When the laughter finally dies, we get down to business.

Kacie Ji

Venus turns to me. "Ava, I don't think you have to worry too much about Juno. You have us to keep an eye on you. Besides, if she was going to do anything, I would have thought she would have done it by now."

"Gee, that's comforting." Noah snorts, drawing the goddesses' interests.

The Goddess of Love scrutinizes him now, studying him from head to toe.

The three of us turn to gawk at him. It doesn't take long before he starts to blush under our combined gazes. "What? Have I grown another head or something?"

I don't want him to get skittish and run off, so I answer, "I think they're doing the same thing I am. Wondering how come you can see gods and stuff too."

He shrugs. "I don't know. I was thinking that it was something to do with you. But then I remembered that I started seeing people on your birthday, too, only way before I even saw you. So that can't be it."

"If even Morta doesn't know how you are able to see us, I doubt we'd be able to do much more." Fortuna sighs.

"Doesn't mean we can't guess, right?" I look at the three goddesses. "I mean, if he can do the same thing I can, doesn't that kinda lead us in the same direction? That at least one of his parents is divine?"

"It makes sense." Venus seems quite agreeable tonight. She snaps her fingers and we've got a selection of really fancy food laid out before us on a beautifully opulent blanket. Trust the Goddess of Love to do something even as mundane as eating in style. She leans back on her pile of conjured pillows and reaches for a pretty cake. The rest of us do the same.

I eye Noah, who seems to have a moral objection against eating such dainty, feminine-looking food.

Flora nibbles at a beautiful pink confection. Though it all seems heavenly, and I'm sure it tastes just as good, she's scowling. "But then that just brings up more questions."

Fortuna nods and I find myself doing the same.

Whose kid is he and why is he being kept secret?

Chapter Nine
Demigoddesses Get Spammed Too

We spend a lot of time discussing the possibilities and come up with a list of ideas.

His divine parent abandoned him.
He's a god who has lost his memory and is stuck in human form.
He's a seer and was born with the ability.
Noah is an illegitimate child of a god, like me.

And my least favorite— *He's another of Jupiter's illegitimate kids.*

I can live with any of the other as long as Number Five isn't true. It's a possibility I just can't deal with. *Nope. Not going there.* So I push it to the back of my mind.

By the time we decide to call it a night, it's nearly three a.m. I'm surprised Mom hasn't decided to check in. She has to be wondering what I'm doing in here.

And what about Noah's mom? She must be frantic, wondering where he is at this hour.

Flora and Fortuna escort him home while Venus stays behind to help clean up. Not like there's much help needed. She just clicks her fingers and *poof!* All gone. I'm getting a vibe from her that tells me she didn't stay behind just to help.

The incredibly beautiful goddess stands silently near my window, deep in thought. Or so it seems.

"Venus? Are you all right?"

She nods. "I'm fine."

Should I push it? She doesn't look fine to me. If I keep asking, will I end up a spinster? What if I annoy her so much she makes my soul mate a sludge beast or something? Wouldn't that be wonderful?

So I quietly go about my business. If she wants to tell me she can. If not, then I'm going to guess what it is that's bugging her, but won't confront her about it. I won't.

I decide to check my email. I haven't done that in a little while. Until all of this happened, I used to check my mail compulsively. I've totally forgotten about it, to be truthful. But with what's been going on, how could I not? I sit down and turn on my monitor, still marveling at the size of the thing. I notice that the little lightning icon in the corner is blinking and click on it to see what's wrong with it.

The moment I do, several windows pop open. The cool thing about this system is that messages are made in video so I can immediately see who the message is from. There are about a dozen windows waiting for me. Wow! Who could be sending me messages already? I didn't think anyone in that world knew me besides the obvious few. I see one from Mors and immediately move that one to the back. I really don't want to deal with his strangeness at the moment. There are a couple that intrigue me. They don't have any faces in the window so I have no clue who they're from.

Curious, I double click the windows. A move I immediately regret as a deep booming voice yells, "Feeling low? Virility in question? Cirrus is the answer! Feel like the Adonis you know you are!"

I'm struggling to find the volume control. I can just imagine Mom coming, charging in to get yelled at by my computer. Another voice starts shouting now. It's feminine this time and sounds breathless and husky, "Lonely? Give us a call! We pleasure all. Gods, goddesses—"

I manage to shut it off before the rest of the message can be screamed through my room. Then I realize I'm not the one who managed to turn off the sound. I look over and see Venus with a handful of cables in her hand. It looks like she just grabbed and yanked until the shouting stopped.

"Sorry about that," she mumbles. "I'm not familiar with that particular machine, but thought that I'd better do something before your mother comes in here wondering what's going on." She throws them back at the computer and they quickly re-plug themselves.

"Thanks. I would have probably ended up doing the same thing." I'm still a little shell-shocked from the messages and my hand is shaky when I push the mouse around to the other windows. I'm not so sure I want to hear the rest of them now. I can't believe even gods and goddesses get spammed. And what spam it is. I shudder again just thinking about it.

Venus pushes me gently aside. "Let me." She taps the screen and several windows close. "Don't worry, I got rid of them. They shouldn't be able to send you any more, at least for a little while. Until they manage to get past the protections I just put on your computer. When they do, let me know and I'll do what I can." She grows silent and snaps her fingers.

It is several seconds before I realize there's someone new in the room with us. Standing behind my chair is a god I've never seen before. He, of course, is handsome. I don't think the Romans did anything but beautiful deities. He has a shock of dark brown hair that stands up and back from his face as though he spent all of his time hanging his head out of a car window. His toga is short, almost indecently so. It's so bad that I keep my eyes away from the hip area completely. My eyes go straight to his feet and I smirk when I see a pair of Nikes. At least they look like Nikes. Then it dawns on me which god would be wearing a pair of running shoes. "Mercury, I presume?"

"Huh?" The handsome god squints at me before his gaze sweeps to Venus then back again. He pulls a couple of buds out of his ears that look suspiciously like earphones and repeats himself. "Huh?"

"I said, you're Mercury, aren't you?"

He nods, impressed. "I am." Mercury holds out the buds in his hands and grins sheepishly. "I was testing out my new invention. It's called MyMuse. It enables anyone to listen to their music anywhere." He shows me a small rectangular piece of machinery that appears on the back of his hand. "Get the name? It helps inspire you on the go like your own personal muse."

Should I mention to him that he's pretty much ripped off the iPod? Although his is much more beautiful than any iPod I've ever seen. Seeing as I don't know him that well, I simply smile and nod.

"Aren't you the least bit curious about her, Mercury?" Venus prods. "It's not often you see a mortal with her ability."

He waves her off when he sees my computer. "I know all about her. Who do you think set her up with this sweet system?" Mercury sits his lean frame in my chair and starts clicking away on the screen. "Is it giving you any trouble?"

"She's getting obscene messages that I want you to permanently block."

Mercury gives me a smirk. "They've got you, eh? What was it? Virility enhancement or pleasure offers this time?"

"Both! Now get them to stop," replies Venus hotly.

He puts up his hands in supplication. "Calm down. I'll do what I can. Those virility ones should be easy. The Sirens, on the other hand, are a trickier bunch. I'll see what I can do."

I can't help but be amused by what's going on in my room. I have the Goddess of Love bossing around the Messenger of the Gods, who is surprisingly handy with technology. Who would have thought?

Mercury is mumbling away as he works. I'm pretty sure I hear him swearing as he jabs at the keys. How weird is that? I listen in complete delight as he continues doing his thing. It isn't until he turns to stare that I realize he's talking to me.

"Okay, I think I've fixed it so that they can't get you with their messages. If somehow they manage to get through, let me know and I'll come back and block them again. Like I said before, Sirens are shrewd. They'll keep trying until they get to you one way or another."

"Thanks for your help. This is the most amazing machine I have ever seen." I pet the monitor reverently, a move that seems to please Mercury to bits.

He smiles handsomely and bows. "It's a pleasure to provide something of use to someone who truly appreciates it." He winks and disappears.

"That was so cool."

"I think he likes you." Venus laughs. "It's not often he gets that kind of validation. I'm sure you'll be seeing him again soon." Venus purses her lips and grows silent again.

"What's the matter, Venus? You look troubled. Is there something I can do to help?"

She puts a sweet-smelling hand on my cheek. "You really are a kind soul, Ava Goddard. That's why this is so hard to say. I really hate to hurt you."

That worries me. What she has to say is going to hurt me? I don't like the sound of this. I take a deep breath. "Tell me."

"This isn't going to be easy for you, but I need you to stay away from Noah." She puts up her hands when I start to protest. "Just for a little while. Until we find out who he is, it would be better to limit your interaction with him."

My heart sinks. "You're asking me to stop talking to the one person who knows what I'm going through. He's the only other person on this planet I can talk to."

"It's for your own good, Ava. You have to understand that I don't want anything bad to happen to you." She gives me a slightly pitying look. "Would you like me to bring Beth back?"

I think about it for a moment. It's very tempting to bring her back. I need her more than ever with all this going on. But, if I'm going to be unselfish, it's not safe for her. What if Juno blasts me and Beth's right next to me because that's where she would inevitably be? I can't in good conscience do that to my best friend. "No. She's safer away from me right now." Time to change the subject before I start crying for my best friend like a two year old missing her blankie. "Who do you think Noah is? A spy for Juno?" I say it almost jokingly, but from the look on Venus' face it's certainly a possibility.

"We're not sure. That's why I want you to be careful around him."

She still looks shuttered. There's something else she wants to say. "What else is there? I can see there's something else on your mind," I prod as gently as I can. Don't want to push her too far, now, do I?

"I know it's going to be tough to stay away from him. You are going to feel drawn to him. Likewise, he will be drawn to you. It's your shared destiny. For the moment, you cannot give in."

"Shared destiny? Can't you tell me more? Why do we have to keep apart? If you told us then it'd be easier."

She smiles sadly. "Perhaps I will later. Until then, heed my warning."

I'm left staring at the spot she was in, inhaling fragrant smoke. Better than any potpourri I've ever smelled. It did little to rid me of the icy fingers of dread spreading through my body, though. What the hell was going on out there? I hate feeling helpless. I hate not knowing what's happening.

Feeling completely unsettled, I decide against trying to sleep. It'd be pointless anyway. All I'd be doing all night long would be tossing and turning as I try to figure things out in my head. Instead, I sit at the computer and start doing what I do best.

Research.

* * * *

I spend most of the night looking up variations of the words—soul mates, destiny and gods. And what I come up with can only be called complete and utter crap. All I keep getting is *Romeo and Juliet*, like they're the only soul mates in the universe. That's when I get an idea.

I click on the lightning link and search through until I find Mercury. Luckily for me, he's there. I double-click and wait until I see his face.

"Mercury? Are you busy? It's Ava."

His smiling face appears in the window. "Ava! I always have time for you! How can I help?"

"I was wondering if there was a search engine on the computer that searched...outside of the World Wide Web?"

"Of course! Just look for a little cloud icon. You should be able to figure it out from there. Just be careful what you click on."

I don't get a chance to ask what he means by that. The window is closed before I can even form the words. "Right, then. It can't be that complicated."

A quick search on my gigantic desktop and I finally find the icon he was talking about. I click on the cloud and wait. A window opens up that looks very familiar. It has the buttons and search box I'd expect from Internet Explorer, but it's a much better version. A Hyper Internet Explorer, if you will. I shake my head. Mercury really has a lot to learn about copyright infringement. But then again, who are Microsoft going to sue? I'd love to see them try.

I start searching and, even in the beginning stages, I know I love this program. It's so much better! Whenever I search for something it comes up with links and information just like it normally would, except now there is also a 3D representation floating in the middle of my room. How awesome is that? Not only that, but it seems to intuitively know what it is you are searching for. No more wasting time slogging through wrong results. You get it the first time, every time. I'd love to see Google beat that.

I give it a few tries, entering this and that to see if it would get what I was thinking about. I typed in roses, thinking of a specific kind, and it found them. I pictured a bird of paradise while typing in bird and it found it. *I'm never using Google again.* Curious, I decided to try something a little more exciting. 'King Tut's tomb' leaves me standing right in the middle of the room with his stone sarcophagus. Definitely creepy. I quickly click off of that. How about the Amazon jungle? I stare up at the huge trees in complete awe. The one thing that I'm not so happy with is it should take me where I want to go, not just plunk me in the middle of a representation. Now that would be incredible. But I can't complain. What I've got is light years ahead of everyone else.

So I type in 'soul mates' and think about Noah. Closing my eyes, I hit enter. It is several moments before I can open my eyes and look. I hope whatever I see is not going to freak me out. With a death grip on my mouse, I open one eye first then the other. I see two old people sitting together on a porch, rocking on their rockers, looking into the distance. The gentle smiles on their faces say it all. I watch them for a little bit and can't help but smile when he reaches over and takes her hand—my hand—in his and just holds it. That is so sweet.

So we're destined to grow old together. That's fabulous news! We look adorable. I watch us for a little while longer before clicking off.

Okay, so Venus said we were destined to end up with one another, but to stay away from each other for the moment. So something bad is going to happen if we're ignore her warning? Like what?

I type in 'soul mates trouble' to see what I get. There's a scene playing out in front of me. I'm there, older, more sophisticated, thankfully wearing some very nice-looking shoes, talking to a very handsome man. But he isn't Noah. He appears urbane and witty, as I laugh at something he says. Noah appears from the side and takes a swing at the other guy. I feel like I've been thrown into a soap opera or something. I watch them tussle until Noah emerges triumphant and drags me out, leaving the guy a fallen, Armani-clad heap. Not quite the trouble I had in mind. I shake my head. I never figured Noah to be the hothead type.

What else could I search for?

'Soul mates kept apart' came up with nothing interesting. Neither did 'Ava and Noah'. I get the feeling that my searches are being blocked. The who and the why of it, I'm not so sure. All I know is this isn't helping me find out what's going on.

Then it hits me. How much of my future can this thing show me? It's already showed me bits of my future. Why can't it show me more?

I type in 'Ava Goddard' and wait.

I'm given a whirlwind tour of my life so far. The baby years, childhood, even the puking incident is in there. By the time it reaches my teens, it slows significantly. I see it all clearly flashing past right up until now, so I'm watching myself looking at myself. How strange is that? I swivel back and forth, watching it do the same. It's like watching myself in a 3D mirror or something.

I turn back to the screen and notice there's a little message.

If you would like to see Ava Goddard's possible future, click a link.

There is a massive list of possibilities. I'm talking *massive*. They weren't kidding when they said that there were an infinite number of ways your life could turn out. Here I am staring at the proof. Of course I want to see more. Who wouldn't want to see their future? So I click the first link. I remind myself that this is just one possibility, most likely the one if I continue on the course I'm on now.

The window goes blank.

I hit enter a few more times, but nothing happens. Great. It seems that this isn't going to work for me either. Come on! I have all this stuff available to me and I can't use it at all. It's so frustrating!

I close the window and try to think of another possible way to go about this. How else can I find out what's going on?

Who could possibly know about my destiny? Jupiter… But considering I haven't even met the guy yet, I doubt that I could ask him. Morta… She was the only other one who I could think of. Maybe one of the other Parcae? The thought of dealing with them wasn't so appealing. I'm pretty sure that if I meet another god or goddess right now I'll overload. Hell, I don't even know if I've got the strength to deal with Morta at the moment.

However, I do know someone who could contact her for me.

I scroll through the list of gods in Mercury's messenger program and click.

It takes a second before the pallid yet still handsome face I'm searching for appears. I stare at him for a bit. He almost appears vampire-like. Pale. Beautiful. If this is what undead bloodsuckers are supposed to look like, then I can totally see the appeal in those novels with the guy dressed as a vampire groping some swooning woman on the cover. It takes me a second to realize that he's talking.

"Ava? I did not think I would be the one hearing from you." His amazing eyes seem as though they can see straight through me, even through a computer screen. "Why have you not replied to my messages?"

Crap. I'd forgotten about those. "Hi, Mors. I'm sorry. I've been a little distracted lately."

He nods. That's a good sign. He's not reaching through the screen to reap my soul, either—another very good sign.

I press on. "I was wondering if we could chat for a bit."

"I can understand the distraction. I suppose with all that is going on you've been a bit overwhelmed." Mors clicks his fingers and settles into the beautiful chair that forms behind him. "What can I help you with?"

"Remember how you wanted to live here with me? All that stuff about wanting to learn about humans?"

"Yes."

I can't tell if he's interested or not. He doesn't give away a thing in his expression or his voice. "I was thinking it over. How do I know that you're going to be an honorable guy? You could be some perv for all I know."

"I assume you have some sort of trial in mind to help me prove myself to you." He seems almost amused by this. Almost. I mean, would it hurt the guy to accompany his remarks with some facial expressions that go further than an eye gleam or an infinitesimal quirk of his lips? Still, I think I'm getting better at reading him... I think.

Now to get him to ask Morta about my future. "I was hoping you could help me with something."

Mors sighs. "It will not be easy. Morta is no fool."

And of course he's read my mind. Why do I even waste my energy talking anymore? Must be the human in me. "But with you on my side it should be a bit easier, don't you think? I'm sure you can think of something."

"Very well. But if we succeed, I will move into your home immediately." He pauses when I flinch. "I do something for you, you do something for me. Is that not how things work?"

"Uh, sure." I don't want to annoy him so I don't push it further. Hopefully, he'll find me to be a less than stellar roommate and move on quickly. "Fine." I close the connection and he appears near my window, staring out at my tree. Let's hope he's not a slob.

"We must find a way to rid your tree of that dryad. They are quite the nuisance."

Okay, my opinion of the god is quickly revising itself and moving from 'creeped out' to 'I love him'. If he can get rid of her, he'll do more than prove himself a worthy roommate. He'll earn my undying admiration and devotion. Well, maybe not total devotion. But close.

And idea sparks in my mind.

"I think we should just talk to Morta instead of your insane little ploy. She will know if you try to steal your thread. Besides, how will you read it?"

It doesn't even bother me that he continues to read my mind. It moves things along faster. "That's where you come in. I figure you'll have something up your dark and mysterious sleeves that can help me out."

He shakes his head, sending his long bangs swaying over his eyes. Somehow he manages to pull off emo hair *with* a toga.

"Didn't you like the other clothes?"

"Excuse me?"

He's going to have to learn to get used to my rapid changes of topic.

"I just meant your clothes. You were in different clothes earlier. Didn't you like them?"

He nods, understanding what I'm talking about. "They were fine. I am just used to my clothes. I will probably try them again sometime soon."

I got his meaning. He'd be wearing them if and when he was with me and other people were around.

"As I was saying, before we started talking about fashion, Morta and the other two Parcae are the only ones who can read the threads. I, personally, don't see how they do it. They just run it between their fingers and they know everything about the person it belongs to. To you or me it would be just another thread."

"Wonderful. I guess we'll have to go with your idea then. You'll just have to talk to her."

"Me?"

"Yeah, you. You're the one with the rapport with her."

"She finds you fascinating. I think that will work in your favor more than my 'rapport' with her."

"Are you scared of talking to Morta?" I almost start laughing at the idea that this imposing god is frightened of little old grandma Morta. I know I am frightened of her. More than frightened, actually. That grandmother act doesn't fool me. The fact is I'm not a god. The only ability I have is to see things going on around me that others don't and that's hardly going to protect me from her.

Mors bristles. "I am not afraid of anything. I am what others fear."

"Yeah, but she's pretty scary too."

"Morta does not frighten me," he intones.

I smile brightly. "Are you trying to convince me or yourself?"

There was only one thing left for him to do — prove to me that Morta doesn't scare him. He mutters to himself as he prepares to meet her. I hear the words stubborn and fool. I'm not sure if he's referring to himself or me. But it does make me smile a little. I've managed to confound Death. How often does anyone get to say that?

My room quickly dissolves, and Morta's overpoweringly floral living room appears.

"Morta? Are you here?"

"Just baking some cookies, Mors! Make yourselves comfortable. I'm glad you've come back to visit, Ava!"

Mors raises his eyebrows in a way that says 'I told you so'. I guess nothing happens without her knowing. At least, not in her living room. Mors sits himself on the edge of a chair as if he's afraid that the flowers are somehow going to contaminate him.

I sit across from him and do my best to make myself comfortable. I'm still uncomfortable in this place. It's just so neat and tidy. It's like I'm a little kid again, visiting the house of one of my mom's friends with the very grown-up house and I'm not allowed to touch anything. Only this is a million times worse, because I know that if I destroy something here I can expect something much scarier than a severe scolding.

We sit silently staring each other down for a few minutes before Morta comes in with a huge tray of cookies.

"Sorry for the wait. I expected you" — she looks at Mors — "to last longer in an argument with her. Maybe you two are well suited after all."

Well suited? What? "Excuse me?" I'm not sure if I heard right. The moment the cookies came into the room the wonderful fragrance overwhelmed my system. She really does make the best cookies.

Morta gives me a mysterious little smile and sets the tray down right in front of me. "Please, help yourself."

I rein in my impulse to grab two handfuls and shove them into my mouth. Instead, I delicately choose one and take a nice-sized bite. Not too big. Not too small. I chew it, enjoying the flavor bursting over my tongue.

"As I was saying, I know why you two are here." She scowls at Mors. "You know I cannot let people have their threads." Morta then turns to me. "Mortals shouldn't know about their futures. Besides, there is nothing concrete. It's all mutable. I've never known a mortal to stay on the same path for long."

I'm too busy enjoying my cookie to answer. I chew manically as I want to reply without spewing the contents of my mouth onto my hostess.

Mors puts up his hand and replies for me. "Remember, Ava is not some mere mortal. She is the daughter of Jupiter and cannot be classed in the same way."

I nod in agreement. He really is going to try to help me out!

Morta seems to consider his words for a moment. "Perhaps. But she is not ready. Maybe one day I will show it to her. For now she must wait."

"Wait. Hold on a sec. I'm not ready?" This is serious. So serious, in fact, that I put down the cookie.

"No. Your mind is incapable of taking in something like this at the moment." Morta gives me a small smile.

"Sure it is." A childish protest, but it's true. At least from my point of view. Unless she can give me something other than 'you're not ready', I'm going to keep arguing.

"Child, I would be one of the first to let you know if you were primed, but you are not. I cannot risk damaging your fragile mind with something like this until I know you are prepared. You are too valuable."

Her smile doesn't waver.

"I need to know what's going on." My eyes meet hers, I plead with her without saying a word.

"And you will. When you are ready."

She waves her hand and I'm sitting on my bed. Mors is on my chair in front of the computer, looking smug.

"What are you smirking about?"

His smile grows. "I am thinking about where to put my things."

"Oh no. You didn't get me my thread. You're not moving in here."

He shakes his head slowly, his increasingly annoying smirk still present. "No. You only said I had to get her to agree to give it to you and she has. When you are ready. Thus, I have fulfilled my end of the bargain. Now you will fulfill yours."

"That's not fair! You know what I wanted!"

"You should have been more specific."

I want to wipe that smirk off his face. *You have got to be kidding me.* Not only did I not get what I wanted, but I still have to give up half my room. Wonderful. But a deal's a deal. I'd rather be on his good side than not. I get the feeling that Mors makes for a terrifying enemy.

He considers me for a moment. It looks like he has a bit of a conscience after all. His smile turns gentle. "Think of it this way, Ava. If something does happen, who would you want at your side?"

Mors is right. Who better to protect me, right? No one is going to go up against him. At least, not willingly. And if I have death on my side, I can't lose. It really is win-win. Besides, I'm sure it won't take long for him to figure out that he's only going to learn about feminine stuff. Once he gets sick of that, he'll be out of here. I give him a week tops. I can put up with him for that long. Not sure how he's going to hide from Mom, but I'm positive he has something up his sleeve. I'll leave that all up to him.

"Fine. When do you want to move in?"

"How about now?"

He smiles and snaps his fingers.

Chapter Ten
My Life after Death (Moves In)

Apparently gods don't need interior decorators. They don't even need time to think or plan. They just do. And Mors just did. The room seems to have expanded about five miles. Okay, well maybe not five. Maybe not even miles. It's closer to twelve feet, I think. He's erected a wall to separate our halves of the space. It's not bad. I still have my privacy, he has his.

I walk around to the door to his room and watch as he decorates. Well, I watch as objects appear and attach themselves to various parts of the room. It's a strange sight. Who would have thought that Death likes knick-knacks?

The room isn't as gloomy as I'd expected. It's monochromatic, black on white — or white on black? — I'm not sure. It looks nice, if a little spartan. He has a little woven rug on the floor next to his bed that has a beautiful black and white pattern on it. It's so intricate and the design's so complicated that I marvel at it. There are a few black sculptures that don't look like anything in particular, which amuses me because I never would have pegged him as a lover of modern art. A desk appears. Does he have to do paperwork as part of his job? A shelf follows then an endless stream of books that find their places on the shelves. He's a reader. I guess it won't be so bad having him around. I'm already drawn toward the books. I wonder what kinds of books could be gracing Mors' bookshelf. Maybe if I'm nice he'll let me read them.

I sweep my eyes around his room once again before I notice him watching me with an amused little smile on his lips.

"What?"

"Nothing." He falls back onto his bed. "Thank you for letting me into your life."

"You're welcome." What else am I going to say? He has helped me a little so far. And with Death literally at my side, nothing bad can happen to me, right? Why do I feel the need to keep repeating this? I feel the urge to giggle bubble inanely up my throat. Instead I start searching for things to keep me busy. Like keeping Mors happy. "Need anything? Are you hungry?" I ask, because I realize I am. I take a look at the clock and see that it's nearly morning. As a matter of fact, I see the sun rising. Well, I see a goddess in breathtaking robes the colors of the morning sky flying past. She turns to me and smiles before continuing on her way, her golden hair streaming behind her.

Mors waves a lazy hand at her in greeting before letting it fall to his stomach once again. "Aurora doing her rounds," he explains.

"So explain to me why you're here again?" I'm a little fuzzy as to the reason he even wants to live with me in the first place. I'm blaming it on the fact that I haven't slept. Or it could be because I didn't get it the first time around.

"I think it would be mutually beneficial. There is much we can learn from one another."

"So you expect me to teach you? About what?"

"Life. Humans."

Yeah, because I know all about life. "How do you expect me to do that when I haven't even lived half my life yet?"

"It is not as though I am going to be living here for a short while."

"Just how long are you planning on staying here?"

"As long as is mutually acceptable."

Should I tell him that it's not acceptable to me? I did make up the terms of the agreement, so it would be stupid of me to bring it up. I just nod and smile.

"I'm going to see if I can find something to eat. I'll bring you something."

"Do not worry yourself." He snaps his fingers and there's a table in the middle of his room with a delicious breakfast laid out. "I hope you do not mind me taking a quick peek inside your head to see what you like."

I shrug and sink into one of the two chairs. He follows suit and settles in the other. "This is wonderful! Don't let me eat too much, okay? My mom will expect me down for breakfast."

He nods.

We share a smile and tuck in.

I immediately go for the pancakes, sandwiching a blueberry one in between two pecan ones. I can't help the smile that spreads across my lips as I take a bite. So, so good. It practically melts in my mouth. "My compliments to the chef."

He nods and shoves a piece of toast in his mouth. "I have never had a breakfast like this before."

"Never?"

"No."

I smile at him and continue to eat.

* * * *

By the time I have to go down for my real breakfast, I'm half asleep and stuffed full of pancakes and various other foods that I barely remember. But I'm happy.

Mors is dozing. I think the breakfast was too much for him. He managed to try a bit of everything, but seemed to like the pancakes best. We had a fun time trying to divvy them up in a way that pleased us both.

So far, having a roommate isn't all that bad. At least I won't get lonely—I'll always have someone to talk to with him around.

Then I hear the words I've been dreading.

"Ava! Get up! Your breakfast is ready!"

I wait a moment to make it seem like I'm just getting up.

I'm about to walk out of the door when a sleepy voice says, "You are still wearing the same clothes from yesterday."

I groan. I'm so tired I completely forgot. I dive into my closet and look for something suitable to wear. I settle for some sweats and a T-shirt. It's not like I'm having dinner with heads of state, right?

Slowly, I make my way down and fall into a seat at the kitchen table. It's all I can do not to flop all over it.

"Late night?"

Mom drops some blueberry pancakes in front of me and, for the first time in my life, the smell nauseates me.

I know she knows they are my favorite so I make an effort to look like I'm enjoying myself when I'm already stuffed full with enough blueberries to make Violet Beauregarde freak out.

I manage to swallow and smile. "Yeah, I was out with Flora and Fortuna for a bit."

"Oh? What did you end up doing?"

"We went to the amusement park." I take another small bite, chewing slowly, hoping my stomach won't rebel.

"That must have been exciting. Did you hear about the gold dropped in the parking lot? It was all over the news."

I manage not to snort. "Yeah, we saw the helicopter drop."

"I'm glad you didn't get hurt in the fiasco." She sits across from me and looks at me levelly.

I immediately know something's up. I try my best to eat the pancakes calmly.

"You're spending a lot of time with the goddesses. Shouldn't you be spending time with Beth?"

"Beth was over last night too. You know she was, you let her up."

"And that's another thing. What were you doing with all that food? All the excitement about your father hasn't triggered an eating disorder, has it?"

"No!" Slightly hysterical. Let's try it a little calmer this time. "No. I'm fine."

Her eyes narrow. "Who's up there with you?"

"No one." Oops, answered just a little too quickly.

"Who is it? Apollo? Bacchus?" Mom is seething and already starting for my room.

It's obvious what she thinks is going on. She's got it into her head that some god is trying to seduce me. *Ew. Just ew!* "No, Mom! It's not like that. Mors is up there."

Her eyes widen, unnaturally so. "What's he doing up there? Are you in trouble?" She pales visibly.

Afraid that she's going to pass out, I shoot out of my chair and usher her into one. "No. He's here as a friend. He's got it into his head that I'm the best one to teach him about life."

"That's ridiculous. He's a god. He knows *everything*!"

That stops me short. That's very true. Was he lying? Why else would he be here? I realize I've been silent just a little too long when I start to see the whites of Mom's eyes. "Maybe he just wants to see it in action, you know? All he gets to see is the end of a person's life. Anyway, he said while he's here he's going to teach me about who I am, which will help me out a lot." I make a mental note to get some clarification on the matter from the god himself.

She relaxes a little but her color doesn't come back. "I'm a little relieved, I must say. I was really worried about what was going on in there."

I realize she must have heard Mors moving in and had been having kittens in her room wondering what was going on. She gets *major* points for not charging into my room to find out what was going on. I'm not sure if I would have had the same restraint if I had been in her place. As a matter of fact, I'd probably have gone in, accusations flying.

"It's fine. Really. He's not so bad once you get past the dreariness. Mors can actually be quite funny when he wants to be."

Mom nods slowly as she tries to accept what I'm saying. "So when is he leaving?"

Uh… "I'm not sure. He says he's staying as long as it's *'mutually beneficial'*."

"What does that mean?"

"From what I understand, he's staying until he's ready to go."

"So he's staying in your room." Her voice is quiet.

I shake my head. Time to make this seem normal, as absurd as that sounds. What part of having a god living in my room is normal? I'm going to need a spin doctor permanently attached to me soon, I think. They'll help me get through my day.

"He's created his own area. He has his own room, his own bed… Everything."

"I want to see."

What self-respecting mom wouldn't?

"Okay. Come with me. I'm sure he won't have a problem with that."

Mom starts laying down the rules as we head upstairs. "He's to sleep in his own bed. No wild parties. You are to come down for meals. I want to at least see your face from time to time. I also want to see him as well. I don't want him hiding in your room all the time…"

As she drones on, I lead the way up the stairs. Her requests are reasonable enough. I can also be sure she's going to barge into my room when she feels it's warranted. Again, I can't blame her. It must feel weird for a parent to relinquish control to their kids. But then again, she's never been the overbearing type of mother. Something I've always been thankful for.

She finally stops when we reach my door. I can tell she's even holding her breath. Is she that nervous? Well, he is Death. I suppose anyone with half a brain would be worried about being in his presence. I guess that means that either half of my brain is in serious trouble, or I'm just used to him now. Well, as used as you can get to him.

Mom follows me in and immediately her eyes scan my room. What is she looking for? Telltale signs of an orgy, perhaps? I wonder if mothers have a sixth sense about that sort of thing? Like a Spidey-sense that alerts her to impure thoughts. And if they do, does that mean mothers of teen boys are driven to distraction? I smirk at the thought, but quickly wipe it away. Now's not the time.

Mom seems satisfied that there's nothing untoward in my room and starts walking toward the new door.

I at least want to give him a warning, just in case we're catching him unawares. Not much chance of that, but there's no need to be rude, right?

"Mors? Are you in there?"

"Yes. Tell your mother she is welcome to come in."

I give Mom a smile and wave her through. I'm not sure if I should follow or if I should give them some privacy, so I hover near the door and wait. This gives me the luxury of hearing what's going on in there while still maintaining an appropriate distance. No harm, no foul.

The moment Mom gets in there, I can hear her interrogation. Why is he here? Does he think it's appropriate to be living with a girl? What does he hope to learn from me? He calmly answers each question. Since the questions eventually stop, I'm assuming that she's satisfied. Then she starts laying down the rules. Pretty much the same ones she instigated on the stairs, but with, "You will not touch my daughter," added. He nods, and Mom strides out looking like a lioness that's made a kill.

"If he gives you any trouble, let me know, okay?" She straightens my bedcovers. "I'll call you when lunch is ready." And with that she heads back downstairs.

That went a lot easier than I thought it would. I hadn't been sure what to expect, really. But this seemed much better than any scenario I could have put together in my head.

I stick my head in Mors' door. "Can I come in?"

"Of course." He puts down the book he's reading and sits up. "Your mother is quite the woman."

I smile proudly. "Yes, she is. Even if she is a little embarrassing sometimes."

"I am sure you will be the same one day." He smiles weakly. "So what should we do today?"

"Um, I don't know. I thought you had…work to do or something."

"That is simple. A little time manipulation can solve that. I can be there and back within moments whenever I want. Now what shall we do? I want to do something exciting."

He sounds like a kid let loose for the first time in his life. I suppose he's in the same boat as me. I'm free of school and can do pretty much anything I want. Almost. No, wait. I can do what I want. I have the goddesses and now Mors to help me with that.

"Exciting, huh? What did you have in mind?"

"I am up for anything. How about sky diving? Oh! Or diving with sharks?"

I'm now of the opinion that Mors has some serious thrill issues. "How about we start small and work our way up to those?"

He shrugs. "Okay. What do you suggest?"

"I've always wanted to travel. How about we do some sightseeing? There are a million places in the world that would be worth taking a look."

Nodding, he stands. "Very well. Where would you like to go first?"

"First, you have to change your outfit." I give his toga a pointed look.

"Of course." The cloth shimmers and transforms into jeans and a severely tucked T-shirt.

"Better. But your shirt needs work. Do you mind?" He shakes his head and I reach over and pull the shirt out of his jeans. "You don't want to look like a nerd, do you?"

"Not if that is a bad thing." He holds out his hand. "Where is the one place you have always wanted to go?"

"Machu Picchu." I take his hand tentatively. I was almost afraid that it was going to be cold and clammy, but I find it comfortingly warm, which is nice. His grip isn't too tight or too loose. It's just right. I feel like my hand should belong to Goldilocks or something.

"Machu Picchu it is, then."

There's a strange tingling sensation as the world drops away for a second. The next thing I know, we're under a brilliant blue sky. The air is thin, so fresh I take a few breaths, as deeply as I can. We're standing on a stone wall overlooking the entire city. It's astounding. It's like someone built the city on top of the world. The mountains surrounding it are almost like silent guardians watching over the quiet ruins, hunched in mourning over the lost glory of the city.

I try to let go of Mors' hand, but he won't release me. Instead he hops down to the mossy floor of the city and steadies me as I do the same.

"I am afraid I would never forgive myself if you did damage to yourself."

His eyes flick over to the wall we were standing on and I realize that if I we had toppled backward, I would have plunged to my death.

"Thank you."

"It was my pleasure." He smiles and leads me through the ruins. "This city is at an altitude of seven thousand nine hundred seventy feet, or two thousand four hundred thirty meters, if you prefer. The name itself is from Quechua for Old Peak."

There are a couple of facts I didn't know. I'm sure he's about to educate me a little more. I'm actually holding my breath waiting for more facts. How much of a geek am I?

"It was built at the height of the Incan Empire, around 1450. There are one hundred forty buildings, including temples, sanctuaries, parks and residences."

He is really quite knowledgeable. I doubt I could have found a better guide to the city. But this is stuff I can learn from any guidebook. I want something only he can tell me.

"That's all very interesting, but I want to hear about the real stuff."

"Real stuff?"

"Yeah, tell me about the sacrifices. The first thing I think of when I hear Inca is sacrifices. Did they really have blood rites and sacrifices?"

He looks at me like he's not sure if he should tell me or not. "Why are humans so bloodthirsty?"

"Don't ask me. All I want to know are the facts."

"But you asked specifically about the blood rites. So obviously you are interested." His smirk dares me to tell him otherwise.

He's got me. Damn it. "Okay, so that's one of the main things I want to know about. You know that scientists have a history of getting things wrong."

"They did believe that blood was needed for the continuation of their world. As wrong as that was, the belief was the center of their world."

I'm confused. "So if what they believed was wrong, why did it continue?"

Mors looks at me and smiles wryly. "We do what we do because it is our reason for being. We do it whether or not mortals do anything to encourage us."

My stomach turns. "So all that stuff that the books say they did is true? Why didn't anyone stop them? All those lives that were lost could have been saved. All that potential wasted."

"Then what? Another so-called holy man would have made up something else, something that could have been much worse. And how would we have persuaded them? We cannot stop what we do."

"And not stopping perpetuated the belief." It was a sick cycle but I could see where he was coming from. "Still, you'd think that gods would be able to do something about it."

Mors' expression is closed but his eyes look sad. Time to change the subject, I think.

"Let's explore." There's so much to see I can't decide what to look at first.

"As you wish."

For the rest of the day, Mors led me around the ruins pointing out interesting buildings, sharing information and anecdotes. I couldn't have asked for a better guide.

I have no idea how much time has passed when my stomach rumbles.

"I'm getting hungry. I guess there isn't a *McDonald's* anywhere near here, huh?"

He smiles at me thankfully. With a wave of his hand he conjures up a meal. Only I don't recognize anything I see.

"I thought your curiosity would like to try an ancient Incan meal."

Since he so kindly offered, I can't really turn my nose up at it. I survey the feast laid out before me and reach for the least threatening thing. I think it's some sort of bread. I manage to chew and swallow the small bite I take. And I can positively say that I won't be craving any of that ever again.

There is laughter from next to me before an entirely new feast is spread out before us. "You are a brave one." He smiles at me. A big, genuine smile. The sight of it totally throws me off balance. It's amazing how something so simple can totally change your perspective of someone. If this was the Mors that I had met first I think things would have been very different between us. The harshness of his face is gone. Melted away. I can't believe I'm about to think this about the God of Death, but he's handsome. Like really, really I-could-stare-at-him-all-day-long handsome.

"You are staring. Have you never seen a smile before?"

"Not on your face." I don't care that he knows I'm studying him with open interest. He's magnificent. "You should smile like that more often."

"Not if you continue to stare at me like that. Please stop. It is unnerving."

"You have nerves for me to mess with? This is interesting news." I feel the smile on my face growing.

"You can stop that right now. I know where that mind of yours is going. And if it continues along those lines, I will make sure to never smile in your presence again."

"Fine. Just ruin my fun." I stick out my tongue and watch as he smiles again. Wow! I'll do this all day long if it keeps him smiling. Of its own volition, my hand reaches out to touch his. There's a slight zap of power that makes my fingers tingle. Something clouds his eyes for a moment, but it's gone in a blink.

"Put your tongue away and have some fish."

Mors waves his hand negligently at our makeshift table. Instantly, a tablecloth and two delicate silver candelabras appear.

Who would have thought that I would be ending the day sitting at the top of the world eating a fabulous candlelit dinner with a god, who turns out to be pretty dreamy when he's not being scary? All in all a good day, I'd have to say.

He waves at something behind me and I turn to see a beautiful black-winged goddess flying across the sky. It seems as though she is dragging a dark mist behind her, slowly turning day into dusk. She slows overhead, observing us openly, so I wave shyly at her. She smiles in return as she picks up the pace once again.

"Nox," Mors offers helpfully. "She will tell everyone about this, you know. By the time Dawn sweeps away the dark, the whole pantheon will be talking."

"Does that bother you?" I spear another piece of fish. "Did you...cook this?

"No and no." He sips at his wine. "Does that disappoint you?"

"What? That you can't cook or that divine gossip doesn't create any drama?"

Mors laughs. "I like talking to you, Ava, now that you have gotten over most of your fear."

"Are you kidding me? I'm still shaking in my boots. You just can't see it because it's getting so dark. Besides, you seem to have gotten over the whole awkward never-talked-to-a-girl thing you had going." I nod over at the horizon. "I can actually see a chariot." The dazzling light dims as it starts to dip behind the mountains. I can make out the shape of horses and a chariot just before it goes dark.

"How do you like being able to see...everything?"

"It's weird. Definitely weird. I don't know if I'll ever get used to it. But I do like being able to see stuff that no one else can. Present company excluded, of course."

"Of course. The things you will see now... I can't imagine how it must make you feel. Are you confused? Does it frighten you?"

"Honestly? It makes me feel special, empowered even, to know that I can do something that no one else can."

Another knowing smile from Mors.

"What?"

He shakes his head. "Eat your dinner."

I don't think I've ever had a better time. I had no idea that Mors could be so charming or such good company. We eat quietly, me watching him, him watching me. The food, the stars, the candlelight. It's all so romantic. Or it would be if this was a date. And if my date could stop staring off into the dark. "What is it?" I nervously study our surroundings and can see nothing out of the ordinary. What does he see?

He puts his hand up and motions for silence. "Stay there. I will be right back."

"What? You can't just leave me here."

Mors pats my hand reassuringly and leaps off the wall and into the darkness below. Yeah. That makes me feel better — a pat on the hand before he goes and chases something that is so much of a threat that he jumps off a mountain to go after it. I feel *totally* safe right now.

I grab one of the candlesticks that Mors conjured and use the feeble flame to cut through the enveloping darkness. Not that it helps much, but I figure it can double as a weapon if I need it. Staring out into the darkness isn't doing anything to help my increasing fear. Seeing nothing isn't helping my imagination. What would get Mors running like that? It must be bad. Otherwise why would he rush off like that? If he had to work wouldn't he just excuse himself? He did see something out there. I know he did. I huddle down with my back to the stone, hoping that he gets back soon.

An animal hoots, stopping my breath, my muscles, my heart. It's answered by another and another and is joined by others. Many others. It's just the sounds of the jungle. It doesn't mean that they're going to eat me. I hold my breath as I wait for fate to prove me wrong. Or whatever god or goddess who's in charge of that sort of thing.

I start to feel better after a few minutes of nothing happening. I'm sure Mors has got whatever he was after and he'll soon be back. Relaxing a little, I sit down fully and stretch my cramped legs out in front of me. I don't care that the stone is cold against my butt. Fatigue starts to wear away the fear until my eyelids feel like they are weighed down with three-pound weights.

I feel myself drifting closer and closer toward the land of the unconscious when I hear a masculine voice whisper, "Ava, wake up."

I open my eyes to see two glowing yellow eyes peering through the darkness at me. I realize that the candles have gone out. The eyes are glowing on their own. And they're getting closer. A low rumbling growl is coming from the direction of the eyes, freezing the breath in my lungs. I try to will myself to get up, but I can't do anything other than stare back at the eyes that are boring into mine.

My hand convulses around the candlestick as the eyes creep closer. I can almost make out a shape in the darkness now. It looks like a big black cat. A panther. I'm about to be eaten by a panther with preternaturally glowing eyes!

When the eyes are close enough for me to reach out and scratch, I swing the candlestick, catching it in the head.

"Mors!" I can't scream more than that one syllable as I get up and start running. "Mors!"

I don't know if the hit was enough to incapacitate it, and with what I know about big cats I realize that there is going to be nowhere I can hide from it. Their sense of smell is acute and it'll be able to track me down wherever I run. Plus, now it's going to be royally pissed at me. Clutching the candlestick a little tighter, I try to find somewhere to hide.

I turn a corner and run straight at a wall. The growling behind me prompts me to turn around. I can see the eyes floating not too far away. They're looking right at me so I know that it knows where I am. It probably knows it's got me trapped as well. I haul myself up onto the wall. If it's going to eat me, I'm going to at least make it work for its meal. With both hands gripping the candlestick baseball bat-style, I wait for it to make its move.

Slowly, it slinks toward me. I readjust my grip. It's going to get one hell of a beating before it takes me down.

There's a moment where it stops and stares at me. I stop breathing and, when it leaps at me, I'm knocked backward. As I scream and fend off the teeth of the panther, I notice that we don't hit the ground. I must have been on an outside wall. I continue screaming and slamming the panther as we fall, not giving up.

Suddenly two arms close around my waist from behind. "I have got you, Ava."

It takes me a second to realize I'm no longer falling. I'm on my bed with a death grip on a candlestick with one hand and I'm nearly strangling Mors with my other arm.

"Are you okay?" He gently extricates himself from my octopus hold and quickly checks me over. "You have some nasty gashes." With his finger, Mors taps my skin in various places.

I'm in too much shock to register pain or if I've managed to get relief from any. Instead, I cling to him and start crying, all the fear and relief flooding out of me.

I register his arms closing around me and him whispering something to me. Then nothing, as blissful sleep overrides everything else.

Chapter Eleven
You Can't Get Away from Death, Taxes or Mothers

Sometime during the night I awaken to someone screaming. Not screaming in terror. It's high-pitched shouting. And it's hurting my ears, not to mention ruining my blissful slumber.

I freeze when I feel arms tighten around me and hear the even louder screaming that it seems to trigger. This is going down as my absolute least favorite way of waking up. Somehow I manage to open one gritty eye and turn my leaden head toward the source of the shrieking.

Mom.

My body reacts for me and jolts upright. Everything comes flooding back, including the fact that I'm curled up in bed with Mors.

"What's going on in here? What are you doing in bed with him?" Mom's already dragging Mors from the bed, screaming blue murder.

"Madam! Unhand me!"

I try to stop Mom, but she's on a mission. Her objective seems to be to tear Mors limb from limb.

"Mom! Stop it! It's not what it looks like!"

She doesn't stop until Mors lands on the floor with a thud. According to her grin, my mom is happy with what she's just done. Hopefully, she's satisfied enough to start listening.

"Mom! Leave him alone!"

"I knew this was a bad idea. I never should have let it happen!" She's pacing the room in rapid circles now. She glares at Mors with steely eyes. "Despicable."

He's still lying on the floor and, from the looks of it, has no intention of moving. Mors points a finger at Mom and she goes silent. She doesn't stop talking, she just stops making noise.

Thankful for the respite, I let out a relieved sigh. By now Mom's realized that she's been silenced and starts to yell. Not that it's having any effect on what Mors has done to her. She screams until she turns an ugly shade of red before she stops.

"Are you ready to listen now, Mom?" I calmly ask.

She glares at me, but doesn't open her mouth.

"Mors saved me. He *saved* me, Mom."

She stares at him for a moment longer before tapping her throat. She wants to talk.

Mors has his eyes closed, but still knows what she wants and points his finger at her.

"Saving you doesn't mean you have to jump into bed with him." She's practically snarling. She whirls on Mors, looming over him menacingly. "And you! To take advantage of a young girl! You're disgusting!" She swings her foot back, and I leap in before she can connect.

"Mom!" I grab her and hold her back, turn her around to face me. "Does it look like we...did...that?" I tug pointedly at my clothes and point at his.

Her eyes narrow when she glares at Mors. "He could have used his powers to put them back on." She lunges at him again.

"Mom! Get a grip!" I keep a secure grasp on her clothes. "It's nothing like that. I was attacked by a panther...or something. Mors got me away. I was freaking out. He held me until I fell asleep. That's it. If he's guilty of anything it's of being a good friend."

Mom's eyes finally clear a little as she focuses on what I'm saying. "What happened? Did *she* attack you?" Mom is pacing like she wants to tear the face off of someone. Who am I kidding? It's Juno Mom wants to pulverize. We've got to defuse this quickly.

"Mom..."

"A panther?" She snorts. "Juno's never been very discreet."

Huh? "You've dealt with her before?" This is news.

"Once. At the beginning." Mom's eyes flicker toward Mors and she hesitates for a moment. His expression is blank as he motions her to continue. Apparently nothing she has to say will shock him. "We had a confrontation."

My mother took on Juno? I can almost feel my eyes bulging out of my head as I stare at her. "You had a confrontation? Are we talking 'walked into the same party' type confrontation? Or, like, 'punches were thrown' type confrontation?"

"It didn't get that far." Mom smirks. "I did manage to throw a drink at her. Well, before your father intervened. I still maintain that if she was human, I could have taken her."

Go Mom! I've never thought of her as a scrapper before. I can just imagine her taking Juno down. Now that's one thing that I want to see. I'd even pay to see that. I glance over to see what Mors thinks of this. His face is as stony as ever, but I notice a slight trembling at the corner of his perfect lips. He's loving this as much as I am.

Mom's still going, but thankfully she's calmed down. She kneels next to Mors. "Thank you. I'm sorry I jumped to conclusions. But a mother has a right to be worried. Especially when her daughter is special. And when a mother sees" — she waves her hands around — "all that." Mom shakes off the image, or at least that's what her head shaking looks like to me. "I'm grateful that you saved Ava, Mors. Now, I expect you to return to your own room. I never want to walk in on something like this again, okay? I'll see you both in the morning." She straightens, spins on her heel and exits.

Wow. I think she said that all in one breath. I'm actually surprised that she leaves Mors where he is. I half expected her to tear him a new one and send him on his way. Does this mean she trusts me? I snort inwardly. More like she realizes he's a god and there's nothing she can do to get rid of him even if she wanted to.

I flop over to the edge of the bed and peer down at Mors, who appears to be sound asleep. I know better.

"Are you just going to stay down there?"

"I cannot be bothered to move." Nothing but his lips move when he speaks and if I had missed that I would be sure that he was in a coma or something.

"Fine. I'm not going to stop you." I roll back onto the pillows and close my eyes. "Mors?"

"Ava?"

"That panther that attacked me..."

"Yes?"

My heart is thumping wildly just thinking about it. "That wasn't a normal panther, was it? I mean, its eyes..." I shiver. "They weren't like regular cat eyes. I don't have much experience with panthers and stuff, but I'm pretty sure cat's eyes don't glow when there's no light to reflect."

There's a sigh from the floor, as though he's given up on the idea of getting more sleep. "You are correct. That was no regular animal." He grows silent again and that worries me.

"What's that mean then?"

"What do you think?" His replies are getting short.

"I think that my mom's right. Maybe my time's up and Juno is out to get me." There's a grunt of agreement from Mors. "What's with you?"

"Nothing."

He sounds really upset so I roll over to the edge of the bed again. "Mors? Are you all right?"

"I am fine."

He didn't sound it. Why? Did he feel guilty about leaving me there? I'm sure he had a legitimate reason for running off. "Don't worry about it. I'm okay. See?" I wiggle my fingers in front of his closed eyes.

"That is beside the point," he mumbles.

"What is the point, then?" I'm getting impatient and I don't even try to hide it from my voice. Not that I could. I'm sure if he wanted to, he could pick through all of my thoughts and emotions without breaking a sweat.

Mors sits up so suddenly and looks so angry that I scoot back a bit. "The point is that I was chosen to take care of you. Me. The pariah. The one godforsaken creature in the universe that has never been trusted with the living. And rightly so. I couldn't even do a simple thing like keep you safe."

So that's why he was so insistent on moving in. "I'm safe. Don't worry."

"But for how long? What if I make another mistake and you are attacked, but this time successfully? What then? Jupiter will have my head."

"He sent you to do this?"

"Who else is insane enough to trust me with someone's life?" he mutters. "I am sorry. I am not mad at *you*. I am just disgusted with my own ineptitude. For once, I am entrusted with something of this magnitude and I fall at the first hurdle."

So. Much. Information. So my father has sent him to keep an eye on me. That whole 'I want to learn more about humans' was a total fabrication. Mors is my own personal bodyguard. How cool is that? And yet, incredibly ironic. Maybe this is his sense of humor? Jupiter thinks that having the God of Death protecting me from…death…is funny? I don't spend much time thinking about it. The fact is Mors is here and he's miserable. The poor guy is beside himself with guilt over what happened. Which is sweet, but also misguided. I'll have to straighten him out on that point. And most frighteningly of all, Juno is out to get me. How scary is that?

"Mors, get up here."

"I don't deserve to sit with you."

"Are you kidding me? You saved my life. You deserve a ticker tape parade." I reach down then drag him up by one arm.

"I failed."

"You didn't fail." I shove him onto the bed. "I'm still alive so I don't think that counts as a failure."

He mumbles something incomprehensible and buries his face in the pillow.

I just leave him there for the time being and fall onto the pillows on the other side of the bed. I'm still so tired. But somehow I don't think that I'm going to get much more sleep. Not if the past couple days are anything to go by.

I close my eyes and pray that I'll get at least another hour.

* * * *

I wake up to someone knocking on my door.

I roll over unimpeded and realize that Mors isn't there anymore. Which is fine by me, I just wish he'd told me first. Seems kind of rude. Especially since he's supposed to be guarding me.

I get up and shuffle to the door and to find Mom waiting, arms crossed and foot tapping impatiently. The moment the door opens, her head is in and she scans the scene. It's so obvious she's looking for traces of Mors. I roll my eyes and swing the door open wide.

"He's not here, Mom. Calm down."

She snorts, her eyes still rapidly sweeping the room. I swear if the FBI had this woman, they'd get their man every single time.

"I just came to tell you that breakfast is ready and a boy named Noah is here to see you."

"Noah?" My stomach flutters. What's he doing here? I get a glimpse at my reflection in the TV. I look hideous. "Stall him, Mom. I've gotta fix myself up." I shove her out of the door and run to the bathroom. Time for the quickest shower known to mankind.

I manage to shower, brush my teeth and tie my hair in about fifteen minutes. Once I dash to my room, I pause a moment before I dive into my closet for something simple yet cute to wear. I settle for jeans and a baby tee with the word 'Princess' emblazoned with glitter across the front. Within moments, I stroll into the kitchen appearing, I hope, as though I always look like this at this hour of the morning.

"Hi, Noah." I keep my voice as breezy as I can.

"Hey, Ava." He smiles with a mouth full of waffles.

I sit and Mom serves some up for me. I see her set aside a few for Mors as well. Her maternal instincts have obviously overridden the fact that she wants to tear his arm off and beat him with it. I smile at her and cut at my waffles with my fork.

"Thanks, Mom."

She knows I'm thanking her both for the waffles and for saving Mors some.

She smiles wryly and shoves the plate she's holding in the microwave. "I'll be in the living room if you need me."

Noah quickly polishes off the rest of the waffles. "Your mom can really cook."

"She can when she wants." I laugh as I take a bite. Mom did good this morning. I guess this is her way of making up for jumping to conclusions last night. "So what are you doing here?"

"I was in the neighborhood and thought I'd drop by."

I gulp some juice. He wanted to see me? That's fantastic! Then I remember Venus' warning about me spending time with him. Does she really think that he is dangerous? He doesn't seem dangerous to me. Not at all.

"Well, thanks for dropping by."

I notice his eyes are drawn to the table and his ears have gone red. What's up with that?

"Are you all right?"

He doesn't answer, but nods. For a few seconds he's fascinated by the table.

"I...uh... I was wondering..."

"Yes?" I'm not sure if I should be amused or worried, so I adopt an I'm-concerned expression and keep listening.

"You want to do something today?"

"I'd love to!" The words are out of my mouth before I can think about it. What about staying away from him? I ponder this for a moment but come to the conclusion that I'll have Mors with me just in case so nothing really bad can happen.

"Just give me five minutes, okay?" I run out only to run back in again. "What are we going to be doing?"

He shrugs. "Just wander around town, I guess."

"Okay." I head up the stairs again. What I'm wearing is good enough for wandering around town so I don't need to change. I have two goals at the moment. First, to put a little makeup on. Second, to let Mors know what I'm doing. After that guilt fest last night I don't want him to freak out again if I can avoid it.

I head straight for my vanity. "Mors? Are you here?" The makeup comes out and I get to work, remembering again Venus' disdain for heavy-handed cosmetic techniques. I apply a little mascara to my eyes and some gloss to my lips. "Mors?" He's not around. So much for him being with me at all times.

I run a brush through my hair as I click on the god messenger thing on my computer. I find his name and click. "Mors?" There's no reply so I leave him a message. "I'm going out with Noah." I feel a blush creep into my cheeks when I say his name. "I'll tell you about him later. I'm not sure where I'll be, but I'm sure you can find us easy enough. Just wanted to let you know. See you later!" I smile cheerily, wave and close the window.

I take one last look at myself in the mirror and grab my purse before going back down.

"Mom, we're going out," I say as I pass the living room.

She's out in the hall in a flash. "Where are you going?"

"Just out." This is going to be another interrogation, isn't it? I sigh inwardly and wait for the torrent of questions.

"Are you sure that is such a good idea after what happened last night?" She tugs me into the living room. "Where's Mors? I thought he was going to keep an eye on you."

My jaw drops. "Were you eavesdropping?"

She stares at me stubbornly. "I was worried and rightly so, it seems. So where is he when he's supposed to be your watchdog?"

I shrug, hoping to downplay that I'm heading out without him. "I...uh...think he's working."

Mom's face pinches even more. "Don't you think you should wait for him?"

"Since when are you part of his fan club?"

"I'm not fond of him, but he's all you have. If it were up to me there would be more than just him watching over you."

If it were up to Mom, I'd probably have an army following me around everywhere. "I'll be fine, Mom. Noah and I will keep an eye out."

"And how is he going to do that?"

"He can see them too."

Mom grabs my shoulders and squeezes just a little too tight. "What? He can see them too? Who is he? Who are his parents?"

Oops, wrong thing to say. I wanted to be reassuring, but it seems like it backfired. "I'm not sure. But I'm hoping I can find out if I spend some time with him."

"That's not a good idea. What if he's dangerous?"

"He's not." I break her grip and pull back. "I'll be fine okay? Relax."

She holds on to my hand, "As long as I live and breathe, I will never relax when you are out there...doing whatever you do."

"Thanks, Mom." I give her a hug that I hope is reassuring. She clings to me for a moment before reluctantly letting go.

Noah is standing by the kitchen door, waiting patiently for me to make my appearance. I think he seems a little relieved when he sees me walk in. Did he think I was going to change my mind?

Grinning, he puts his hand on the doorknob. "Ready?"

I do a quick check of my purse, making sure I have everything I need in there. Phone? Check. Wallet? Check. Gum? Check. All the other stuff, like gloss, are lumped together in the 'just in case' category and are going to be tagging along for the ride. "Yep."

"Great. See you later, Ms. Goddard!"

"I want Ava back before dark." Mom still looks stressed, but least she's not keeping me locked up in the house. She waves feebly as we walk away.

"So we're just going to wander?" I ask.

Noah nods. "Yep. Just me and you and wherever our feet take us."

It actually sounds like fun. I don't think Beth and I have ever just wandered. I don't think we've ever gone farther than it takes for us to shop and head back.

So we walk. This time I'm wearing flats so I'm pretty sure I can handle any distance as long as we don't have to cross lava or something.

We stroll along silently for a while. I wonder which one of us is going to break the ice. I guess we could always talk about what's going on. There never seems to be a good time for us to just chat. This is as good as it's going to get.

"So... You're the daughter of a god, huh?" he hedges.

I guess he's going to go first.

"How does it feel? Is there anything new you can do yet?"

"It's weird. I mean, it's only been a couple of days and I've already done more things since finding out than I have in my whole life. But it is really weird. How about you? Seen anything out of the ordinary lately?"

He shakes his head. "Not really. I've been trying to see if anything strange is going on out there, but I haven't seen anything weird since... Since you saved me." Noah's brown eyes meet mine. "I think I can only see Venus and the others because they let me."

"You think so?"

"Yeah. I get the feeling that it only happens when I'm around you guys. Or at least it does now. But I suppose it's a good thing. I'm not sure if I can handle it as well as you are."

"Uh, yeah." If you could call what I'm doing handling it. "Well, I have a mini support group to help me through it. I don't think I'd be able to cope otherwise."

"So what's it like? Who else have you met?"

"I've met a few goddesses. It's great. So far."

He stops. "So far? You're expecting it to get bad?"

I can almost hear Venus' warning booming in my head. I'm not too sure it isn't. Is it possible for your eardrums to thrum from an imagined sound? Whatever. I'm taking heed. Um... How much to tell him?

"Well, yeah. Let's get realistic here. Nothing good lasts forever." I think about last night and can feel the goosebumps prickle my skin. "Didn't you see my mom and how stressed out she was? It's like any minute now the world is going to cave in."

Noah looks stricken. "That's...uh...not good. What's going to happen to you?"

I shake my head. Like I know. "I have no idea. Everyone might just be worrying over nothing." I wish I was able to believe that. But with Juno after me there's no doubt that things will end in a pretty messy manner.

"It must be horrible waiting for something to happen."

"Yep, it sucks all right." I know I sound flippant, but if I dwell on it too much I'm going to end up having a nervous breakdown. And that just won't do.

He lets it drop and we wander silently for a while. I wish he'd just say something so we could get out of this funk that we've fallen into. I would say something, but now I'm obsessing about where my life is going. Is it actually going to go somewhere? Or am I destined to be toast? I remember the images of me as an old woman after that search on the computer and the sassy looking me in awesome shoes. Those are my possible futures. Obviously, I will grow to be that old woman *if* I chose the right path. But what's the right path? If Morta would just give me my thread this whole thing would be a lot easier.

Our wandering takes us to the edge of the woods. Which is weird, considering we were headed in the opposite direction when we started. At least we were while I was paying attention to where we were headed.

"How did we end up here?" Noah looks just as confused as me.

"I was following you."

"*I* was following *you*."

Apparently, we're like the blind leading the blind. It's a good thing the town isn't that big or we'd be lost for sure. I don't like it here. The gloominess of the forest creeps me out. How can it be gloomy on a glorious summer morning like this? Yet it is. It looks like the backdrop from a Hollywood horror film that would have me hiding under my seat.

"Uh, Ava?"

"Yeah?"

"Do you see fog coming out of the trees too?"

A closer look proves that he's right. There is a mist coming from the trees. And it's not light, either. Picture London in those horror movies where people are walking through cotton-like fog with Big Ben towering overhead and you'd have an idea of what's pouring out of the forest.

"I think we should get out of here."

Evidently Noah agrees. Grabbing my hand, he starts dragging me away — very quickly.

I'm all for it and am about to break into a run when I hear a deep growling from my right. What I see turns my knees to jelly. I stumble, falling forward, dragging Noah with me.

An enormous white wolf leaps into our path, snarling ferociously. It's as beautiful as it is feral. The top of its head easily reaches my shoulders.

"Get behind me." Noah gets in front and spreads his arms, making himself a bigger target. "Hey, wolfy. What're you doin'?"

"Noah! Are you crazy?" As chivalrous as Noah is being, we have to get out of here before he gets himself eaten. "This way!" I get up and latch on to Noah's arm. "Come on!"

We only manage a few steps before it bounds our way. We turn and run in the opposite direction only to be thwarted once again. We switch directions again and again, but it jumps in the way every time. The only way it doesn't seem to impede us is toward the forest.

"I think it's trying to herd us into the trees," I hiss at Noah.

He nods. "Let's try splitting up. You go right, I'll go left. Ready? Go!"

We make a break for it and run in opposite directions. I sprint as fast as I can, searching for somewhere to run where the wolf can't get me. There is nothing but open field and the sidewalk we came in on. I keep running, peering over my shoulder to see how Noah is doing. The wolf is closing in on me.

I change direction, skidding as I do.

"Ava!" Noah's running toward me too, brandishing a stick like a baseball bat. "Duck!"

I do as I'm told and I can hear the branch *whooshing* over my head as well as the bone-crunching collision it makes when it hits the wolf. It gives us a few seconds' head start.

I'm slowing down. I can barely breathe. Noah doesn't look like he's faring much better, though he's not breathing as hard as I am. He leads the way, frantically seeking somewhere to go.

Amazingly, the blow to the head doesn't seem to have affected the wolf at all and it bounds in front of us. We barely have time to register the sudden movement when it leaps again.

Straight at me.

Chapter Twelve
A Sheep in Wolf's Clothing

The collision knocks me clear of Noah and straight into the forest. The wind is slammed out of me as I hit the mossy floor. I roll a couple of times until I crash into a tree. Aching and barely able to draw a breath, I struggle to get back on my feet.

Noah shouts for me in the distance and is running toward me. I reach for him, but he runs straight past.

"Noah!" I stare in stunned amazement as he runs wildly through the trees as if he's searching for me.

"Ava!"

He *is* looking for me! Can't he see me?

"Noah!" I realize for the first time that my breath is condensing and comes out in little cloud-like puffs. "What the...?"

The forest is gone.

Noah is gone.

I'm alone on a mountaintop and I'm going to freeze if I don't find some shelter soon. Wrapping my arms around myself, I stumble through the snow. I pivot using my vantage point to survey my surroundings. Being at the summit of a mountain has its advantages. On my second spin I see a valley not too far below. Should I head for it? It's got to be better than staying up here, right?

I start toward it, but the wolf is back and standing in my path once again.

Teeth chattering and shivering uncontrollably, I glare at it. "What do you want from me?"

Its beautiful blue eyes hold mine.

"If you were sent here to finish me off, you'd better do it fast because the cold is going to beat you to it."

It tilts its head as it studies me. And not like a predator staring down its prey. It's really looking at me, sizing me up. It drops its head and lopes away. It stops when it's a few feet away and looks at me. Is it waiting? I shuffle forward to see what it does. I take a few steps toward it, it continues on its way, slowing to wait again when I stop. The moment I move, it turns and walks again.

Since it's established that it wants me to follow, I creep along behind. It slows and huffs a breath that sounds suspiciously like a sigh. I freeze when it circles me and shoves me along, its hair warming me slightly. It isn't long before it brings me to a hollow in a snowdrift. I never would have noticed it otherwise. It pushes me toward it and I realize it's more than just a hollow. It's a cave.

It shoves me into a corner, knocking my near-frozen body to the ground and winding itself around me.

The cold envelops me and pulls me into the dark.

* * * *

"Ava!"

Someone's slapping me. I want to slap them back, but I can't get my arms to move.

"Ava! Wake up!"

I manage to open my eyes a crack. I think I see Fortuna hovering over me. She smacks me again.

"Quit it."

"She's awake!"

I'm not sure who she's shouting to, but she's dragging me into her lap and hugging me a bit too tightly.

I'm warm and cozy. Definitely not in the cave anymore. I blink a few more times to get my eyes to focus. I'm not in my room either. What am I wrapped in? Bear skins?

"Where am I?" My voice sounds scratchy even to me.

"Never mind that." She swats me. "How in the hell did you get here in the first place?"

I push myself up so that I'm sitting up and can survey the room. Fortuna is practically on me while Flora is messing with a bouquet. Mors stands silently in one corner watching everything sullenly while Venus and Mercury are chatting quietly in another.

"What's going on? Where am I?" Maybe if I ask it enough someone will answer me.

Mors looks even paler than usual and when I turn to him, his attention is immediately pinned to the floor.

Not again.

"You guys, can I talk to Mors alone?"

They look a little baffled by my request, Mors most of all, but they agree and step out of the room.

I have to handle this gently. I know how skittish the guy is and more than likely he's feeling guilty enough without me freaking him out.

"What happened?"

Still unable to look me in the eye, he mumbles, "I failed you again."

"Would you quit that?" I grab his hand and sit him down next to me. "Just give me the facts and leave out the self-pity for the time being, all right?"

He flinches. "You are in Vanaheim. Fortuna brought you here after I found you."

"Vanaheim?"

"It is a place in Asgard. I do not suppose you know anything about Norse mythology."

I'm in the Norse mythos now? The thought of exploring another world clears my head a little more.

"Why here?"

"It was the closest place. You were dangerously ill."

"What happened to the wolf? What about Noah? Is he okay?"

"Wolf? There was no wolf. As for your friend Noah, he is fine. He was very worried about you. Venus calmed him."

I'm relieved to hear that Noah is fine and that he's not freaking out. But thoughts of the wolf confuse me. It might have stranded me, but it also found me shelter and kept me warm. But what was the point of the whole thing? If it wasn't there to hurt me then what had it been doing? It didn't make any sense.

"I'm so confused, Mors." I'm dangerously close to tears now. It's obvious to me that Juno is truly out to get me. "Why does she want to kill me so bad? I've never done anything to her. Why is this happening to me?"

He puts a comforting hand on my shoulder. "I wish I could tell you."

"You *could* tell me?"

Looking sheepish, he shakes his head. "I meant I wish I knew so I could tell you. I think I'm just as clueless as you are." He stares into the distance for a moment. "I couldn't protect you," he whispers.

"Mors, with what we're up against, I think you're doing pretty good."

"That is exactly the problem. I am a god. *A god*! And I have no idea what is going on. Do you realize how frustrating this is for me? I was asked to protect you and I can't do that because something is clouding my mind. There is always something drawing me away when you need me."

It's true. It's all too convenient. Only someone with major power and who is omniscient would be able to pull off something so complicated. How else would you fool a god?

But enough is enough. I can't take much more of this. I need to know what's going on. So I'm going to do what I always do in this type of situation. I'm going straight to the source of my misery. "Mors, can you do something for me?"

His black eyes grow wide as he looks at me for the first time since we've gotten here. "No! I will not take you there."

"Please! This is the only way. I can't take much more of this and you definitely can't. Please. Take me to Juno."

"Ava, do not make me do this. It is suicide."

"Mors, please. If you don't do it, I'll get one of the others to help me. At least this way you can keep an eye on me." I can see him wavering. "Please!"

He stands. "Fine. But I do not like this one bit, Ava."

"Thank you." I try to stand too, but find that my strength hasn't returned. None at all. "I need help."

"No." He almost looks joyful at the fact that I can't get up.

"Mors," I say warningly. "Please help me."

He sucks his teeth. "I'd rather not. You need to regain your strength before you embark on an endeavor like this."

He is so frustrating!

"Fine! If you're not going to help I'm getting Fortuna!"

Mors puts up his hands. "Fine. Fine. You are the most stubborn person I have ever encountered." He scoops me up in his arms.

He does it so easily that it makes me feel like I'm as light as a feather. A nice feeling, I must say. Mors' body feels strong next to mine. I'm thinking this is a great way to travel. I'm relaxed, comfortable, and I'm sure that if I want intelligent conversation I'll get it. What more could a traveler ask for? I hope we do it again soon.

Within seconds, we're standing in a glorious room. The columns reach up into the cavern, melding into the concave, silky looking marble high above. Between the pillars gauzy fabrics of every conceivable color flutter in an unseen breeze. There are tinkling bells somewhere that react whenever the wind blows. The air is thick with incense. I spot huge vats that look like vases, prickling with long burning stems, strewn all over the room without any discernible pattern. The pungent odor is strong, but not completely unpleasant. Floral and spicy all at once. It wouldn't take long for me to get used to it. I'm surprised I can see anything, really, considering how much of the stuff is burning. The place is incredible. *Arabian Nights* meets the Hippodrome.

"Where are we?" Stupid question, really. Where else would I be? I asked him to take me to Juno. I appear in this new place. *Hello, logic? Ava calling.* I'm hoping that he'll forget what I just asked. I take a look at the room around me. I'm staring up, wondering just how high the ceiling actually is. "It's like an ultra fancy, super huge airplane hangar in here."

"Yes. Well, you know how it is. We like our creature comforts." He wanders over to a table laden with food and drink set out on platters of gold, silver and bronze.

Juno definitely does if this place is anything to go by. There is a dais at the far end. Statues dressed in gold cloth line the path up to it. Everything is reflected in the polished marble floor, making it look as though the room is much larger and much more ostentatious than it really is. Not that it could get much more opulent.

"Come, eat."

Mors offers me a plate and I stagger over to take it from him.

"I'm sure she won't mind. You need to regain your strength."

"Are you sure this is such a good idea? I mean, I'm probably not on her favorite person list."

He shrugs. "She's hardly going to poison you in her own home. It's not her style."

I'm getting nervous now. My stomach is churning just looking at the food, but I continue to hold on to the plate because it gives me something to do. Something to occupy the tiny part of my brain that is not panicking. This isn't a good idea. There's a very clear voice in my head screaming that at me right now.

"I want to go."

"Whatever for, my dear? You've only just arrived."

The voice is very feminine, very sweet, but somehow still manages to creep me out.

I turn around to see a gorgeous auburn-haired woman on the dais now. She glides her hand over the back of the throne as she makes her way around it to sit down delicately on the wrought gold.

"I understand that you are anxious to meet me. I go through all the trouble to get food and drink in, the least you can do is stay for a short chat."

She's glowing, radiant. Her hair is coiled and pinned to her head with jeweled pins that glitter with every movement. The diaphanous toga she sports looks as though it's been spun from sunlight. She exudes power. She truly is a sight to behold. And most definitely a force to be reckoned with. There's no need to tell me that I'm standing face to face with the Queen of the Gods.

"Yes, I would like that." Did I just say that? And so calmly? I can't believe I did that! A little coffee table appears and two velvet-covered chaises. What had I expected to appear? Two rickety wicker chairs? She motions for me to take one and waits until I do before she seats herself. At the moment this seems, at least to me, nothing more than a couple of women sitting down to afternoon tea. Nothing to worry about. No need to be shaking like a leaf in a hurricane. I just wish my body would listen to my mind.

"Tea? Wine?"

"Tea, please." A gilded cup with my requested drink appears in my hand. I wriggle a bit, trying to get comfortable. This is the first time I've ever attempted to drink tea while lying on my side.

"Please help yourself to some cakes. I took the liberty of finding out what you like." A plate filled with delicate-looking cakes hovers before me. "Everything there should be to your liking."

"Thank you." I take one and nibble at the icing, taking just enough so that I can taste the sugar.

She laughs, sounding like tinkling bells. "Come now. You must be ravenous after your ordeal." She looks over my shoulder. "Mors, tell her no harm will come to her here. She will listen to you."

"I do not know that she would," he replies quietly.

The poor guy is standing in the corner again. Doesn't anyone treat the guy like the god that he is? I sit up and shuffle over. "Come and sit."

"So compassionate." She sips a little tea. "I wonder if you would be so, if you knew his true nature."

Is she challenging me? I wait until Mors is perched precariously on the edge of my chaise. "I would treat him the same no matter what. He has been a friend and has watched over me." To punctuate my words, I hand him a cake.

"But not very well," points out the goddess.

My chin goes up. "It's not his fault that he has to run off and do things. He's still managed to come through for me every time."

She arches her eyebrows, but she says nothing. She finishes off a cake and with a flourish produces a napkin, which she proceeds to use delicately at the corners of her mouth.

"You are very pretty. But willful and outspoken."

"There's nothing wrong with speaking my mind. This isn't the first century BC."

She looks a little surprised, but she manages to contain any real reaction.

"Indeed, it isn't." She studies me a bit longer. Her gaze performs a long sweep over me. "I like you."

I certainly wasn't expecting that. Fire bolts. Lightning aimed at my butt, perhaps. But not an admission that she likes me. I stare at her. It's rude, I know. But there nothing else I can do. Is she messing with me? Is she trying to lull me into a false sense of security so that I'll be easier to take down? I'm searching her face for any signs of lying. Her eyes hold mine steadily. She's not flushed. No telltale signs whatsoever.

"You are confused."

"Well, yeah. I was under the impression that you were out to get me."

"Because of those stories? Because certain gods and goddesses think they are omnipotent?" Her tinkling laugh rings from her lips once again. "I have no interest in that. As you said, this is not the first century BC. My husband has illegitimate children. You are simply the latest of a long line. I bear you no ill will. It is not your fault."

Is it me or does she sound like she's channeling some TV shrink? I glance at Mors. He looks undecided. His eyes meet mine and I get the feeling that he wants me to go along with it.

I turn back to her and force a smile, trying to keep my head blank. She's probably in my head right now. Bunnies. Flowers. Kittens. I do my best to think about useless stuff. "Thank you for not wanting to get rid of me, I guess."

"You're very welcome. From what I understand about you, I would be doing the world a disservice if I did."

The heebie-jeebies are back. I can feel the hair on the back of my neck standing on end. "What? What are you talking about?"

"Nothing, my dear." Our tea cups disappear and she gets up. She circles the table and stands right in front of me. "I said nothing. I am, however, going to give you a gift."

Juno presses a kiss to my forehead. I fight the urge to recoil. Despite all that's gone on here, I still don't know if I should trust her.

Heat spreads from where her lips touch my skin. It's soothing at first, then it warms even more until it feels like she's poured molten honey over me. It slowly seeps over my entire body, heading creeping toward my toes. Just as it reaches my tips of them the sensation disappears.

"Wha... What did you do to me?" Shaken, I reach for Mors' hand and grip it tightly. Somehow, I hope sheer willpower will help me gain some of his strength through osmosis.

"You will find out soon enough, child." She smiles and she fades away.

I'm still clutching Mors' hand like a lifeline when I find us in my room sitting on the bed exactly as we had been sitting on the chaise. Our hands are still linked, each tightly gripping the other. At this point I'm not sure if I'm holding on to him or vice versa.

"What did she do to me, Mors?"

His hand tightens on mine even as I'm asking. "I'm checking." He's silent and holding my hand sandwiched between his. Mors' blank expression soon turns into one of intense concentration. It's nearly a minute before his eyes lose the glazed look. "I don't know. As far as I can tell there is nothing different."

Venus, Fortuna and Flora appear in quick succession.

"What's wrong?" The three say the words as one, peering around the room, searching for danger. Their gazes fall upon Mors gripping my hand.

Fortuna fires something that resembles lightning at Mors before she launches herself at him, knocking him aside bodily. "Mors! What in Hades are you doing?"

Flora seems to want to tackle him as well but resists, though the expression on her face could curdle blood.

Venus rushes to my side and takes my hands in hers. I feel warm and there's a sudden flash of light that envelops us both before dimming into a shining cocoon. She keeps it up for a full minute. Venus looks a little less than radiant when she releases my hands. Her gorgeous face is baffled.

"There's…nothing to heal. You're perfectly well."

Everyone stops to look at me. Mors shoves Fortuna off of him while she's distracted and gets up to dust himself off.

"Well, yeah. Mors isn't trying to hurt me or anything. He was just checking me over." They stare at me agog. Yes, agog.

Jaw slack, Flora shakes her head at me. "That's not possible. No one can touch Mors and not lose…something of themselves." She takes my right hand and studies it as if she would be able to see a telltale sign.

"I'm fine." I wriggle my arms and legs in a show of health. "See?"

I look over at Mors, whose expression is mutinous. "She's fine. I wasn't hurting her."

"But you touched her!" Venus steps in between us so we can't make eye contact.

"I've touched him lots of times. And nothing has ever happened."

"When?" Fortuna looks horrified by the very idea.

"All the time. Like when I'm scared, he'll hold my hand. Or…" They're all staring at me like I'm crazy. "What?"

"You willingly let…him touch you?" Flora glares at Mors. "How could you touch her? You could have killed her!"

"But I did not. Can you not see? Ava is *different*. That is why Jupiter left me in charge. I am the only one who can take care of her properly."

"What are you talking about?" I've joined in with the other three now and have started talking at the same time as them. What *is* he talking about? He knows what I'm destined to do? To be? "Why didn't you tell me before?"

"You are not meant to know yet. But these three insist on meddling." The scorn is evident when he glares at them.

"Mors." Venus stands in front of me, flanked by the other two. "What's going on?"

"The end of our world."

Chapter Thirteen
It's the End of the World as They Know It

"What?" What do I have to do with the end of the world? "Like the end of the world? The *end*, end? Like fire and brimstone type end of the world? Or are we just talking hyperbole about ruining someone's day?" *Please, please let it be exaggeration. Please!*

The fear on Mors' face wipes all hope away.

"The end of our world, Ava. The world of the gods. Your father's world."

All at once I'm relieved and afraid. My world isn't in trouble. But then again, the other world is a part of me as well. And what would happen if the gods and goddesses weren't around to do their thing anymore? After seeing how involved they are in our day-to-day lives I'm jumping to the conclusion that things are not going to end well for this world either.

"So what do I have to do with it?" I hadn't intended on saying it out loud, but now that it's out there, I'm glad. I want to know if I'm the cause of the end of the world. And even if the pivotal role doesn't go to me, it's still good to know how I have a hand in it. Maybe I'll be able to do something about it?

As pathetic as me hoping to change fate sounds, it gives me a little hope. Just a smidge.

Mors glowers at the three goddesses. "You will all find out in good time, so if you would please excuse us." It wasn't a request. He didn't bother waiting for them to comply and snapped his fingers, banishing them.

"You're scaring me, Mors." That's a bit of an understatement. I'm pretty much terrified.

"Ava." He takes my hand in his and cringes a little when I flinch from his touch.

I don't know why I do. It's already proven that his touch has no effect on me. Reflex, I guess. After hearing all the hoopla about his touch and the end of the world, I guess you could say that I'm just being cautious.

Mors closes his hand around mine, holding it tightly. "I had hoped that this wouldn't happen. I wanted you to get used to the idea gradually."

"What idea? You still haven't told me anything!" I try to pull my hand back but his grip is like iron.

"Ava. You are the last hope for our world. You are the key."

"How can I be the key? It doesn't make any sense."

"Think about it, Ava. Have you not wondered if you have no other siblings? If the other gods might have children your age too?"

It hadn't occurred to me. Maybe in the back of my mind, but I hadn't actually sat and thought about it. "I've been busy with other things." It comes out a bit more sarcastically than I wanted. Mors doesn't look like he minds, but I can't insult the one person on my side. "I'm sorry, Mors. I'm just so confused. I'm freaking out.

I have no idea what's going on and I feel like I'm on the verge of a nervous breakdown."

"It is okay." He looks at my expression and amends, "All will be well. I will be here with you through whatever is thrown your way."

That makes me feel a lot better. The anxiety boa constricting around my chest eases up a little and I manage to take a few deep breaths. "All right. Lay it on me." I take his hand and grip it. At the moment it's the only thing keeping me from either keeling over or running screaming.

"Think very carefully about all the people you know. Everyone you have interacted with. Did you not find anyone a little different? Anyone that stands out?"

Of course, the first person to come to mind is Noah. "Well, yeah. Noah. We have this thing… This connection."

"Anything other than rampaging hormones?"

I feel a blush creep over my face. "Well, yeah. He can see you guys too. Not all the time, but he can. We were talking about it before I was tackled by that wolf."

Mors' hand convulses on mine. "Why was I not told? Why did you not tell me?"

"I assumed you knew! You guys know everything that's going on. How could you *not* know?"

The god's handsome face darkens. "Yes. How could I not?" He pauses for a moment, his other hand patting mine in a thoughtful manner. "Do you mind me summoning your boyfriend?" There's a touch of scorn as he says the word boyfriend.

"He's not my boyfriend. I was hoping he was up for the job, but now I'm not so sure."

Mors says nothing. He flicks his hand and Noah appears. He's disoriented at first, but he quickly focuses his gaze on me and Mors and our joined hands.

"Ava? What's going on?"

I pull my hand from Mors' grasp—not an easy task. "Noah…"

"Do not look at her. Look at me." Mors is up and on his sandaled feet and circling Noah like a vulture over dead meat. "Who are you?"

"I'm Noah—"

"No. *Who* are you?"

Noah stares back at him blankly. "What the hell are you talking about, man?" He starts to swivel toward me, but Mors twists his hand as if he was holding a toy Noah and I watch as the real Noah wrenches around to stay where he was.

"So be it. Ava, turn away."

"What?"

"Do as I say."

I've never heard Mors sound like that before. His voice is cold. Hollow. Scary. It actually sends shivers skittering up my spine. What is he planning on doing to Noah? I hope he's not going to hurt him.

"Mors—"

"Ava!" Mors points to the far side of the room.

It's more than obvious that he wants me to do as he says and go over there. My first impulse is to rebel and stay put. The more rational part of my brain is karate kicking that impulse and telling me to shut up and do as I'm told.

My legs seem to be in accordance with my brain and slowly propel me to the far side of the room. My eyes, however, are riveted to the two figures on the other side.

"Ava, for the last time. Turn away."

"Fine." I turn and face the wall. Luckily for me my mirror's there and I can see them clearly. Good thing Mors is so caught up with Noah that he doesn't notice. I do my best to make it appear as though I'm staring at the wall while watching them from the corner of my eye. I want to know what's going on.

Mors glances over at me. Noah does too. I quickly stare at the wall. When I no longer feel their gazes on me, I turn my attention back again. They're ignoring me now, lost in an argument. Only I can't hear it. It's like they're inside some sort of bubble that blocks out all the sound. I watch Noah's mouth because Mors has got his back to me. He's talking too fast for me to make out the words.

I freeze when Mors raises his arm like he's about to strike Noah. I'm not sure how I'm going to react if he does. I know I should be wary of him. Haven't I been warned? But I just have this instinct to protect him.

I force myself to stay put, but I watch everything that's going on as if my gaze is riveted on them.

Mors' form seems to shudder then shifts until he appears to be a dark blur. I can see through him pretty well. Noah is writhing on the other side of him. He doesn't seem as though he's in pain. Just agitated. Mors' upraised hand begins to glow, and Noah goes still.

I watch as Mors pulls something away from Noah. It's transparent and looks like him, from what I can see of it. What did he just do? It appears painless. Noah is staring at it just as hard as I am. Mors doesn't notice that he's under our scrutiny and studies the transparent thing like a captain plotting a course on a map. He does this intently for what feels like an hour before shaking it out like a rug and throwing it back at Noah. It gets sucked into him and he recoils from the impact.

I release the breath I'd been holding and realize too late that it was a bit too loud. Obviously their anti-sound bubble doesn't work in reverse.

Mors jerks around. My lungs freeze. I can hear my heartbeats slow to a stop. This isn't Mors. It can't be. His handsome face is gone. Instead, two hollows where his beautiful eyes had been glow red as they peer at me. His flawless skin is gray and shriveled tight to the bone. The sight petrifies me so that I'm incapable of moving and can do nothing but gape back.

Shock sends my blood everywhere else but my head. I feel myself wobble. The skeletal thing once known as Mors lunges forward, catching me as the room lurches sickeningly.

Next thing I know I'm gazing up at the beautiful Mors I've grown used to, and Noah is on the other side of me, looking both concerned and ready to tear Mors' face off.

Noah takes my hand. I don't think a hand as warm and comforting as his can belong to someone evil. Or could it? I don't know anymore. I'm just so confused. "Ava? Are you okay?"

Am I okay? Am *I* okay? I wasn't the one who had a part of him ripped out by the God of Death. "I'm fine. What about you?" I can't help the accusing glare I flick at Mors before looking over Noah again.

"I'm all right."

Now that that's established, I focus on Mors. "What did you do to him? What was that you pulled out of Noah?"

"It is best if you do not know." Mors' expression is sad. No. More than that. He's lost something very important to him. Before I can say anything, he continues, "What is important is that I know who this boy is."

I look at Noah. He looks at me. We both turn to Mors.

"Care to share?" Noah blurts it out a mere nanosecond before I do.

Mors seems like he's about to answer, but before his mouth can form the words he doubles over. He closes his eyes, grimacing and moaning in pain. The only thing that leaves his lips is a groan. "I have to go." He is already fading from view as he grinds out the words. "Noah... Lock..." And he is gone.

What the hell does that mean? Lock Noah up? Keep him away from me? A lock of his hair? What?

Noah turns his wide eyes to me as if to ask what the hell just happened. I'd love to share with him, but I would need someone to explain it to me first. "Ava. What just happened?"

Wonderful. Why did he have to ask? Can't he tell from my gaping mouth and vapid expression that I have no clue what's going on?

When I don't answer he takes another course of interrogation. "Who was that guy? Why was he here? Why was he holding your hand?"

I kind of wish he'd stuck to the questions about what was going on now. I sigh. "That was Mors. He's keeping an eye on me."

"It looked like he was keeping more on you than just an eye." Noah snorts.

Is he? Could it be? Is Noah jealous? I think back to every article I've ever read in *Teen Vogue* and *Cosmo Girl*. Yes, I do believe he's exhibiting signs of jealousy. The urge to grin is so strong that I'm pinching my thigh *and* biting the inside of my mouth in an attempt to thwart it. Maybe if I give myself enough pain the compulsion to rejoice will just go away.

Nope.

Can't stop it. The smile creeps its way over my lips until they split apart and I'm grinning like that cat from *Alice in Wonderland*. You know, the one who doesn't stop smiling even when Alice is going crazy. Kind of like what I'm feeling right now. The whole world is going crazy and here I am grinning like an idiot.

"What are you smiling about? You think it's funny letting me know you have a boyfriend like that?"

"Whoa. *Boyfriend*? Did you miss what just happened here?" Had he just missed what Mors did to him?

I can't believe that he's acting like this. On the one hand, I'm loving it. But Feminist Ava is screaming at that part because she doesn't like being objectified and being treated like a possession. Where does he get off asking me these questions? I don't belong to him. Sure, we had that moment at Morta's, but nothing else since. I had hoped in the beginning, but because nothing's happened, not to mention the whole to-do about who he is, the attraction's kind of dwindled.

"So? What's going on with you two? What the hell kind of name is Mors, anyway? It's a stupid name."

"Noah. Weren't you just here? Didn't you see what he just did to you? He snaps his fingers and things happen. Or haven't you noticed?"

Noah considers this, I think. At least he looks like he is. The ugly expression on his face slowly fades until there is only a sheepish-looking smirk in its place.

"He's a god, eh?"

"Yeah."

"And he's watching over you, huh?"

"That's what I said, and have been saying for the past, oh, I don't know, ten minutes?"

"Uh, right. Sorry."

So now we're sitting here watching each other fidget since we have nothing else to talk about. Fun. Well, maybe not nothing to talk about. Just nothing we *want* to talk about. Or are willing to...

So we sit and trade tight smiles for another few minutes, though it feels like eons.

This is stupid. I might as well return the treatment he's giving me with the same.

"Did you feel any different after Mors...did his thing? Do you know anything new? Did it do anything?"

"It didn't feel like anything. Didn't even tickle." He flips his hands over, examining them as if he was expecting there to be something written on them telling him that there's something different about him. "It was weird, though. You know, seeing myself...outside myself."

I am going to blame the strange situation we're in for that little foray into the 'most useless thing anyone has ever said' territory. If it happens again, I'll have to call it a personality fault and use it as a strike against him as possible date material and maybe even as a human being. I nod, hoping that it will prompt him to say something a little more intelligent.

"What do you think he was talking about when he disappeared?"

I had almost forgotten about Mors. Almost. Then I remember what happened. What happened to Mors? He'd looked like he was in a lot of pain, as if he was being dragged away against his will. The thought causes my stomach to flop over. Who would have the power to drag the God of Death away? And why would they want to?

Unless someone knows about me and the job he is doing. Which is probably the truth. I mean, I'm dealing with gods here. The big question is which one? Juno, of course, is at the top of the list. But, if I remember correctly, Jupiter had a fair number of enemies too. How many of them would pass up the chance to get to him through his helpless mortal daughter?

I've read about people going cold from dread or fear. I've never actually done it until now. I actually feel like I've been tangoing with an ice block or something. Not the best feeling.

"Ava? What's the matter?"

He winds an arm around my shoulders, but it does little to make me feel better. It's like I'll never be warm again.

"We've got to find Mors. He's in danger. I know it."

"Uh. Sure. How are we going to do that?"

Good question. I scan my room for some sort of inspiration and my eyes automatically go to my computer.

"I'm going to try to contact someone, okay? While I'm doing that, see if you can remember exactly what happened when he was fading away. Can you do that?"

"Sure. But I don't think your computer is going to be any help. It's cool and all, but unless you've got some super special hotline on that thing, I don't think it's going to get you anywhere."

I smirk at him and fire up my juiced up computer. Noah will just have to wait and see, now, won't he? This might not be one of my greatest ideas, but Mors' life may be hanging in the balance. I don't have time to play *Spy vs. Spy*. Besides, when I get him back he can always erase Noah's memory, right?

Within a few seconds, I'm logging in on Mercury's messenger and searching through the names. A few clicks later and I've got a conference video chat going with Venus, Flora, Fortuna and Morta.

"Ava? Is something the matter?" Morta is back at her most terrifying even though she sounds like her grandmotherly self.

"I was wondering if there was something going on in your world that I should know about?"

They seem deep in thought before Flora shakes her head. "Not that I know of. Why do you ask?"

"Mors disappeared a few minutes ago. It was like it was forced or something. He definitely didn't look happy about going. I guess I'm just a little worried, that's all."

Fortuna's beautiful face blurs for a second as she speaks, as if there is some sort of interference or something. "I'm sure he's fine." She fuzzes out for a second. "Not much can hurt him."

But obviously something can, or else she wouldn't have said the 'much' part. In my gut I know there's something wrong. Even if they can't see it.

"I'm worried. I think something's going on."

Morta seems interested now. "What makes you say that, child?"

"Just a feeling. I'm restless. Like I should be doing something. Like there's something coming that I could be doing something about." Yeah, real specific. It was a strange sensation that I couldn't describe even to myself. All I knew was that if I didn't do something, I'd go crazy. "I... I don't know. I just need..." I concentrate on the sensation and realize that I shouldn't have done that.

The room fades away and so does everything in it. For a moment there, it's as though I'm being pulled a million different ways at once. Just as my limbs are about to tear off, the feeling stops and I'm left standing in the middle of a very bright...place. I can't quite tell what it is at the moment because my retinas are being burned out.

Then, as quickly as it happened, the sensation reverses itself and I'm back in my room, once again gaping back at an obviously bewildered Noah. He's pale and his eyes are huge and wary, but at the same time he's interested in what just happened.

Hell, *I'm* interested in what just happened.

"Can someone tell me what just happened?" I look at the three faces on my screen. They're the ones who are supposed to be teaching me about this stuff. So why aren't they teaching? Come on, goddesses! Hop to!

Fortuna attempts an explanation first, as usual. "It looked as if you had a go at teleporting."

"I can't do that." Can I? Had Juno's kiss done something to me? The thought of developing new powers is a little frightening, but also gives me a jolt of vigor. Teleportation would definitely come in handy.

"Try it again," urges Flora.

"Try what? I don't even know what I did."

"Try thinking whatever you were thinking," Morta encourages.

Noah grabs hold of my hand and squeezes, knowing that there isn't any advice that he can give. Still, moral support counts for a lot.

I grip his hand like a lifeline and try my best to remember what was going through my mind before my little excursion.

I was thinking about Mors. How worried I am. How I wish I was with him. He'd seemed to be in such pain when he disappeared that I want to be there to hurt whatever it was back. Twice as much.

I take all that frustration, worry and fear and blend it all together into one gloriously potent mix of emotion as I think about Mors again. There's a slight tingling. Then nothing.

"Nope. Not gonna happen."

"Is this how you were in your lessons, girl?" Morta isn't at all pleased with me right now. She is peering at me in a very angry, very scary manner. "Try it again! You did it once, you can do it again. Now concentrate!"

I fight the urge to pout and stick my tongue out at her. Childish, I know. And it certainly wouldn't help matters. So I try it again without fussing, but all I get is tingling once again. Though this time it's a little stronger.

I think about what Morta said about my lessons at school. How did I learn the stuff I did and make it stick? The answer comes to me right away. I study everything from every angle I can think of until it makes sense. I need to tackle this a different way. "How do you guys do it?"

"What do you mean how do we do it? We just do!" The other two nod in agreement with Fortuna. "I don't know how to explain it. I suppose once you're born with the ability it becomes second nature." Her expression grows thoughtful. "Just concentrate on where you want to be... Though seeing as you don't know where that is, maybe you'd better just

concentrate on Mors. Think about being with him…"
She sighs heavily. "Try it again. Think about Mors." She
smiles at me knowingly.

"That's what I've been doing," I grumble. Shaking
out my arms, I give it another try, this time willing
myself to be with Mors.

The tingling starts again, first at the top of my head
and quickly making its way down my body. The instant
it reaches my toes the room fades. *I'm doing it! I'm really
doing it!* The room sharpens again and I concentrate
harder, afraid that the brief moment of celebration
ruined it for me again. The room fades faster this time,
becoming nothing more than a blur within seconds.

This time, instead of a blinding light, I see nothing.
No light. There is no sound. Just a void.

"Mors?" I'm on solid ground and I turn, hoping to at
least hear something that will lead me to him. "Mors!"

"Ava."

Mors! But his voice sounds so weak. I spin again,
trying to pinpoint his location. "Where are you? Are
you okay? I've been so worried."

"I will come to you. Stay where you are."

Too late, I'm already heading toward his voice.

"Ava! Stop!"

I freeze. "What's wrong?"

"Do not move."

This is where I notice that his voice is worn. He
sounds raspy, tired. He sounds as though he's been
shouting for hours. "Are you okay?"

"I am fine." He pauses for a deep breath. "Now stay
where you are."

"All right."

He sounds stressed out enough without me screwing
things up. If he says to stay here, I'm staying here. If he

tells me to stand here and wait for him while hopping on one foot, I'll do it... Well, maybe.

Standing here in the dark isn't settling well with me. I have a thing about not being able to see my surroundings and therefore not being able to prepare myself for whatever might be heading my way. Call me a control freak.

"Mors? Are there any lights in this place?"

"Trust me. It is much better this way."

His voice is much closer, but why is it taking him so long to get to me? Is he hurt? Is he somehow incapacitated or something? I start moving toward him.

"Stop!"

I'm balanced on one foot. "Can I at least put my foot down?"

"I would not."

He's next to me now and winds an arm around my waist. There is so much weight behind it that I'm a little scared.

"Mors? Are you hurt?"

"No, not exactly. But this is not the place to talk. Now, do exactly as I say." He nudges me to the right and uses his weight to propel me.

It's strange. All the times we've touched he's felt solid... But there is no weight behind him now. He seems light, ethereal. He feels...real.

"What happened to you?"

He shushes me and continues to push, turning me this way and that every few steps. It dawns on me that he's steering us through a maze of something. And considering how carefully he's doing it, it must be pretty serious.

Finally he stops and breathes a sigh of relief. I feel my own muscles un-bunching. Somehow we manage to keep each other up. It doesn't last long. Mors is too heavy for me and falls rather ungracefully to the ground.

"Mors, what happened to you?" I hit the ground too and gently pull his head onto my lap. "What can I do?"

"I honestly do not know." His turns toward me and clings to me like a teddy bear. "One moment I was talking to you and the next I was here. I cannot leave. I cannot do anything that I used to. I have been going crazy trying to get out of here." A slight pause before he continues, his voice quieter, his arms tighter. "I was worried about you. What might have happened to you."

My face heats up a little. Thank goodness it's dark. "I was worried about you too. I had no idea what happened. Didn't know if you were hurt…" It's at this point that my stomach flops over and I realize that I really do care about Mors. As strange as he is, I've grown fond of him. How is that even possible? Now is not the time to figure this out, though. I file it away for later and focus on Mors. I can feel the gentle smile on my face. I wonder if he can tell in the dark.

"Come on. Let's see what's wrong with you. Can you manage at least a little light in here?"

"I can try." He tenses, and after a few seconds the room begins to lighten a little.

It's enough for me to get a look at our surroundings. I can see why he didn't want me wandering around. There are pits and jagged rocks everywhere. I'm amazed that there's even enough space anywhere for us to sit. My gaze drops to Mors. He's all banged up. Cuts and scrapes everywhere, some still oozing.

"What happened? Who did this to you?"

His little laugh is a cross between a chuckle and a cough. "I am afraid I am a bit clumsy."

I bite at my T-shirt and tear strips off of it to try my best to bandage the worst of his wounds. He banged himself up? "But how? You're a god."

He looks up at me, his bottomless eyes peering into mine. "I do not think I am anymore, Ava."

Chapter Fourteen
Between a Rock and…More Rocks

"Mors? What do you mean?" The light in the room is dimming. The last thing I see before it goes completely dark is the sad glint in Mors' eyes. Once again we're enveloped in the darkness. "How is that even possible?"

"I do not know. All I know is that I can no longer do the things I used to. I cannot even light up this room anymore. I think the last of my divine power has been drained now."

I can feel him wriggling around trying to get up, but I hold him down. He struggles again, but in his weakened state he soon gives up.

"This cannot be happening. How are we going to get out of here?" His voice is hard, angry. I know that if whoever is responsible were here right now, they would be in danger from Mors, powers or no powers. He rubs my arm. It feels apologetic. "How did you get here? I know I was reaching out for you, but I did not think I would actually be able to bring you to me. I actually hoped it would work the other way around."

A surge of pride rises in my chest. "I did it myself. I concentrated on finding you and I did."

Shock must have stunned him because, for a few seconds, I hear nothing but his ragged breathing. "You came here…on your own?"

"Yeah. I figure it's just the rest of my abilities coming out. Why? Is it a bad thing?"

"No! Not at all. This is good news. Do you think you can try to get us both out of here?"

I only barely made it here myself. "I can give it a try." I start thinking about the places we could go. I just know I want to get out of here. "Where do you want to go? Is there somewhere you want to be?"

"Anywhere but here will be fine." He relaxes in my arms and appears to be waiting for me to transport us magically out of this place.

"Okay, but just to warn you, it might take a few tries."

I feel him nod in reply before concentrating on my room. It seems as good a place as any to go right now. Mom keeps the first aid kit well supplied so I'll be able to patch him up a little too.

I think about my room, piecing it together in my mind until I can see if perfectly. I focus my energy on going there and taking Mors with me. My hands convulse on his clothes. I don't want to risk leaving him behind and not being able to come back.

I feel a surge of power as we lurch upward. We float for a second before we drop back down again. There's a slight moan from Mors. Poor guy. I'm not making this any easier on him.

"Sorry. Are you okay?"

"Fine. Try it again."

It doesn't help my nerves that it sounds like he's saying that through gritted teeth. It just proves what kind of state he's in. I really need to get this right.

Come on, Ava. Concentrate.

I can see my room forming around us. Somehow I manage to get it so that Mors and I will end up on my bed when we get back. Which is really a good thing since I don't think I'm going to be able to get him up there on my own. The shocking thing is that not only is Noah still there, but the goddesses are there as well, not to mention my mother. It startles me so much that we end up back on the hard ground of Mors' prison once again. Colliding with the dirt annoys me almost as much as not being able to pull this teleportation off.

"Sorry." I'm not sure if he even hears my muttered apology. Mors isn't moving at all and for a second I'm terrified that I've hurt him. "Mors?"

"I am okay… Try again."

He sounds even worse now.

Clutching him to me, I try again. This time my attempts are thwarted by a *whooshing* sound. The next thing I know there's someone groping my arm. Afraid that it's someone here to hurt Mors, I flinch away and pull the fallen god in my arms a little closer.

"Get away, whoever you are!" I have half a mind to start making empty threats, but chances are whoever this is will have some sort of ability that will make my seeing gods and almost-teleporting abilities look really, really pitiful.

"Ava?"

I know that voice! "Noah?" He hugs me clumsily in the dark. "How did you find us?"

"I did that thing you and the goddesses were talking about."

He teleported? On his first try? I'm jealous. "That's incredible…" Why did he come?

"You don't sound so happy." He feels around with his hands and traces down the length of my arm to find Mors' head in my lap. "So you found him." His voice has lost the 'I just teleported to find you' happiness to it. "What's the matter with him?"

I want to remind him that *he* has a name, but now's not the time to get into it. "I don't know." I shrug uselessly into the dark. "When I got here he was fine, but weak. Now he's practically unconscious. I'm really worried about him."

"You must be. You're practically breastfeeding him." He sighs after the snide remark. "I'm sorry. I thought that something bad had happened to you. And for the second time today I find you cuddling up with this guy."

I've had it. "Noah, you have no right to be jealous. It's not like we're dating or anything. Mors is a friend. He's taken care of me and been there for me when I've needed a shoulder to cry on. So unless you've got something you want to say, just stop with the jealous act, okay?"

The body at my side slumps a little. "All right. Fine. Whatever. Want me to take him?"

What? His tone totally puts me off. There's no way I'm going to let him drag poor Mors around. "I'm all right. We have to figure a way out of here."

"Just teleport."

Like it's just *that* easy. I don't want him to know how hard it's been for me to get a handle on that particular trick. "I don't know if it's such a good idea. Mors…"

"Just let me take him and we'll head for your room again."

I look down at Mors uselessly. In my mind's eye I can pick out his features as he lies there helpless. What the hell is going on here? How... What could do this to the God of Death? And what the hell happened to Noah? Where's the sweet, mild-mannered soccer playing guy I've been interested in all year? Certainly not here.

I know Noah is waiting for my answer, but I really don't want him taking Mors. Something in my gut is going haywire at the suggestion.

"Take my hand and we can both take him back. It's the safest thing I can think of." Not to mention the most neutral answer I could come up with.

Noah releases a burst of air. I can almost see him scowling.

"What's the matter with you, Noah? You're not yourself."

"I'm fine. Let's get back."

Alarm bells are pealing in my head now. Whoever this guy is, he isn't Noah. I shuffle back a little, taking Mors with me. "Who are you?"

"It's me, Noah. What's the matter with you? Has this guy done something to you?" His voice hardens with the accusation.

I hug Mors defensively. "That's not what I'm saying and you know it. Who are you? What have you done to Noah?"

There's no answer, but there's a different energy coming from whoever it is next to me. It's like the air around him has chilled and the vibe is now menacing. This guy really doesn't like me. Then again, he might be full of hate for Mors. Either way, it's not looking too good for either of us. Mors seems incapable of doing anything to help and I can't control anything I do. It seems that this would be a really good time to learn. Talk about being thrown into the deep end.

Panic starts to creep into my system with icy fingers clawing up my spine. What the hell do I do now?

Mors grabs hold of my hand and squeezes it reassuringly. It's weak, but it's enough to let me know that he believes in me. It's nice to know that someone does, even if I'm lacking in self-confidence at the moment. Thankfully, as small a gesture as it is, it grounds some of the anxiety.

I knead his hands restlessly. I can't help it. At the moment, it's either that or screaming in frustration. And I don't think anyone here would appreciate that. I take one hand away from Mors and press it over my chest where my heart is trying to thump its way through. I need to do something before I have a heart attack or something.

I let my hand slowly drift down until it rests against the same spot on Mors' chest. I concentrate on the slow beat against my palm. I need to make sure it keeps beating.

What do I do? Do I try to get us out of here? What if this guy tries something in the meantime? What do I do then? Would it be better to hang back a bit and see what happens? A million different scenarios flash through my mind. I wish I could ask Mors what to do.

He squeezes my hand again. Is he still able to read my mind? That would at least be something going my way. Of course, him reading my mind doesn't help me out when I'm the one needing guidance.

How do I make this work for me? I squeeze his hand to get his attention and think about making a run for it, aka trying to get us both back to my room. If it's a good idea I want him to squeeze my hand twice. If not, to squeeze it hard once.

I wait.

Come on, Mors!

After a breathless moment, Mors clamps down on my hand. Okay. Bad idea. What about trying to find a way of attacking him?

Another hard squeeze.

I fight back a frustrated squeal. This would be so much easier if I could read his mind. Normally, I'd be giving up just about now. If I wasn't so worried about this guy hurting us I would have. Mors groans. Getting up and walking out is not a choice.

Okay, Ava. Think!

My mind starts going in another direction now. Is this really Noah or just someone taking on his likeness? Has he been possessed?

Mors squeezes hard at that thought. Not possessed.

If he's not possessed then what the hell is going on? I've never been patient enough to play Twenty Questions. And this is a hell of a lot worse. I like getting straight to the answer. I could always ask him directly. I could ease into a conversation and work up to the questions. Perhaps that would help. You know. Talk some sense into him along the way. Remind him who he really is.

I get two slightly hesitant squeezes.

Okay, since I have Mors' blessing, sort of, I decide to give it a try. What to talk about...

"So... Noah... How's your summer going?" I'm glad no one can see me cringe. How lame was that? *Quick! Think of something else!* "It's so weird what's been going on, eh?"

Even in the dark, I know the guy formerly known as Noah is staring at me. Well, at least I've distracted him. Might as well just keep going. "How do you feel about what's going on?" No answer. My brain tells me to keep pushing. To get more personal. "It's so weird, isn't it? I mean, to have powers like we do… It's kind of cool and scary at the same time." I look him straight in the eyes. "I'm glad you're going through it with me. I don't know what I'd do if I was alone in this." I know it's risky, but I take his hand in mine and squeeze.

His hand is rigid and cold. I'm afraid that he's going to either drop my hand or squeeze too hard. I'm not sure which would be worse. But after a few seconds his fingers twitch and closes over mine.

"Noah?"

"Ava? What's going on? Where are we?"

I know we don't have much time to play catch-up so I dive right in.

"I have no idea where we are, but more importantly, something is going on with you. You just appeared here and I don't know what to do. If you know what's going on, you have to tell me. Mors is getting weaker by the minute and unless we do something fast I… I don't know if he's going to make it." The last words are hard to get out and tears are threatening to spill.

Noah puts his arm around me and he gives me a reassuring squeeze before it quickly slides away. Is he afraid to hug me? Maybe in this instance it's the right thing to be.

"Let's just focus on how we're going to get out of here."

"Agreed. But if you zone out on me again, I'm going to have to clobber you. Just so you know."

"I wouldn't want it any other way."

Now that's the old Noah I remember.

Noah seems to be trying to look around. I hear him shifting back and forth. "What if we pick him up and start walking?"

"No good. Before he passed out, he managed to light the room enough so that I could see. Nothing but a horrible death awaits if we try that option."

"Great. Okay." He's silent for a few seconds. "How did you get here in the first place?"

"I teleported."

"Great. So just teleport us out of here."

"I'd love to, but it's not exactly a skill I've mastered just yet."

"Right. What about getting the goddesses to help?"

I ponder that for a bit. Wouldn't they have helped before now if they could?

"I get the feeling that they can't. I mean, look at Mors. He can't even talk let alone teleport."

His hand finds my shoulder. "It's all up to you, then."

He's right and I know it.

"I'll give it another try. You know, I almost got us back before you got here."

"This time actually do it."

His voice sounds strained, like he's fighting something. No time to chat now. Maybe if I get him back to the goddesses they'll be able to help him.

I focus on my room again, aiming to get Mors on the bed. Gripping Noah and Mors to my sides, I go for it. Success! I can smell the potpourri that Mom liberally sprinkles in cute little dishes all over the house. It's a relief from the dank mildew smell of wherever we were.

Just as the room crystallizes, I feel Noah wrench away. Only Mors and I fall onto the bed.

The moment we land everyone pounces.

"Where were you?"

"Are you all right?"

"What happened?"

"What's wrong with Mors?"

My mind rejects their questions as I try to comprehend what just happened. As far as I can tell, Noah voluntarily stayed behind. But why? Was that thing coming back? Could he feel it taking over again? What if it was something else? What if there was a monster that grabbed hold of him?

I have to get back to find out what happened to him.

"Keep an eye on Mors. I have to go back."

Mom latches on to my arm. Obviously she's not too keen on the idea of me just teleporting willy-nilly. Especially into an unknown situation.

"Hold on. What's going on?"

Even government agents trained in the art of doublespeak wouldn't be able to help me now. Time for the truth.

"Noah's still there. I have to return and get him."

"What?" Her grip on my arm tightens as she looks at Mors. "Are you sure that's such a good idea?"

"I have to. Besides, I'm getting the hang of this teleportation thing. If I get into trouble I can just come straight back."

"What if you can't?"

Great, Fortuna just has to jump in. It's bad enough having my mother hovering over me. Goddesses are much harder to shake.

"Don't worry about me. Just take care of Mors."

"We're coming with you." Flora and Fortuna look pretty adamant, not that I could stop them.

"It might not be such a good idea. Look at what happened to Mors. What if something like that happens to you guys?"

"We won't let that happen." The two goddesses flank me, grabbing an arm each. "You take the lead."

Mom is livid. I don't think I've seen her this angry before. Ever. But her voice is steady. Quiet. Scary. "You are *not* going."

I know she's worried about me, but this is something I've got to do. "Mom, I've got to go." I didn't say 'don't worry', because it's a mother's prerogative, so how could she not worry? I know I would if it was my daughter going out there. "I'll be extra careful, okay?"

I don't get a go-ahead nor do I get a scream forbidding me to go. She just stands there, looking as though she is willing herself to let me go.

"Thanks, Mom. I'll be back soon." I give her a peck on the cheek and think about getting to Noah.

This is getting easier. As the darkness closes in around us I give the goddesses' arms a squeeze. "Light up the place!"

They immediately do as I ask and the crevasses and jagged rock appear with startling clarity. I can see that it's more like a dark world than the cave I had imagined. At least with a cave it would eventually end. This looked like some desolate alien world or something. I almost expect some weird *Star Trek*-like being to pop out from one of the holes. What a horrible place.

I carefully aim us at a particularly wide section where we settle. There's no sign of Noah anywhere.

I don't think that it's a good idea to be shouting for him, so I settle for scanning the darkness for a Noah-

looking shadow. I think I spot him a couple of times —
at least I think I see his hair — but no. Not him.

Weird. He should be around here somewhere. I was
thinking of getting right back to him, so I should have
gotten close. I don't think I'm skilled enough in
teleportation yet that I can just appear in random
places. Although my abilities might just be bad
enough...

Fortuna and Flora have both let go and are scanning
the terrain. From the expressions on their faces, neither
of them knows where we are either.

How disconcerting is it when *two* goddesses, beings
who are supposed to know everything, don't know
where you are. How knee-shakingly scary is that? But
who else could block a divine being's sight but another
god? A much more powerful god. But who and why?

I look over at the goddesses to see what they think.
Only they're not paying any attention to me let alone to
what I'm thinking. Strange. They're usually so in tune
with what I'm feeling.

A quick wave of my arms have them looking over.
Shrugging at them, I think about my question again.

They stare back blankly.

It's occurring to me that whatever happened to Mors
might be because of this place. And now it's happening
to them too.

"We've got to get you both out of here."

They seem a little perplexed about what's going on,
but nod in agreement. They look a little more than
confused if you asked me. Weakened. Wobbly even.

I lunge for them, but find that my hands pass right
through theirs.

"What the —?" I make another grab but the same
thing happens again. "What's going on?"

"Ava!"

Noah's back and running toward us... Well, me. Within the millisecond it takes for me to turn and look at him, Flora and Fortuna disappear.

He skids to a halt next to me. "What's going on? What are you doing back here?"

"I came back for you. What happened? Why did you let go?" I automatically start checking for any wounds that could have resulted from him staying behind. He's all in one piece. What's more, he still seems to be himself. So now to wait for a reason why he stayed.

He shrugs and has the grace to look a little sheepish. "I thought I saw something."

Okay, so all sympathy for the guy just went out of the window. "You thought you *saw* something? So you just decided to find out on your own? Are you crazy? You have no idea what you're up against!"

He puts a hand on my shoulder, supposedly to calm me down a little. It doesn't. Shrugging it off, I step back. I need my space after all.

"Calm down. I'm all right. Nothing happened." His smile morphs into a mischievous one. "Want to see what I found?"

"That depends. There isn't anything out there made out of one or more animals, is there?" Mythological monsters are famously purported to be made of everything horrifying all meshed into one. "Nothing that could be classified as a monster?"

"Nope. Nothing like that." He grabs my hands and we're off.

I realize that the place is still lit up. I'm not doing it and the goddesses aren't here anymore. Is it Noah? "Hey, are you making it so we can see?"

"I don't know. I guess so." I can see a cheeky grin over his shoulder. "I got sick of fumbling around in the dark and just thought about making it light in here. And it worked. The light's been following me around since."

So, on the plus side we have light. On the minus, Noah's gaining more powers. Does this mean that Scary Noah is coming back? Will I even know if he does? What if he's getting better at disguising himself?

Noah takes my hand and walks us down a winding path through a few trees. I let him. I don't want to risk freaking him out.

Even in the darkness I can make out the shimmering surface of a lake. The silvery moonlight is reflected on the still water to make it appear as though there are two moons kissing on the horizon. The air is as still as the water, but there is something not quite right about it. It's fresh, but there is something else in it. In a few wafts it smells a little like someone has been burning matches. One breeze in particular gusts something that smells a little like rotten eggs through a few skeletal trees. Weird.

"Isn't it beautiful?"

"Breathtaking." It's true. The smell might be a bit weird, but the sight itself is spectacular. It might be because of the amazing things the moonlight is doing to the scene spread out before us, but it really is incredible. "Where are we?"

He shakes his head. "I have no idea." He starts walking again. For someone who's in a place he doesn't know, Noah's pretty sure about where he's going.

It's got alarm bells pealing in my head again now. How can I be sure this is Noah? And if this isn't him, where is he taking me?

The unsettling thoughts slow my feet a little. Noah notices immediately and turns to me. I can see half of his questioning expression. It's really creepy.

"What's wrong?"

I tug my hand from his grip. "Don't you think it's a bit weird for you to be charging into the dark without knowing where you're going?"

Noah slows. Apparently he hadn't thought of that. "It is a little weird, isn't it?" He stops completely and scans the area. "I just feel like I know this place."

"Really?" I suppose this could be a good thing. "Why are we headed this way? Any idea where we're going?"

He shakes his head. In the darkness his hair and eyes are black, only shining silver when the light penetrates the trees to hit him. "I just want to walk in this direction. No idea why. I just do."

I guess there's nothing to do but go with it. Cautiously, of course. I'm hoping that whatever we end up doing or facing, it will answer at least a few of the questions I have whirling around my mind.

Like the question first and foremost on the tip of my tongue — what the hell is going on here?

Our pace is slower when we resume our trek into the darkness. Thank goodness for the light Noah is producing. Otherwise, we'd be in serious trouble. It's too bad that it doesn't reach too far. I look over at him. I think he's just as keyed up as I am about this whole thing. Who wouldn't be, right? He still seems to know where he's going but he's being a bit more cautious about getting there now.

Noah doesn't stumble once, but saves me more than a few times from falling flat on my face. Thankfully, before I can injure myself, we find ourselves standing in front of a cave, staring into the eerie darkness.

"What's in there?" A stupid question, I know. But maybe Noah's suddenly picked up on something I haven't. *Yeah, fat chance.*

"Don't know. I'm going in. You can stay here if you want."

He's already walking forward when I snag his hand and drag him back. "Are you sure that's a good idea? You don't even know what's in there."

Turning slowly, he takes my hands, squeezing gently. He says very simply, "I'm going."

I watch him saunter off into the dark, left with two choices — wait out here alone in the dark with who knows what or follow him in there into the unknown. There is a third choice, of course — teleport the hell out of here and back into my nice, cozy room. But I'm not going without Noah.

Sucking in a deep, slightly stale breath of air, I force my feet to follow Noah into the yawning cavern.

"Wait up." I feel safer knowing that I'm not alone in the inky black.

"Glad you decided to join me."

He takes my hand and we inch forward, feeling our way along.

I keep peeking back at the entrance, wishing that the light could somehow follow us. But it doesn't and all too soon the glow isn't there anymore. Noah is nothing but a warm hand attached to mine and the darkness is starting to suffocate. I'm not liking it. The longer we spend in here the more panicked I feel. Nothing good can live in a place like this.

We walk for about a week — well, it feels like a week — when I finally hear something. It sounds like running water. A lot of running water.

His hand tightens and I know he hears it too.

"Is water a good thing?"

I hear him chuckle. "How bad can it be?"

Another few seconds of trudging and I start to see illumination. It's not natural, at least I don't think it is. It's not firelight or moonlight...though it's got a silvery tint to it. But it's too blue to be moonlight, not to mention that we must be half a mile under the ground.

I'm curious enough to move faster toward it. Noah is too. He has an excited glint in his eyes now and in turn it's making me more anxious to get there too.

It becomes a race and we're running, leaping over rocks, zipping in between and around the ones we can't jump.

Noah gets to the mouth of the cave just a split second before I do. I skid to a halt behind him. The dust clouds around our feet, drifting down the gentle slope toward a river of what could be dark, liquid mercury.

We trade a look as our breathing returns to normal. Somehow we reach a mutual agreement. We both want to get closer and start moving toward the wide expanse of rippling fluid. At a crawl we step toward it as though if we moved faster we'd somehow disturb its peaceful pace.

Noah reaches forward first, intent on touching it. I haul him back by the arm he has outstretched behind him as a counterbalance.

"What do you think you're doing?" *Is the boy insane?* "We don't know what that stuff is. Whatever it is, it's definitely not water."

"We won't find out what it is unless we get nearer."

"That doesn't mean touching."

"It does when you want to find out what something is. I thought you were into the science stuff."

"Sticking your hand into unknown liquid isn't a technique used in science, Noah."

He shrugs and reaches for the river again.

"I would rather you not do that."

A shadowy figure detaches itself from the cavern wall and drifts up the shore toward us.

Points for chivalry goes to Noah, for stepping in front of me, shielding me from the newcomer.

"Who are you?" He took the words right out of my mouth.

The new guy smiles and edges closer, but stops when he's just over an arm's length away. I get the feeling he wants to give us a chance to study him while he scrutinizes us at the same time. Reassuring? Maybe a smidge. But seeing as we're in yet another situation where we don't know where we stand, I'm going to have to say that all I want is to just go home and call it a night.

I peek at him from around Noah's shoulder. This guy seems pleasant enough, and his dark robes remind me a little of Mors' usual choice of attire. Like all the other divine beings I've encountered so far, his face isn't hard to look at. Quite the opposite actually. He's almost pretty. Which of course could be a good thing or a very bad thing.

While I'm trying to figure out his deal, the two males are sizing each other up. Noah is watching his every move while Pretty Guy is outright gauging us. He's not even trying to hide it. His apparent interest in Noah piques my own curiosity. I wonder why he's so focused on Noah. I'm the one who's the daughter of a god.

The moment the idea passes through my mind, he looks at me. Can he read my thoughts? He grins hugely. I guess he can.

"I am to ferry you across the river."

He bows. His arm swept grandiosely back is aimed at a boat that I'm pretty sure wasn't there before. The black wood of the hull is polished and looks strong enough. I'd get into it readily if I wanted to. But right now I don't want to. I want to know a little more before I head blindly into the unknown…again.

"Who wants you to ferry us across?"

"It is my reason for being." The answer flows off his tongue easily. "All I ask for is payment for my troubles. Just a coin. A trifle, really."

This whole thing is starting to sound really familiar to me. Wasn't there a scary, ugly, creepy guy that was supposed to take people on his little boat across the river to…?

"Nope. No. No way." Grabbing Noah, I start hauling him up the slope, fully prepared to push, pull or drag him out of here.

"Ava? What's going on? What's got you all stressed?"

Apparently Noah wasn't in the other Ancient Civilization class or he might have clued in to what's 'got me all stressed'.

He's dug in his heels but it's not going to stop me. "Noah, we have to get out of here. That guy isn't exactly offering to take us on a pleasure cruise."

"What're you talking about?"

"That's the ferry man for the dead. He's offering to take us into…Hades." The last word comes out as a hissed whisper. It's as if saying it aloud would condemn us to it.

He yanks, catching me before I stumble back down to the place I'm trying to get away from. "Are you sure? I've seen movies. He's supposed to be scary, like a skeleton in ragged robes and all that stuff."

"Don't you get it? They can look like whoever they want." I take a deep breath and can't hold back the exasperated release. "That's not the problem. I don't care if he makes himself look like Mickey Mouse, it's the fact that he wants to take us into the Underworld." Again, the word comes out as a whisper. "That's not somewhere I want to visit."

"Hades?" It takes a moment before comprehension dawns. "Hell? He's taking us into Hell?"

"Not if I can help it."

I'm about to practice my Noah-dragging technique when Ferry Guy steps in front of us. "If I may interject."

"No, you may not, and I haven't got any money for you either. So you can just forget about taking us across."

"That's very well, my dear." He wedges himself in between us. "But I know for a fact that he has a coin for me. You can stay here if you like."

"What?" This is new. For the past little while it's been all about me. I'm not sure if this is a nice change or not. I'm not one of those girls who needs attention twenty-four-seven, but it's been nice to be the center of it all for once.

"You. Can. Stay. Here." He enunciates as if I were a two-year-old.

"Yeah, I get you." To prove that it doesn't miff me that he's more interested in Noah than in me, I sit on the rocky shore and draw my knees up to my chest. "Fine, I'll just wait here."

Noah reaches for my hand. "Come on. Don't be like that."

"I'm not being like anything. I'll be waiting right here when you get back." And here's the moment when he's supposed to say, 'I'm not going anywhere without you, Ava'. *Come on. Say it.*

"All right. Are you sure?"

Am I sure? This isn't going how it's supposed to go!

"I'm fine. I'll see you when you get back." I'll just sit right here and wait, thank you. Noah gives me one last hesitant glance. Yep, that's right. Feel guilty. Swim in it until your fingers get all prune-y.

They start back toward Charon's boat. I'm glad I finally remembered Pretty Ferry Guy's name. It was beginning to bug me. There are other things about this area that I recall from class as well. According to a thousand years of myth, there are supposed to be the souls of people unable to pay the ferry price wandering the shores for eternity. I don't see any.

Charon and Noah are getting into the boat. As he gets Noah settled in, he smiles up at me, displaying his teeth in a slightly predatory manner. "You will soon enough."

The words have barely stopped echoing before I start to see silvery wisps whisper past me. As I draw a startled breath, they solidify... Sort of. It's enough so that I can make out features. I can see their clothes, their hair, even the horrifyingly pained expressions on their faces.

They drift close to stare at me. Near enough for icy-coldness to lash at my skin whenever they pass a little too close.

Yep. That's enough for me.

"Wait for me!" Lurching to my feet, I all but fly to the boat. A deft leap and I'm over the side of the boat just as Charon pushes off. Noah catches me...awkwardly. He manages to keep me from propelling myself over the other side while simultaneously keeping the boat from rocking. One arm is around me securely while his other hand is wedged in between us and spread over my heart. For one long moment we're stuck that way.

"Payment, if you will." Unfortunately, Charon has incredibly bad timing.

Noah untangles us and flips him a coin before easing himself over so I can sit.

"Sorry." There's nothing like a mumbled apology to make a girl feel better for being accidentally groped by the guy she likes.

Oh, it's awkward.

I wave him off. "Don't worry about it. You saved me from going head first into the river."

My hand goes to my chest before I can stop it. My shirt is wet through where he touched it. He must be stressing out more than he's letting on.

I keep my eyes on his face as we slip into the darkness.

Chapter Fifteen
What Lies in the Dark

I expected him to take us straight over the river. That assumption is dashed when he steers us into the current and we start to follow the swift flow. I didn't think there would be much by way of scenery. But looking around there are a few things that make my breath hitch in my chest.

There's light everywhere—though I can't find a source. Just like where we came in, the glow is silver laced with blue. It's bright, yet it only provides enough illumination to see what I'm looking at—nothing more. It's like a warped version of tunnel vision and is incredibly infuriating. However, what I do see at the end of the tunnel is incredible and completely wipes away the irritation at only being able to see a portion of it.

I suppose when imagining a world of the dead you tend to think of the dark and dreary. This place certainly has dark undertones, but it definitely is not dreary. It's not cheerful by any means. It just is. There's no real feeling attached to it. The spirits are slashes of gleaming white in the gloom. A closer look reveals that at the center of each is a different color. I wonder if it's the color of their souls.

Some drift. Some flash from one spot to another. Others swirl about in groups. But that's not what catches my attention. Not too far away, on the side we haven't gotten to yet no matter how hard Charon seems to be working, there is a building. No, to call it a building would be an understatement.

Part palace and part fortress, it looms above the rocks, above the spirits, like a beacon in the night glowing from within with a dark light. The river we're on seems to flow around it, surrounding the mesa it's perched upon, gleaming and glistening like a sword warding it.

My guess is we're heading for that.

Time to wrack my brain for everything I know about this place and its inhabitants.

The Underworld. Hades. The not so cheery place where the souls of the dead reside. It's ruled by Pluto, who I'm assuming lives in the big scary palace that we're drifting ever closer to. He's the not so personable brother of Jupiter and has tried more than a few times to take over the throne of the King of the Gods. Why in the world would we be headed to see him?

My gaze is drawn next to me. Noah is looking around, his expression as wide-eyed as mine. Charon said that I could stay behind, meaning that whomever we were going to see wasn't interested in seeing me. Which leaves Noah. Am I right? Yes, I do believe I am.

The icy hand of fear squeezes at my heart. We're not replaying that episode with Morta, are we? Does Pluto want to finish off the job? To take what he considers his? How scary is that thought?

I nudge Noah. "I don't think this is such a good idea." I know Charon can hear us even if he is pretending to be looking at the scenery he's probably seen a million times before.

"Why not?" He turns to stare in the same direction as me. "Does it feel like you're looking through a telescope too?"

"Yes. And it's a hunch. I'm not getting good vibes right now."

"I'm not getting any bad vibes. Maybe it's just you." His eyes glaze over as he stares in awe at the palace. "Look at that place. It's incredible."

"Incredible is one word for it." Not the word I'd use for it, but whatever.

Noah's entranced by the view. He leans back and stretches his arms along the side and back of the boat. He's so at ease and relaxed you would think he's in a gondola in Venice rather than on a cruise in Hades.

He finally notices my scrutiny and frowns. "What?"

"You're so comfortable. Doesn't it bother you where we are?"

"Not really. Nothing bad has happened."

"So far. That doesn't mean it's not going to happen."

"Relax a little. Just enjoy it." He pats me on the shoulder like it's nothing.

Enjoy it? I'm about a breath away from teleporting the heck out of here. I suppose knowing that I can get out of here any time I want is part of the reason I'm even here in the first place. Well, that and my curiosity. Imagine all the mythology books I could rewrite from my experiences! Not that it would ever happen. It's just nice to know I have options.

And my mind is running away with me. I have got to keep focused on what's going on around us. We're getting steadily closer to the citadel and, if possible, it gets even more imposing.

The sharp angles are jagged yet fluid all at the same time. It's as if it was expelled in a violent blast from a volcano to freeze for all eternity in a tall, multifaceted tower. It's not that hard to imagine with the glow coming from within the walls as if they're made out of white-hot magma just cooling into glass.

No one else seems to think it's strange that there is this beautiful building in a place like this. If they do, they're not letting on. My eyes are drawn to how it glistens like shards of obsidian. Beth is always telling me how I must be part magpie, the way I instantly focus on anything that sparkles. Thinking about her makes me smile a little. I miss her, but I'm glad she's not here right now. I have enough to worry about without Beth getting involved. She would be having one hell of an adventure, though.

Charon steers us into a passage that leads to the moat. Looks like I guessed right. We are headed to the big, pretty glass-rock building.

With my fears confirmed, I'm feeling a little nervous. I've read a few myths about Pluto. I know that he's a rival of Jupiter and tried, according to the stories, to take over the throne a few times. What will Pluto be like? I hardly think that the Lord of the Underworld will be the joke-telling type. But hey, I can be wrong. Why does he want to see Noah? What are we even doing here? How is he going to react to me? The fear starts to build now, an ugly gooey mass in my stomach that is threatening to take over. Every fiber of my being is screaming to get out of here.

"What are you doing?"

I've grabbed Noah's hand as I would Mors' without thinking about it. I start to pull away, but he grips it tight.

"I wasn't complaining, was I?"

Okay, so he's holding my hand. And now I'm worried about two things. Meeting an enemy of my father and hoping that my hand isn't sweaty. I do realize that it's completely inane to be worried about two such things at the same time and to give them both the same importance. Still, it feels a bit strange. A few days ago I would have been thrilled to be palm to palm with Noah. Now it just feels…weird. Still, it's nice to know that I'm not alone here.

Charon is still pushing the oar gondolier-style and hasn't even worked up a sweat. He's watching us. And it's not in an 'oh, I just happened to look your way' kind of thing. It's creeping me out. The way he's smiling isn't making me feel any better.

When we're a stone's throw away from the shore, I have to try at least once more to change Noah's mind.

Tugging on his hand a little, I remind him, "I can still get us out of here."

He shakes his head. "You can go if you want. I'll catch up with you later."

"We're not at the mall, Noah. We can't just split up and meet up again later."

"I don't see why we can't. If you're so worried, go home, and once I'm done checking things out, I'll meet you there."

He's talking like he's going to peruse a display at a gallery or something. How can he be so calm? There's no way I'm letting him go alone.

"I'm going with you."

Noah squeezes my hand in what I'm assuming is supposed to be a reassuring way. It just serves to remind me that I'm all cold, clammy and losing the fight with my nerves.

"Thanks."

"No worries." I'm only about to throw up, that's all.

Charon docks at a very elegant looking jetty. Very gothic. Very cool. Lots of black. Charon gets out. Then Noah. Both reach back to help me. With no struggle whatsoever they get me up and on land without mishap. They actually make me feel light and delicate. It reminds me of when Mors picked me up. It's a sensation that I am growing to really like. Something I could definitely get used to. Well, maybe without Creepy Boat Guy. And a lot less brimstone. And a certain dark-haired, dark-eyed god instead of Noah...

Whoa! Where did that come from? I shake it off and push the thought aside. Not the time to let my brain wander off on these crazy tangents.

Charon releases my hand and bows, allowing us to take the lead. It's not as though there's any confusion as to where we are headed. There is one path, adequately lit so that there is no way we can mistakenly stray. It would be even easier if my legs would move without having to be forced by my equally rebelling brain.

I'm tugged along by Noah, who is still showing no fear. If anything, he's eager to get into the palace. I hurry up to walk beside him. Better being close to Noah than the creepy Charon. I keep a tight grip on his hand. The first sign of trouble and we're gone. Why am I not convinced?

Noah, on the other hand, is straight and tall, like Prince Charming about to enter the ball. All he needs now is the Disney treatment and all the spangles to go with it and he'd be all set.

The enormous doors carved from the surrounding glass-rock swing open without a sound, beckoning us in. I get the impression that this is how krill feel before they're swallowed by a blue whale.

As we walk torches flare, adding to the already adequate lighting coming from the walls. The whole place shines, gleams, not just with light, but with power. I can feel it practically oozing from the walls, barely contained. It's like electricity crackling around me, zapping my skin, buzzing in my very soul. It's amazing I don't just pop from the sheer intensity.

The vast antechamber gives way to an even bigger hall, the end of which is completely empty except for a throne and a dark figure lounging on it.

"Talk about minimalist."

His smile cuts through the gloom. "I prefer my surroundings to be unfettered, Miss Goddard." He stands, unfurling a tall, lean body. His hair is long and black, hanging to his shoulders. Long patrician nose, high cheekbones, full lips, dark eyes. Wow. Gods definitely don't come in ugly. He catches my eyes and his growing smile causes a burn to start in my cheeks. "Welcome to my home."

Home. He talks about the place like he's sitting us down in his cozy little kitchen and feeding us stew. "Thank you."

"Sit. Please." The word sounds rusty. But I barely have time to think about it before two mini thrones grow out of the floor, just as glossy and jagged as the one he's sitting on. A table pops up. Two silvery wisps appear to attend. I'm surprised they are even able to carry the stuff, they look so intangible. Food is laid out and it looks good.

"Help yourselves." He does as he says as if trying to lead by example.

Smiling, I pluck a grape from one of the bunches piled on a highly polished silver tray. I nudge Noah, hoping that he'll do the same. I don't think it'd be wise to upset this particular god.

Instead he stares at our host with blatant, slack-jawed interest. I try again, but give up when he doesn't stop. Grabbing another grape, I pop it in my mouth and chew thoughtfully. What are good conversation topics to have with the Lord of the Underworld? The weather? Gardening? How many souls moved in today?

"I can see you are curious about why you came to be here."

"I can see that you're very perceptive." Instant cringe. The snide retort had flown out of my mouth before I could stop it.

Instead of the smiting I'm expecting, his smile grows wider and he actually laughs. Not like an evil 'I'm going to get you now, my pretty' type laugh, but sincere amusement. I'm not sure if that's a good thing or not, to be honest. This guy could really be into the morbid. Oh, the freaky things that could be bringing that smile to his face. It's too scary to let my overactive mind go where it wants to. *Get a grip!* If I don't I'm afraid I'll end up on the floor in the fetal position.

"Have a drink." He gracefully waves and two spirits immediately float into view. If the decanters they are holding look like they are made of crystallized moonlight then what was poured out of them could be liquid sunlight.

I take a goblet and swish its contents around. The way it glows golden from within when there is no warm light in here is amazing.

"Please, try it. You'll like it," our host encourages as he lifts his own goblet. I don't know if I want to drink the stuff. It looks a little *too* special if you ask me. There's no telling what it's going to do to us. What if it kills us or turns us into pigs or something? I've read the myths. I know what a simple drink can do. I'm not stupid. Noah and I both swirl the drink around in our respective goblets. While I'm weighing up whether or not to drink it, I think Noah's mesmerized by how amazing it looks. I bet the fact that it could be dangerous doesn't even factor in his decision to drink the stuff.

Another moment and the god's going to get insulted. Okay. It wouldn't make sense to poison a daughter of Jupiter, right? As powerful as Pluto is, he still can't take on Jupiter. Can he?

Great. Now I'm second-guessing myself. It's now or never. I hope Jupiter's got his omniscient eye on me right now.

I lift mine, and Noah finally jolts out of his drink trance and does the same. The three of us clink glasses and drink. Some more deeply than others.

It's sweet—warm and cool at the same time. I can feel it going down. Holding my breath, I wait for something to happen. One. Two. Three. Nothing... Four. Five. Six. Still nothing...

"Miss Goddard, you look as though you are expecting the wine to turn into acid."

"To be honest, I'm not sure what I was expecting."

"Read a few stories, have you?"

"This is good stuff!" Noah interjects as he takes another enthusiastic swig.

Pluto's eyes drop from mine and he smiles warmly at Noah. "It is my own blend. I am glad you like it."

The way the god is staring at Noah, and I'm not saying there's anything wrong with one guy taking an interest in another, but he's just a little *too* interested. Like he's studying him, searching for something.

I look down at the wine. Nothing's happening to me. At least, nothing I can feel. But just a glance at Noah and you can tell something's going on. Something more than just getting buzzed on wine. He's got a growing smile on his face and his cheeks are starting to flush. Strange. Considering he's a soccer guy, I would have thought that he and the rest of the team would have found a way to sneak a few drinks on their many trips. It's like this is his first drink and it's going straight to his head. Weird when it's not even that strong.

But yeah, he's flushed and giggling away. I'm starting to envy what he's feeling. Obviously it's really good. Why isn't it doing the same for me?

That's when I see it. There's a glow surrounding him. A deep sparkling orange.

"What's going on?" I'm panicking a little now and I reach for Noah, hoping I can shake him out of it. Pluto's hand clamps down on my arm before I can even get close to him.

"Leave him."

The elation on his face evaporates and is replaced by pain. Extreme pain. Convulsing, he keels over in his seat and tumbles to the floor.

"Noah!" Breaking Pluto's grip, I lunge at Noah only to be thrown back by some invisible force. I try again, but it rebounds me farther. The harder I try, the harder it repels. "Help him! He's in pain!" I try again and get flung into the stone wall. Pluto hasn't moved, though he looks on with open interest. "How can you be so cruel?"

I can't catch my breath. Between the blasts from the barrier and witnessing Noah suffer, fear has caused my throat to constrict. "What are you doing to him?" I watch in horror as his body bows back, almost bending in half as he lets out a silent scream. "Stop it! You're killing him!"

"I am not."

Pluto's expression is rapt as he watches Noah's pain. That's when I notice something weird about the dark god. It's like there are two faces I'm seeing. One on top of another. Now that I've taken the time to study him, he's like that all over. It's as though there's someone underneath, projecting a hologram or something, and the projector is on the fritz. It flickers again, but not long enough for me to get a full look at what's underneath. But it is enough to prove that this isn't Pluto we're dealing with.

"Who are you?"

That gets his attention. He turns to me with a perfectly pleasant smile on his face. "Whatever do you mean?"

"I mean you're not who you say you are." I slowly make my way back to Noah, positioning myself between them. If he's going to go after him I'm going to make sure that he has to get through me first.

"Such devotion. And for a boy you hardly know." The smile on his face is hard and his eyes glitter. "Yes, I know all about your infatuation. He might have even felt something for you."

"Might have?" Past tense isn't good. What's he trying to do? I know that I didn't know much about Noah before all of this. I was just interested in a pretty face...and body. Even though I'm not sure if we're a match made in heaven, after going through what we have in the past few days, we have the basis for a very strong friendship. If something blooms from that then so be it. Why does he even care?

Then it hits me. Who else would be interested in a boy's relationships but his parents? My knees wobble a little. Oh. God.

There's a smirk on his face now. "So you think you have figured things out, do you? I can tell you that you are partially right." He takes in my confusion. "I can see I have perplexed you." He taps his chin, talking almost to himself. "How should I remedy this?"

That catches my attention. Suddenly his movements are more feminine. A flick of the hair, the sitting posture... What the hell?"

"Juno? Is that you?" If I'm going to take a stab at it, might as well start at the top, right? Who else would want to mess with my life?

"Juno!" The voice is definitely a woman's. And very amused. Her laughter is husky. Lilting. Haunting. "You *would* think that."

I don't like the scorn laced in that voice. My chin tips up a notch. "If you're not Juno, then who are you?"

"Now, *that* is the ultimate question, isn't it? Who am I? Who are you?" The god or goddess or whatever it is gets up and walks toward me. "You are only now just finding out who you are."

I sidle closer to Noah. I can't see how he's doing, but my guess is he's not doing too well. If I can just get a little closer, I might be able to get us both out of here. I know whoever or whatever it is walking closer to us can read my thoughts. It's time to be thinking of sunshine and daisies and anything else that's not what I'm planning. "Now you're talking semantics. You know what I'm asking."

"And you know that you cannot hide anything from me. At least not in that weak mortal mind of yours. You are easier to read than a sheaf of parchment." He-she-it shrugs. "Very well."

There is a brilliant smile then an even brighter flash.

It's so dazzling that I have to close my eyes, even put my hands over them. Blinking away the spots, I do my best to glare. "Was that really necessary?"

"Yes. If only to see that look on your face."

Finally I'm able to see who owns the voice I've been listening to for the past few minutes.

The woman before me is tall, slender, swathed in a shimmering gold cloth that I'm pretty sure a good gust of wind would whip right off. Her hair is black, long and wild, swirling in its own breeze. Either that or this goddess wanders around with her own private wind machine.

Aside from her obviously divine presence, there is nothing that lets me know who she is. With the others it was pretty noticeable who they were right off the bat. Flora with her flower fetish. Fortuna's finger snapping people's lives into the upper strata of heaven or into the gutter. And Venus—a few more whiffs of her pheromones and I'll be all over her.

But this one is different. At least, to me, she is. There is nothing at all to let me know who she is. So I stare, searching for something, anything, that will give away her identity.

"I can almost see your mind working. Quite amusing, really."

Having her laughing at me is beyond irritating now. If there's anything I hate, it's feeling stupid. It's not something I'm acquainted with, nor is it something I wish to get accustomed to. I'm quickly reaching boiling point.

"Who are you?"

She doesn't answer, but I hear movement behind me. A quick check tells me that Noah's finally recovered from whatever it was that this goddess did to him. Hunkering down, I reach over to give him a hand up.

"Are you okay?" Not trusting him to answer, I check him over. He looks fine as far as my eyes can tell. A more thorough check will have to wait until we're out of here. His hand is still in mine. Noah's preparing to teleport us out of here.

"Surely you're not leaving? Don't you want to quench your insatiable curiosity? Don't you want to know who I am?" She's taunting me, and if I could hurl lightning bolts she would have been fried a few times by now.

I'm picturing my room. Thinking about my nice soft bed. My mom, who must be going out of her mind by now. "It's not like you're going to tell us."

Noah jerks his hand out of mine and glares at her. "She doesn't have to."

"Noah?" I grab for his hand again but forget about teleporting. If he wants to stay, then I am too. I can't leave him here alone with this nutjob. "What are you talking about?"

"I know who she is."

My gaze shifts between them. She's beaming triumphantly while Noah scowls like he's ready to kill. What's going on here?

My eyes finally stop on Noah. "Who is she then?"

"This is Discordia." His lips twist wryly. "My mother."

Chapter Sixteen
Come Again?

Okay. So, in the past few seconds, life as I know it has some crashing down around my ears for the second time this week. I think I'm handling it better this time around. Rather than reeling from his words, I turn to him, gaping like a carp.

"What?" I croak. I'm taking it better, but that doesn't mean that the part of my brain controlling my vocal chords isn't short-circuiting on me. Let's try it again. "What?" *Yeah, much better.*

"What is so hard to understand?" Discordia, purported mother of Noah, looks absolutely delighted at what's going on. Well, why shouldn't she be? She likes chaos after all, and my brain is exactly that at the moment. "Noah is my son. My offspring. My progeny."

I put up my hand. Just this goddess's voice has the ability to raise my hackles. "Yeah, I get that. How is this possible?"

"You think you're the only one around with divine parentage?" She snorts. "You really think you are *that* special?"

"Actually, I do." Pointing at the wine we drank, I ask, "Why all the theatrics, then? Why are you playing games with us? Why not just come out and greet your little boy?"

"My darling girl," she says, the words dripping with sarcasm, "the theatrics, the games are what make life interesting. You can't slog through life without enjoying yourself. Think of how deadly dull it would be." Her lips split into a wide grin and she stares at me. "You think you are so smart, little one. You do not even realize that if you had truly been in Hades the food you had eaten would have been the manacles binding you to the Underworld. Silly child."

Oh, my God, she's right. How could I have been so stupid? I've been so caught up with the wonder and weirdness of it all that I wasn't even thinking. How could I forget the thing with Proserpina and the pomegranate? She only ate four seeds of the fruit and was trapped for four months of the year. We practically ate an entire banquet in comparison. I really am a moron. Wait, we're completely off topic. She's doing it on purpose. "Stop trying to confuse us."

"Yeah, Ava's right." Noah has stepped forward now and still looks incredibly unimpressed. I get the feeling that I'm about to be in the middle of a domestic hissy fit. "What was in that wine?"

She studies her nails. "Just something to jog your memory."

"Just jog my memory? Why don't I believe you?"

"Why would I lie?"

"Yeah, why would you? What are you after?" The accusation flies out of my mouth before I can stop it.

Noah and I are toe to toe with her now, which probably isn't the best idea. It's too late if it isn't. The words are out. Time to deal with the consequences.

"What makes you think I am after something? I am a goddess. I have all that I could ever need."

But what does she *want*? That's the question that immediately pops into my head.

She glides closer. "I *want* to know my son. I *want* to claim him as mine. I *want* him to take his rightful place." With each word she gets closer until she's leaning over us.

She is tall. Was she this tall when we walked in? Definitely feeling intimidated now. I gulp and, though I manage to stay where I am, I reach for Noah reflexively.

"Isn't that sweet? Now, are you reaching for him to protect him, or for protection?"

I have no idea. All I know is that if I'm touching him I'll feel a little bit better. Or will I? It's starting to sink in now that this is *her* son that I'm dealing with. The Goddess of Discord's son. Plus, the drink might have done something to him. He might seem miffed at her right now, but who knows what's going to happen in the next few minutes? The next few seconds, even. I'm getting definite evil vibes from her, which is freaking me out. Noah is tense next to me. I want to believe that he's not taking this well. I know I took the news about my parentage pretty well. But then again, I wasn't hauled to some godforsaken location and tortured with a weird drink. If I had been, I'm pretty sure I wouldn't have been very receptive of Mommy dearest.

I turn to look at Noah and notice that the room around us is morphing. The cold glittering beauty of the obsidian is melting away into a whirl of brilliant radiance. It cascades over us like a waterfall of every hue and intensity. I flinch from the brightest ones and am fascinated by the dark lights. A weird phrase, I know, but that's the only way to describe it. There are flashes of dark...light. It looks a little like the blacklight Mom pulled out of the attic a while ago, but without that weird effect it has on colors around it. A rainbow of hues bloom and flare randomly, zipping past us. It's quite beautiful, if a little disorienting.

Within seconds, I can't tell which way is up. I find myself clinging to Noah, who is standing as steadily as Discordia. He's so busy glaring at her that he hardly notices me hanging off him.

Noah puts a hand over mine and I start to feel weird. Like I'm being pulled away. "What are you doing?"

"Getting you out of here. It's not safe."

I clutch at him, refusing to let him do this. "I'm not leaving without you!" I know it's already too late. I can see my room forming around me. "Noah!"

"I'll see you in a little while."

That's the last thing I hear before I land butt first on the floor.

"Ava!" I'm pretty sure the first body I feel colliding with mine is Mom's. We're quickly dog-piled by the goddesses.

"Are you okay?"

"What happened?"

"Where's Noah?"

I try to answer. I *want* to answer, I really do, but it's a little hard to do when you're being crushed. I wave my arm feebly. They must realize what's going on, as they quickly hop off.

Fortuna grabs my hands and hauls me up. She makes sure I'm steady before she lets go and returns to the circle of females staring at me, waiting for an answer.

"He's back..." I realize I have no idea where that was. "I don't know where we were, but I have to get him."

"No!" Mom practically tackles me. "I'm not letting you go."

This might be a good time to tell her what's going on. But do I really want to tell her? Not like I have much of a choice. I doubt that she'll leave this room ever again if she doesn't start getting some answers.

Where to start?

"Noah's with his mom."

Mom relaxes. I really don't want to burst her bubble.

"His mom's Discordia." I close my eyes and wait for it.

"*What?*" It's said in unison all around the room.

"Yeah, she dragged us down to the Underworld to tell us."

"*What?*" the goddesses shout, looking extremely confused in their gorgeous goddess style.

"That cannot be." A weak voice came from the bed.

Mors! I'd almost forgotten about him! Dodging the others, I rush to his side. He's tucked in my bed. I suppose that's the best place for him, since everyone is congregating in here.

"Are you okay?" I drop onto the bed next to him, my hand automatically going to his face. He feels cool and his eyes are clearer. "Feeling better?"

He waves away the question. "Discordia is that boy's mother? Are you sure?"

"Well, yeah."

Everyone starts jabbering away at once. I can see it's wearing on Mors' nerves and I'm not surprised when he waves a hand and everyone disappears.

"Looks like someone's getting their strength back." I fall onto the bed beside him and stare at the ceiling, suddenly overwhelmed with fatigue. I'm glad that Mors is feeling better. There's nothing more disconcerting than a god losing his powers. Then, of course, there's finding out that the guy that you thought you liked is the child of a deranged goddess. I'm trying to wrap my head around it still. He seems to have taken it well. Plus, it gives us one huge thing in common. That brings a smile to my face.

"I wouldn't be so pleased if I were you." The soft voice chides from my side. "Having Discordia for a mother might actually make the boy less suited to you."

He sounds almost pleased. Rolling to my side, I glare at him. "What aren't you guys telling me? What's up with Discordia? Do you know why Noah got me out of there so quick?"

Mors attempts to mirror my movement, but abandons the idea with a groan. Looks like he's not recovering that quickly after all. I shuffle closer so my face hovers over his.

"Please tell me."

His fathomless eyes hold mine for a moment. I think he's gauging my reaction. In fact, I'm sure of it.

"Just tell me. I can take it." I smile. I hope it's reassuring, but with the emotions warring inside me at the moment there's no guarantee it's not some demented leer.

"Discordia is as chaotic as her name implies. She is…insane, for lack of a better word. She likes disorder, chaos, and wants everything to be like that."

"Okay, I'm confused. Isn't everything about balance? You all function as a whole. Right?" He doesn't answer. Is it wrong to want to beat an ill god with a pillow?

"Theoretically. Ideally. It does not mean that we all want the same thing." His eyes close and he grows quiet.

He's keeping something from me. I can tell. "Open your eyes."

Mors obeys. His twin onyx orbs pin me and for a moment I'm stunned by the sheer force of his gaze. But only for a moment. That's before I delve into those eyes. I'm sinking into memories, sensations. I'm surrounded by everything Mors is. The darkness. The isolation. I can feel it all. I know it all.

The power Mors wields is awesome. I don't know if I'm accessing it all, but it's staggering. I'm so overwhelmed that I can't think, let alone sift through his mind. Thankfully, I feel it being shifted away from me a little. Still, it is a few moments before I can move again. There are countless memories of people he has been with in their final moments. I can feel the sadness in him in many of the memories. He's felt far too much sadness. There are few times he's felt relief and even fewer when he's felt true happiness. I'm stunned to find his happiest times to date are with me. Geez, if I'd known he was that hard up for entertainment I would have done something more. I make up my mind to do something more fun with him in the future.

If we have a future, that is.

The way things are going right now, I'm not so sure we'll have time to frolic. I search around more, looking for memories concerning Discordia specifically. From the few I find I can see that Mors wasn't kidding about her being a bit loony. I remember reading stories about fish falling from the sky and day turning into night and stuff. I'd thought that they were weird legends that had been warped until the truth was lost completely. Apparently stuff like that does happen and it's all because of her and her need for things to work against the norm.

In the process of looking for more information about her, I see a few incidents involving Jupiter. It's pretty obvious from what I'm seeing that he's always been the one to smack her down and put her back in line, which she fell into most of the time. Apparently, an insurgence from her is long overdue.

Satisfied, I start to pull out of his mind. That's when I notice an image mixed in amongst the others. A whispered conversation with Morta. I feel his apprehension. That's what draws me toward it. I can see the scene flickering in front of me like a movie. Morta is holding a beautiful thread. It's not one color like the others. It gleams and glistens like a spun rainbow. She tucks it into a ball and places it into a shadowy figure that I can't make out properly. I can feel anger and resentment as she does this. Mors didn't approve. I'm about to touch the image, step inside it so I can see what happened, when I'm yanked almost violently out of his mind.

I'm back in my room, leaning over Mors like nothing happened. Except it did and I'm totally stunned. I look at him questioningly.

"You were not meant to see that."

"I get that. But how did I do it? How did I get in there?" I tap his temple gently.

"You have the gift, and I let you in."

He makes it sound so simple. But despite his help I'm quite proud of myself. Another new ability. At least it's useful. Well, sort of. At the moment all I'm sure of is that I can look into someone's head... With their permission. Now if I can just get the permission of everyone in the world, I'd be set. The thought amuses me. The things I could see and learn...

"Ava."

I come crashing back to earth with a thud. Right. Not the time to be fantasizing. I need to figure out what's going on.

Now I'm left wondering what I saw in his head.

I stare at him, hold his eyes with mine, knowing that I'll be able to pick up clues if he starts lying. "Whose life thread was that?"

His eyes shift slightly. "I don't know."

"Mors..."

"Tell her, Mors. It's time she knew."

Morta's at the foot of my bed in all her scary glory. Her eyes flit back and forth over the tiny space between me and Mors and she raises a brow, making her forehead crease like silk in a sweaty armpit.

I slide away from Mors and sit up, trying to look nonchalant. Yes, you did just see me with my face inches from Death's. And no, it's not a big deal. From the look on her face, she's not believing it. But she doesn't say anything.

Time to divert attention. I quickly find my voice. "What are you talking about? What were you doing with that thread? Whose thread was it?"

Morta looks at Mors, who looks back at her resolutely. He's not going to be the one doing the talking. She sighs and gives him a withering glance before turning to me.

"There are a few things that you should know."

"About..." I sure can think of a few things I'd like to know.

"Everything."

Finally! Someone's going to fill me in on what's going on. Then again, how can I be sure she's going to be telling me the truth? After all, isn't everything I've heard up until now supposed to be the truth? I look at them looking at me. I'm sure it's one version of the truth.

"It was all you needed to know at the time."

"So what's changed?"

"Everything."

"Okay. You've got to stop saying that and just tell me because it's starting to get on my nerves." I realize who I'm talking to and add hastily, "I'm sorry. I'm just getting a little frustrated."

Mors takes my hand and squeezes gently — a move that doesn't go unnoticed by Morta. Uncomfortable with her watching, I try to pull away, but he grips tighter.

"Of course, my dear." Her eyes slide away from our joined hands and glides up my arm to my face. "That's completely understandable."

She perches herself on the other side of the bed as I kick myself for not offering her a seat. I try to stand so I can at least get her something to eat or drink, but Mors is like a three-ton anchor on the end of my arm.

"Don't worry about me, I'm fine." She fluffs a pillow before smoothing her hand over it. Her gaze wanders over my face contemplatively. "Where to begin..."

"Can we start with the thread? That one I saw in Mors' head. It was so beautiful. Whose is it?"

"Yours."

Well, I wasn't expecting that. I fall back onto the bed, but quickly prop myself up again on my elbow. "What? How is it mine?" Didn't I see mine linked with Noah's that day I first met her? It looked nothing like that. I distinctly remember a silver thread, not something brilliantly multicolored.

"That was Noah's thread connected to you. You two have been coupled for a shared destiny for quite a long time."

The muscle holding my jaw shut fails at this moment. "What do you mean coupled?" Wrenching my hand out of Mors', I get up and stare at them both. "This was planned? And you two knew about it?"

Morta nods.

Mors' stony expression remains unchanging as he watches me. "Discordia intertwined your fates when you were merely a twinkle in your father's eyes."

"She what?" The anger that flares blinds me with a red haze for a moment. "What does that mean?"

"It means that she has made it so that your fates are entwined." I'm about to point out that she's just said that, but she continues. "It means that whatever happens, you cannot do it without Noah's involvement."

"So...?" They look at me. Can they really not know what I'm talking about? "So why? Why do this? So what is she up to? Why does it involve me?"

Morta looks at me like I'm the dumbest thing she has ever laid eyes on. "It has everything to do with you. Who do you think Discordia is trying to get at?"

There can only be one answer to that. "Jupiter?"

She nods gravely. "Yes, Jupiter. No other god gives her as much grief as he does. At least not in her eyes." Right now I'm thinking that Morta doesn't think too highly of Discordia. I don't know — call it intuition. Or maybe the way that she rolls her eyes every time she says the Goddess of Discord's name might be a clue.

"I still don't get it. What's it got to do with me? I'm nothing to her. I'm just some mortal who happens to have Jupiter as a father. We all know he had plenty of those. What makes me different?"

"As far as she can see, you are his favorite. The fact that you are mortal just makes it even better for her. It means that you are vulnerable, which means you are a weak point for Jupiter. One that she can exploit."

Oh, jeez. A very clear picture is forming in my mind. Threaten Daddy's little girl and Daddy does what the crazy goddess wants. "What are her terms?" I rub at the pain in my forehead as I wait for one of them to answer. I'm guessing it's going to be Morta because Mors is doing a fabulous impression of a doormat.

"Jupiter has to imprison himself then relinquish his powers. And to make sure he can't get away he is being guarded by the Titans. Without his power he is helpless."

"Why? Why would he do this to himself?"

"He didn't want any harm coming to you. Surely you understand a parent's love."

This is surreal. So that father that I didn't know I had, my father the *god*, cares about me so much that he would let this happen. "This isn't right. He's got to have something up his sleeve. Otherwise this just doesn't make sense."

"We think he might." Morta is looking at me strangely.

"What?"

Morta is silent and, for a change, Mors speaks. "You were not supposed to have powers."

"What?" I know I'm starting to sound like a track set on repeat, but you know what? I need some answers and 'what?' seems to be the quickest way to get a few.

Morta gives Mors a reproachful look. He returns it with a glum one. I get the feeling that they are communicating silently, but Morta quickly shakes off his glare and turns back to me. "You were supposed to be…like a caretaker of Jupiter's thread. A safe hiding place."

"So that's all I was? A safe?" So much for being special. Then a thought occurs. "What about my mom's reaction? She seemed to think that this was going to happen. It was like she expected it." Well, she had, hadn't she? She'd said as much when I pinned her down and asked her.

"Morta altered her memories," Mors says shortly. His miserable expression turns a little challenging as he tips his chin up at her just a notch.

I turn, gaping, to Morta. "Is he telling the truth?"

"Yes…"

I feel as though the world is trying to spin me off it. "What about that other stuff? The stuff she remembers about Jupiter?" That had to be true. The thought that my mom could be in love with a figment of her imagination is too much. That would be too cruel even for gods.

"Of course the memories are true. What kind of monster do you think I am? I only made it so that this whole charade would be convincing to any observer." Her bottomless eyes shift to the scene around us before settling back on mine again. Discordia could easily have spies everywhere, but I'm sure that the power of these two combined would thwart anything that she could come up with. God, espionage in the divine world must suck. But imagine the gadgets and tricks they'd use. James Bond and his bag of goodies would look pathetic.

At least that was a load off my mind. But now my brain is whirring, trying to process this all. "So all of this was engineered before I was even born?"

Morta taps her chin with a gnarled finger. "I would say that we've known about this for quite a while. A thousand years or so. Who knows how long Discordia's been planning it."

It occurs to me that I need to learn how to think like these gods do. At least I do if I want to continue hanging out with them and not drive myself insane. To them, time isn't linear. I suppose if you can live forever you wouldn't see time as a straight line either.

I glare at Mors. "That's why you didn't like me getting close to him. You knew who he was!"

His eyes hold mine levelly as he nods.

"Wait. It wasn't only you who tried to stop me. Venus did too. I just assumed you were jealous or something..." My words peter out. My eyes meet his apologetically. This really isn't something I want to be talking about in front of Morta.

Mors has already pushed past that. "When did Venus say this?"

"I don't know... A couple of days ago? I'm not sure. Since I've met you guys all the days have started running together."

Mors nodded understandingly. "What did she say exactly?"

"That she wasn't sure if I should get involved with him."

Morta and Mors trade a look.

"What?"

"It sounds like Discordia was playing with you. Do you not think Venus would know if he was right for you?"

Now that I think about it, it does sound strange. I feel weird knowing that she was in my room with me, pretending to be someone I'm so close to. "What's the point in that?"

"Think about it, Ava." Mors shifts hesitantly closer. It's as though he's afraid of me or something. He's a god, for heaven's sake. The God of Death at that. If anyone should be scared, it's me. "You are young, headstrong. What is the best way to get you to do something?"

"Tell me not to do it." I feel like a fool. "She really has had all the bases covered, hasn't she?"

"Not all of them."

I really do feel like a colossal moron at this point. It was bad enough when I first discovered who I am. I finally start to feel comfortable in my skin again and *bam*! The pain in my head throbs again, darkening my vision for a moment. The anger and betrayal that have pooled in my gut during the conversation are starting to spread now. I can feel them seeping, creeping into my veins. My hands are shaking I'm so angry. To think that I actually believed that I was someone special. I've been nothing more than a pawn. A puppet they've been tugging the strings of.

Livid, I start pacing. "So did we amuse you? Were we fun to watch?" Morta might as well not even be here. The anger is completely focused on Mors. All the time I've spent with him, the bond we've forged, it all seems so false now. For all I know he could have been here to watch everything happen from the sidelines.

Frustration and anger reach boiling point and I grab a pillow and throw it at him. Not satisfied, I grab another and start pummeling him.

"Ava—"

I don't even listen to Morta. I thrust a warning palm at her and she disappears. The shock of what I just did doesn't dampen the fury.

Mors sits perfectly still, letting me hit and swear and cry. When I finally wear myself out, he gathers me in his arms and holds me while I exhaust my tear supply. He's silent for a long while. I can tell he's searching for the right words. It's in this moment that I realize, with my face pressed to his chest, that he's not breathing. An odd thing to notice, I know, and even stranger to contemplate. He's been so human to me that I'd forgotten that he's not.

"Ava, it was not like that."

I rub my face on his shirt and look up at him. I'm still angry, but too tired to do any more but listen. I'm pretty sure he's got something to do with that, but I can't be sure.

"Why didn't you tell me?"

He sighs and shifts so that I'm lying next to him. His arm is still around me, his voice soothing. "I didn't want to upset you when we had no idea where things were going. Yes, I knew Discordia was up to something, but things were up in the air... So to speak." He pauses. "Think of it like this. You start at a point and you end at a point, but how you get there is up to you. You shape your own destiny. We can foresee only so far before we have to wait until you make a choice."

It makes sense, I guess. "So what now?"

His muscles bunch. I know he's got something to say, so I wait. If I've learned anything about dealing with Mors, it's that patience is the key.

"I am sorry I did not tell you at the start. We did not know how you would react." His eyes age a thousand years while his face remains youthful. It tugs at something deep inside me, seeing him so troubled. "I was worried about you... Your ability to handle this all. Morta and I, that is. The others do not know anything about it. We tried our best to keep it quiet. They believe the story we engineered."

"Keep what quiet? Her plan? Why? Wouldn't they help if they knew?"

"They would if they knew. However, there is something more to it, and if they knew it would just help to further Discordia's plans for total chaos."

"Okay, what?" His words make sense, but strung together like they are, it's not working for me. Maybe my brain is overtaxed or something, or I'm just stressed out beyond what I can handle, but I repeat, "What?"

"You know perfectly well what I mean." His eyes catch mine and I know he's in my head. I don't mind. If anything, I wish he'd plant everything I need to know straight in there. "We have to be ready for what is coming."

I fall back onto my pillow. I know there's more coming—I feel it—but Mors gives me some time to let that bit sink in. Sitting up awkwardly, he gingerly brushes the hair from my face. I stare up into his eyes and the pieces start falling into place. It makes perfect sense.

"So I wasn't supposed to have any powers?"

Mors' expression relaxes a little. Probably because he doesn't have to try to spell things out for me anymore. "No. Jupiter wanted you to be a normal child. Well, above average, of course—you are his offspring after all—but no more than brilliant." He smiles wryly. I wish he would do that more. But then again, it would ruin his image terribly. "At least that's what we were led to believe."

I'm not sure what to feel about this. He didn't want me to have abilities? That hurts a little. The emotion is quickly superseded. It was all a plan. Aren't the powers I'm not supposed to have starting to show up?

Mors tightens his arms around me. "He did not want you to suffer any hardships. Surely you can understand a parent wanting to spare their child pain."

"Sure, I guess. But I do have powers, don't I? And I seem to be gaining more."

"Everything that you are now able to do is the thread emerging. We thought we bound it so that nothing would escape. But it seems that it is." His eyes peer into mine. "Do you feel any different?"

"Not until you told me all this. Now I'm feeling a little queasy." More like a *lot* queasy.

He rubs my arm. "You will be fine."

"How do you know? You said yourself that you can't see everything that happens. Will I be able to do more? Will I get *all* his powers? What would that do to me? Can I even handle that? What if the human part of me is too weak? Am I just going to explode?" The words tumble out of me, the last ones making Mors wince.

"I will not let that happen." He sounds so sure of that, it actually makes me feel a little better. Not much, but enough to have me sitting up.

"So now what?"

"It is up to you to put Discordia back in her place."

He says it like it's the only thing that makes sense. None of this makes sense!

"You have got to be kidding me. How am I supposed to do that?"

"You can do it, I have no doubt." Again, he sounds absolute in his belief.

"How can you be so positive?"

"Because I'm here to help you. I'm sure Morta will help, if she is not too miffed at your treatment of her."

I can literally feel the blood draining out of my head and into my stomach. "Oh, my God! Morta!"

Mors actually starts chuckling at my panic.

I whack him lightly on the chest. "What did I do to her? How do I...?" I wriggle my fingers frantically.

"Just bring her back."

Why do I get the feeling he's challenging me? Never one to back down from a dare, I tip my chin up. He wants me to bring her back? Fine. I will. I'll figure it out all on my own. He'll see. I go over what I did to make her disappear in the first place. While I was arguing with Mors I wished she would just go away so I could yell at him in peace. Then I threw my hand at her and *poof!* So theoretically all I'd have to do is want her to return. Right?

I give it a try. I think the panic at the thought of offending her does it, because she appears in the blink of an eye.

"Thank you," she says primly. She doesn't look mad.

"I'm so sorry! I didn't mean to. It just kind of happened."

She shakes her head. "I understand. You seem to be progressing much faster than I had thought." She shrugs the thought away. "But what matters now is you stopping Discordia."

I nod, slowly trying to digest all this. There's one thing that's been niggling at the corners of my mind this whole time and it decides now to springboard off my tongue.

Mors shifts, drawing my attention to him. "The day I was hit with this" — he waves at himself — "thing, I had just found out about Noah. We both knew that you and he were linked, but Discordia hid his identity very well. We never suspected that he was related to her until then."

I put up a hand. "Hold on a second. You never liked Noah. But if you didn't know who he was, why didn't you like him?" Mors looks uncomfortable for the first time. I think his pale cheeks are turning a very faint pink. Oh. It's *that* kind of dislike. Mors was jealous of Noah? Wide-eyed, I stare at him. The revelation doesn't freak me out. Actually, it makes me feel a little warm and fuzzy inside. We really have to sit and talk this through when everything settles down. *If* everything settles down and *if* I'm still alive and able to talk, that is.

Morta clears her throat discreetly, breaking the silence. "Discordia. We should figure out what we are going to do with her."

I agree. Discordia first. This thing between me and Mors is willfully pushed to the back-burner. Our eyes hold for a moment more before I drop mine. "Do we have to worry about Noah? Is he going to...be a problem?" I have to go head to head with him and I'm not sure if I will be able to do it. "He did send me back here. He said it wasn't safe for me to be there." I look at them for some hope that Noah is on our side.

Mors slowly shakes his head. "It is up in the air for the moment."

Meaning that Noah is at the crux of a choice. What will he choose? I really hope I don't have to hurt him.

"Ava." Mors' voice is quiet. "You need to focus on a plan."

Yeah, because I can come up with a plan to overthrow a goddess just like that. "Any suggestions?" My gaze alternates between them. They're coming up with plans as fast as I am. "How long do we have?"

"Not long. She is not known for her patience." Mors kicks back the covers and tries to get up. And when I say tries, I mean he struggles to sit up but falls back again.

I practically dive on him and hold him down. "Mors, just lie down. You're not strong enough." I put a hand on his forehead, wishing I could make him better. My hands get warm the moment the thought crosses my mind.

Mors flinches. "What—?"

"Shush." I hold him down and continue running my hands over his temples. "How do you feel?" I'm not exactly sure what I'm doing, but I hope I'm making him better.

"I feel good." He sounds surprised.

He can't be more surprised than me at this moment. I'm starting to like this whole 'being able to do everything I want' thing.

Mors looks up at me, his face a little apprehensive but at the same time appreciative. An interesting combination on his habitually impassive face. He's got some color back in his cheeks now, as much as Mors ever had. His pale hands pull mine from his face and squeeze them in thanks as he levers himself off the bed.

I'm still in shock at what I've done and am looking around for Morta to see if she saw. It's a 'look what I did, Mommy!' kind of moment, and though my own mommy would probably be freaking if she had been watching, I'm sure Morta will be proud.

But she's not sitting on the bed anymore.

This whole time I've been healing Mors, Morta was at my computer typing and clicking away. I find it fascinating that she can work it so well. I can't believe how quickly her arthritic-looking fingers work.

"Uh, what are you doing?"

"I need to contact a few deities. I didn't think that doing it the usual way would be wise."

I suppose Discordia will be listening in on all the communication going on between the gods.

Morta's using Mercury's messenger program and, from the looks of it, is calling up just about every god, goddess and monster she can find. She's got so many windows open that the faces looking at her are Barbie-sized on my giant screen. Suddenly Morta's form morphs, becoming slender. Her gray hair shortens and turns black. Within moments I'm staring at myself in the chair.

"I need your help," the other Ava says. "The daughter of Jupiter commands it."

The moment the words are out of her mouth there's a muted bang and the screen goes blank. I watch as a plume of smoke rises from the tower. There goes another computer.

"I did not expect she would make it easy for us." Morta is back and frowning. "Let us try another approach." Her face creases even more in concentration. She's trying to summon the others. Her eyes open then narrow in frustration. "No use. Ava, try to bring the others here."

I concentrate on bringing Fortuna, Flora and Venus here, but after a few frustrating seconds with nothing to show for it, I give up. "It's not working."

Mors' hand is on my shoulder. "Try bringing just Fortuna."

It's another long minute before she appears. Fortuna's beautiful face is marred by worry.

"Ava? What's going on?"

"No time to talk," I mutter distractedly, already trying to bring Flora here.

It takes me nearly ten minutes to fetch Flora and Venus. I'm exhausted but exhilarated by my achievement. I sit on the bed, reeling a bit from the effort. My head is throbbing with each heartbeat. I vaguely hear Mors filling them in on what's going on. All eyes turn to me, all of them questioning, shocked. I nod weakly. The dull throb has escalated into a crushing pain in the back of my head that threatens to blind me.

The room tilts abruptly and Mors is the first to my side.

"Ava!"

The crushing sensation turns into a tugging, ripping. I'm being drawn away and there is nothing I can do to stop it. I concentrate on its origin. I'm not going to be dragged off like a wayward puppy. I'm going to pounce.

Ever conscious of my thoughts, Mors grabs my arm. "Ava, no."

I smile with more confidence than I'm feeling and look him in the eyes. "It's going to be fine."

And with that, I follow the pull.

Chapter Seventeen
Monologs, Chaos and a Word from Our Sponsor

Noah is nowhere to be seen but Discordia, in all her chaotic glory, is waiting for me as I expected. With her wild hair whipping in the same invisible wind as before, she makes her way toward me. Sashaying as if she was on some casual walk, she steps closer and closer. I'm not feeling too intimidated. I'm a little apprehensive, but not as petrified as I think I should be. I'm not too sure if it's a good thing or not. It's probably for the best. Thinking is not always top priority when I'm freaking out.

Calmly, I watch her walk up to me, tilting my head back just so I can continue to look her in the face. She's like a tree. A big, beautiful tree with flowing hair and a slightly feral smile. Nope, still not scaring me.

"You look different." She slowly circles me. I'm sure she's going for a predator circling its prey, but I'm feeling like a statue in a museum that she's trying to get a better look at.

"I feel different."

Her smile disappears. It looks like my lack of fear is irking her. So now I've graduated from merely not being afraid of her to provoking her. Give me a few more minutes and I'll be poking a finger in her gut. Well, either that or splattered with my body parts spread across the universe.

We'll just have to see how things work out.

And now I'm scaring myself. How can I be so calm? I'm annoying a goddess for God's sake. One who can do some crazy stuff. One who has no opposition but me. Oh, this is not good. What do I know about taking down a goddess? Her voice pulls me out of my reverie.

"A thousand years of planning and everything just falls into my lap. This is absolutely delicious."

At this point I'm wondering to myself if I can get her to do the evil mastermind monolog. You know, the type you see in movies where the villain reveals everything before the hero kicks their butt and gets away?

"Of course I will tell you." Discordia leans down so that we're eye to eye. "But only because I *know* that you won't be getting away to 'kick my butt'."

Okay. That's slightly worrying. She continues to talk. Maybe it'll give me some time to figure things out.

"After the last time, I knew I had to get Jupiter out of the way before I could try anything again. All he cares about is his precious balance. Who needs balance?"

"The world? No, the universe." The throbbing in my head is getting worse. Steadily, agonizingly worse. "Everything has to be balanced. Yin and yang. Right and wrong. Without one, you don't have the other. Don't you get it?" Maybe I'm not being clear. My thoughts are muddled. I'm hoping that I'm getting through to her, but the goddess has a tendency to be a bit arrogant. She's much worse than any other I've encountered thus far.

"That is exactly what I'm hoping. Exactly what I'm willing to sacrifice my son for." Her eyes glint wildly. "Do you know what it's like to live an eternity? To live an eternity striving for—no, *being* chaos? Being essentially useless?" She sighs heavily and her hair falls to cascade down her back. "So I planned. I plotted. When I found out that Jupiter had a daughter." She smiles at my gasp. "Oh, I heard the rumors. I saw Juno raging. You were the talk of the pantheon. But Jupiter kept you protected from us. All of us." She grins widely. "But not mortals. He thought he was so crafty. But I'm smarter."

My eyes feel like they are going to pop out of my head. I press the heels of my hands against them. I need to relieve the pressure. "So you...had Noah and were going to use him against me? How could you use him like that?" For a moment the world blurs horribly. Then, just as suddenly, everything sharpens. The colors are more vibrant, the smells more pronounced. I can feel vibrations in the air. Her feelings are as tangible to me as the clothes I'm wearing.

She's gloating. I feel her bravado. Discordia thinks she's won. And now she's tying up loose ends. Meaning, she's about to get rid of me.

On instinct, I jump out of the way just as she lets loose a bolt of energy at the spot where I was standing. The expression on her face is almost amusing.

The perplexity there evaporates as she snarls. "So, Daddy's little girl has learned some tricks, has she?"

That's not the only thing—I'm careful to try to block some of my thoughts. I know that if I block everything she'll know something's up. A quick look at her tells me she hasn't noticed anything. I do feel her curiosity flowing over me. Maybe if I intrigue her enough she'll want to keep me around for a little bit longer. I teleport next to her, grinning in a way that is sure to annoy.

"Yeah, I picked up a few things. Noah can do that one too. Did he tell you?"

She narrows her eyes to glare at me. I guess he didn't.

"When did he do this?"

"All the time. How do you think we even found you? I was following him around." My grin grows wider. "You mean you didn't know?"

"Of course I knew." Her face still says otherwise.

Her anger surges from her now, lashing hotly against my face. Oh, she's really not happy. Might as well keep going. She did say she was going to tell me everything. I'll make sure she does.

"I have a question for you. What was that drink you gave us?"

My question surprises her. Her emotion pops like a soap bubble on my skin. Weird.

"You received wine. Noah"—she cringes at his name—"received a little something that...reminded him who he is."

"Where is he now?"

"Somewhere safe. You have no need to worry about him." She stops, smiling as she leans forward. The feeling I'm getting from her tickles. She's amused. "You still have feelings for him! Even though I told you that everything about your so-called relationship was fabricated. Incredible. You mortals really are slaves to your emotions."

Okay. That hurt. Though I'm not interested in him *that* way anymore, I still think of him as a friend. But I'm not going to tell her that. I want her to lose her temper and make a mistake. "Aren't you doing the same thing? Poor Discordia doesn't want to be second place anymore. You're the one acting like a little kid who wants her big brother's toys!"

She blasts me again before I can get another word out. I manage to save myself before I hit anything. I've never been more thankful that I'm a quick learner. Hopefully I'll be up to taking on a goddess within the next few minutes. Seconds would be better, but I'm thinking that mastering the powers of a supreme god might take a little longer than it takes me to inhale a mini donut.

I drop back onto the ground and dust myself off. "That stung." I enjoy the anger flaring from her. I think she finally realizes that getting rid of me isn't going to be that easy. Good. If I'm going out, I'm taking her with me. I want her to know that I'm not going to be a pushover.

Her lips curl back and she hurls a few more bolts at me. I deftly dodge them, to Discordia's consternation.

"I guess I should try a little harder." She does an impressive wind-up and hurls another bolt, only this one splits into a dozen deadly fingers that I narrowly dodge before they flicker out of existence.

The intense expression on her face looks permanently fixed. At least I thought it was, until it evaporates and she turns to me with an expression of pure delight.

Okay. That's not how it's supposed to go. The abrupt shift in mood totally throws me off. She's supposed to be angry, not happy. What am I supposed to do now?

"This is very good."

Come again?

Discordia's grin is getting a bit scary now. It's maniacal. How is this any good for her?

"I can use you. Join me and you can have everything you ever wanted." She snaps her fingers and Noah appears. There's confusion on his face for a moment before his eyes meet mine. They widen for a split second before narrowing and glittering menacingly as he turns toward his mother.

My stomach drops. That is not a look that'll give anyone warm and fuzzy feelings. What did she do to him? Whatever it is, it can't be good to have him glaring at me like that. I try to give him a smile, but find that I just can't make my lips work.

"Noah is quite fond of you, for some reason. You could be with him forever if you so choose."

Meaning if I choose her. I take in his menacing expression. Do I really want to be with that forever? Doesn't seem like much fun to me. My chin tips up defiantly when I turn back to her. She's going to have to do better than that.

"Go with what she says."

What the hell? I give Noah the side-eye. It was his voice I heard, but as far as I can tell he didn't say a word.

"Ava... Stop being stupid."

I glare at him.

"Stop looking at me! Play her game!"

My gaze drops away from his face immediately. Wait a sec. Why am I listening to him, anyway? For all I know he's with her and is manipulating me so I fall into his mother's hands. I catch his attention again.

"What will it be?" Discordia's voice is soft, dulcet. Like she's coaxing a kitten to come and play. "Will you join me?"

Should I listen to him? My gaze flickers toward Noah again.

"You would like to be with Noah." Her voice is smug. "Even a poor soul petrified by Medusa could see that."

She's so self-satisfied when I finally look at her again. It emanates from her in hot, sticky waves. I want to knock the smile off her face. My head throbs at the thought. I can do it. I know I can. I can feel energy surging through me as I start plotting.

I need to give myself a little bit more time, so I shake my head. "There's got to be more in it than just getting Noah."

Her eyebrows rise.

"I want power. I want to be able to do anything I want."

Her smile grows. "And you will. It will be glorious. The three of us ruling together. Forever."

Yeah, right. I've only known her an hour and already I know she's not the type to play well with others. I smile a little, hoping it looks convincing. It's hard to keep up since the throbbing in my head is starting to feel as if something with sharp hooves is trying to kick its way out.

Discordia takes my smile as encouragement and keeps talking. I barely hear her now. My head hurts too much for me to focus. I hear Noah through the ache, but just barely. It's like being at the seaside and he's trying to shout over the sound of the waves on a stormy day. It's not going to happen. I catch a few words — *"careful"* and *"hang on"*. Is he trying to encourage me? The expression on his face hasn't changed, though it's hard to tell since a red haze has narrowed my vision so that I can barely see him.

Definitely something wrong here.

My skin feels electrified, as if there is an actual current running up and down my arms. It doesn't hurt. It tingles in my veins and tries to flow out of my fingertips. The sensations from Discordia crystallize. I also feel Noah. His emotions are completely different from those of his mother. He's worried. He's worried about me. How about that? The chills he's experiencing run down my spine for an instant before I clamp down on them. I don't need that right now. What I *do* need right at this moment is a way to stop Discordia. Not distractions.

So I ignore Noah and focus on creating a plan. What could I possibly do to stop her? And if I manage that, then what? I'll have to get to that when, or if, I get to it.

I'm hot. Uncomfortably so. She's planning something. Getting impatient. I need to answer her. I've always stuck to the truth. I don't see why now should be an exception.

"I can't."

To her credit, my reply doesn't faze her at all. Her calm expression stays on her face though that strange wind has picked up in her hair again. The heat of her anger blasts me. Nope, I haven't made her a happy goddess.

"Very well. But I believe that I should give you a chance to change your mind. Or perhaps I should just rephrase my request?" She whirls her hands with a flourish. In the blink of an eye she has Mom in one hand and Beth in the other, holding them by the scruffs of their necks like they were puppies caught doing something particularly naughty. "Join us, or they die."

The pain in my head flares with my anger.

She must see my distress, as her face brightens.

"Or I should just leave it up to chaos? See where it takes them."

The world starts to swirl around us. Suddenly, we're back — on Earth, I suppose, is the only way to explain it. Only it's not the same Earth that I've grown up on. Trees are uprooting themselves and start walking, cars begin sprouting wings and fly, the world tilts until the horizon splits the view vertically. For a second my stomach does the same, doing its best to propel what little I've eaten up my throat. Standing as if petrified, I take a few breaths to keep from humiliating myself in front of Discordia. It's easier to do than I'd thought it would be. That's when I realize that nothing seems to have changed. If the world is shifted the way it looks, shouldn't it make me feel weird? Aside from the visual Tilt-A-Whirl I sense nothing different. So unless having Dad's power makes me invulnerable to universal constants being thrown out of whack, this isn't what it seems to be. Or do I have that backward? I'm confusing myself now.

Glaring at her, I edge closer hoping to get a better grip on what she's planning. Not that I need to. Her anger is like a hot desert wind scorching my face. What I am getting from her, under all the volcanic fury, is something sour, fetid. It's slimy. *Fear.*

"*Attack now!*" Noah's voice urges from somewhere in my thumping head.

Even before his words register, I lift my hands and hurtle bolts of electricity at her. I watch, horrified, as they fly toward Discordia, Mom and Beth. I will vines to spring up from the earth, tangling around Discordia's legs, anchoring the goddess to the ground.

"*Get your mom!*"

I heed the words and run for my mom faster than the bolts, faster than I ever thought possible. Tearing her from the goddess's grip, I plant my foot to change course. Mom, Beth, Noah and I all come to a skidding halt in a tangled pile of limbs at the same time as Discordia is hit.

The Goddess of Discord looks surprised as she evaporates in a brilliant flash, but not before she lets loose another bolt of energy straight at my chest.

The bolt slams into me, hitting me right over the heart. Pain flares and I'm flung back with such a force that I'm sure I hear several snaps of bone.

There are a few seconds during which I can't see anything, can't hear anything. I'm dead. I have to be. Nothing could survive a direct hit like that.

But I open my eyes.

I sit up and look down, expecting to see a gaping, smoking hole in my chest, but there is nothing. Not a stitch out of place. How? I run my hand over the point of impact and it's still slightly damp from where Noah touched me earlier on the boat. Then it dawns on me. The wetness. It wasn't sweat. Noah had touched the water after all. The River Styx supposedly grants invincibility to skin immersed in its waters. I guess that's the river we were on when we were in the Underworld. *Jeez. Looks like it's true.* Thank goodness for that! When I get a chance I'm diving straight into that sucker.

But first I have a goddess to take care of.

"Keep an eye on my mom and Beth." I don't wait for Noah to answer before I teleport, following Discordia.

I know what to expect when I get there. Discordia is trapped in a golden cage suspended in mid-air. She looks like she's been blasted and she knows it. I've overridden her powers so she can't fix herself up. Her fury is like firecrackers popping on my skin. It bothers her. A lot. And I love it.

"You cannot do this to me. I am a goddess! You are nothing! Less than nothing!"

Pain flares in my head, but I smile past it. I feel her anger lashing at me. It's a good thing I took her powers away or I'd be in some serious trouble right now. But seeing as I'm not, I want to play with her a little more.

"Sorry. What was that? I can't hear you." I cup my ear mockingly and am rewarded with a furious rattle of her cage. "I think we need to talk, you and I."

"I do not wish to speak with you. I want to speak with whatever god or goddess dares to do this to me."

Funny, I thought she was more perceptive than that. Smugness curls my lips. "You don't get it, do you?"

She looks down her nose at me.

"I did this."

"One as insignificant as you could never do this…" Her eyes lose that superior sheen. "Jupiter…"

"Yeah, Jupiter. Did you really think that he'd let you get away with this?" It's getting harder to hold back the pain. I close my eyes against it, wishing, willing it to go away, but it only grows worse.

Forcing my eyes to open, I find Discordia smiling evilly at me. "Headache?"

"Not really. I'm just sick of looking at you." Yes, I know I'm being snippy. I can't help it. My head is throbbing with every heartbeat. Besides, as long as I keep her power away, I'll be fine.

That's if my brain doesn't explode first.

She's definitely up to something now. I feel her plotting. Peeking into her thoughts, I see images of different scenarios flicking through her mind. There is one where she is standing on a miniaturized planet Earth with a crown and scepter. Yes, very subtle. Another where she is scrubbing the floor at my feet. I have to admit I like that one. Then there are a dozen or so mixed variations of the two. She has an active imagination.

"Your beloved father is just using you."

"Just like you used Noah?"

She gives me a slow smile. "Of course. Only I have come right out and said it."

"So… That makes you better because you're more honest than another god who's trapped and incommunicado at the moment? I don't think so."

"Just take a moment and think about it. You are a vessel for his powers. Powers that you so obviously cannot contain and will more than likely destroy you. And all because he doesn't want to be trapped for all eternity. How does that make you feel, Princess?" She spits out the last word like it's a curse.

For a second her words send me reeling, but it might have something to do with the infinite cosmic powers threatening to burst through the top of my skull. "He did it to stop you."

"Or so you think."

"Yeah, I do think." And just to prove I'm right, I'm going to stop her. "You know what I've learned from hanging out with you gods and goddesses?"

She stares at me silently.

"You are all part of one big whole. You need each other to exist. I think you've forgotten that." Even before I think about it, power coils around me before whipping around Discordia.

Her beautiful eyes widen. "What are you doing?"

"I'm making sure that you can't use your powers for anything other than they are meant for."

"You cannot do that!" She pulls helplessly at the bars. "You cannot do this to me!"

"I'm doing it, aren't I?"

"Please…"

"I'm not killing you."

"You might as well!"

Wow, is this goddess a drama queen or what? "It's just until Jupiter comes back. Then he can do whatever he wants with you. I know if it was me, I'd smack you down pretty good."

There's a snort from the cage.

"Already whatever powers you have gained are eating you from the inside. I can tell that you will not be able to contain them for much longer. Then they will consume you and you will be dust. Like you never existed. Just like every mortal."

"At least I'll be a mortal who took down a goddess when I go." Fatalism really isn't my thing, but right now I'm not exactly sure how things are going to turn out. Besides, thinking positively takes more energy than I can spare right now.

It's done.

My legs wobble embarrassingly before I fall to the ground. So much for going out with style.

Discordia looks at her hands, flexing her long fingers. She seems surprised that she's all in one piece. "Thank you for not destroying me." She creates a startlingly blue rose with the flick of her wrist. Trust her to come up with the unnatural. "You left me with my powers."

"I told you, I just made sure you can't use your powers against the gods again."

She smiles. It chills me to the bone. "How kind of you. And how stupid." The rose shimmers, disappears. In its place is a gleaming spike of ice.

Which she hurls at me.

Her aim is true and it comes straight for my head. I try to deflect it but my reactions are sluggish. I know I'll never be able to duck it.

I hold my breath only to have it knocked from my lungs as arms wind around me and swing me around.

"Noah!" His name is screamed by both of us as he falls to his knees, the spike sticking out of his back and blood trickling from the wound.

"Oh, my God." My heart aches more than any other part of me as he topples, his body sprawling over mine, jerking me out of shock as I try to hold him up. "Noah."

"I'll...be fine."

He doesn't look it. Far from it, in fact. The rage at what Discordia has done turns my vision red. Anger flares and courses into my hands. Before I can think, I hurl a bolt of lightning at her chest and watch with satisfaction as it blasts her. I don't know if I've killed her or what, but all I care about is Noah at the moment. I'll deal with the fallout of what I've done to Discordia later.

I press my hands on his wound, trying to hold the blood, willing it to stay inside. "What do I do?" I have no idea who I'm asking, or if I'm just trying to get my brain to work. The words keep tumbling out of my lips over and over.

Clutching him to me, I teleport.

Subconsciously I must have been thinking about Mom and Beth because that's who I am standing in front of now. I step forward to herd them all up so I can get us all out of here in one last burst of energy, but my muscles choose this moment to give out on me and we fall back into a heap on the ground. Doesn't look like I'll be getting us out of here any time soon, but I need to do something about Noah's wounds. I just hope I can.

I wrap my hand around the spike in his back and concentrate on healing him. The spike slowly flickers. I hold my breath until it finally disappears and my hand is flat against his back. For a few frustrating moments nothing happens.

"Come on!" I pull my hands off and flex them before returning them. I'm a bit woozy now but force power down my arms and into my hands, then his skin warms. The hole shrivels and shrinks until it disappears completely.

My gaze flits up to Noah's face. His color is returning, and from the movement of his chest, I'd say that he's breathing easier.

His eyes open. "I owe you one."

"Yeah, you do." Relieved, I let myself relax and fall back. Almost as soon as the realization he'll be okay hits me, the relief is replaced with pain. I need to get a grip on myself. Either that or find a way of continuously producing adrenaline. I'm totally willing to be perma-stressed if it will stop the pain.

I sit quietly immersed in my own personal hell.

That is, until I hear a high-pitched scream.

"What the hell is going on?" It's Beth. She sounds…close? I can't really tell through the haze in my head. A hand closes over my shoulder for a second before jerking away again. It's got to be Beth. That's easy to deduce when she's screaming directly in my ear. I manage to open my eyes to squint at her. Yep, it's Beth. "How did you do that, Ava? Same with Noah!" Her wide eyes flick between us. Frightened. Wild.

The pitch of her voice escalates to the point where I'm pretty sure if there was any glass nearby it would shatter.

Her hysterics only serve to cleave my head more. I wave at her, and as she begins to fade away I click my fingers, wiping her memory of the incident. I wave at Mom and she disappears before she can start up too. I'll deal with her later. I lift my hand at Noah and find him shaking his head.

"Don't do it."

I pull my hand back to squeeze my skull. It feels like at any moment it will split open. He scoots closer, but I shuffle back as best as I can with my hands on my head.

"Ava, relax." He reaches for me again, but stops when I flinch. "What's the matter? Didn't I just prove that I'm on your side?"

I can barely see him now, but I feel the drag of concern. He's being honest. At least that's one question down. What's bothering me most right now is my head. And maybe that strange tingling in my limbs. It feels as if there are a million electrified spiders crawling through my pores and over my skin. Not the best sensation in the world.

"Ava?"

I open my eyes to find myself looking up at him. When did I decide to lie down? The ground actually feels pretty comfortable and pressing my head against it makes my head hurt a little less.

"Are you okay?"

Not particularly. I can't seem to make my mouth reply, but I'm pretty sure that he can guess. The ground morphs into something soft and I snuggle into the familiar scent. One of my eyes manages to creak open. Why am I on a bed in the middle of nowhere? Rolling my eyes toward Noah, I see he's just as confused. I'm just hiding it better. But only because I can't make my face form expressions at the moment. Or am I? I don't really care.

"What are you doing, Ava?"

Am I doing something?

"Yeah, you're messing with the environment."

I guess Noah's in my head. Well, at least we're communicating again, even if I have no idea what he's talking about.

"You are. You made the bed. I have no idea what you're doing to everything else, though."

Another eye roll lets me survey the landscape. The terrain is rocky, burned, and the sky is red. If I didn't know better I would have thought we were in hell or something. The ground groans and cracks around us, tracing crevasses over the land. If I could see my brain, I'm pretty sure this is what it would look like. Did I do that? Pretty darn cool, if you ask me.

"What's wrong with you? Your thoughts are all over the place."

I have no idea. I'm too tired to try to find out. The spiders that were crawling on my arms and legs feel as though they've made a nest in my stomach. One that's pulsating and heaving and about to burst out of my gut at any second. I curl myself around the sensation.

"You're glowing. And not in a good way."

Am I? Maybe that's why I feel warm. I just thought that the heat was from me trying to keep my head from exploding. That didn't make any sense. I chuckle inwardly. It doesn't make sense and I don't care. I feel a pair of arms scooping me up. I let myself dangle from them limply.

"I think we should find out what's wrong with you."

Somehow I don't think a doctor is going to be able to prescribe anything for this.

"Don't be stupid. If anyone will know, it's Mors. He's an expert in this sort of thing, isn't he?"

Mors knows about death. Is that it? Does Noah think I'm dying?

"Well, you don't exactly look like a poster child for the living."

Gee, thanks. I curl up against him. This feels nice. It even makes my head feel a little better. The bliss is interrupted all too soon when I'm lowered onto what feels like my bed. A quick sniff assures me that it is my bed. Nice. Warm. Comfy. I snuggle deeper into my pillows, listening to the hushed voices around me.

"Is she okay?"

"What's the matter with her?"

"Quiet!"

The last was from Mors. No doubt about that voice.

Cool hands press at my temples and for a moment the silence is deafening. Or is that the blood rushing through my head that's making me deaf? The coolness of the hands feels nice against my skin. I lean into it, hoping it'll help ease my discomfort a little.

Mors lets me go, much to my dismay, and he shouts at the others to leave him with me. All except for Morta.

"I'm not leaving her." The words are said several times by different voices, last of which is Noah's. Unlike the slightly hysterical versions of the others, he says it calmly, like it's a certainty.

"I do not have the luxury of time to argue with you." Mors sounds really annoyed. I know if I was up against an annoyed Mors, I'd be quaking in my boots. Or sandals. You know, whatever footwear I happened to be wearing... But I digress.

The room is quiet now. I don't sense my mom, Beth or the goddesses but someone is breathing. That must be Noah. The other two, I'm pretty sure, don't need to breathe. Someone's holding my hand and there are a couple of other voices arguing in hushed voices. As much as I find the hand interesting, the voices hold more of my attention.

"There is nothing I can do! You must separate the threads!" Is Mors actually shouting at Morta? Well, shouting sotto voce.

"If I do, I might kill her!"

"If you do not, she will die!"

The hand tightens over mine. "If you at least try, there's a chance she might be okay."

Noah's voice is quiet, sad. I want to say something to reassure him, but I'm hit with another painful spasm. When it finally calms, I feel that my other hand is being held too. The hand holding it is cool, strong. I know it is Mors.

"There must be another way —"

"There is *no* other way. If there were, believe me, I would be prepared to hear about it. Ava has no other chance." His hand tightens around mine as he speaks, the pressure reassuring. It's quickly forgotten when the pain flares again. My muscles feel as if they are on fire. They contract and cramp so tightly that I'm sure it's doing damage. Somehow I manage to produce a cry from my constricted throat.

"Morta!"

"Very well." I sense her leaning down so she can speak directly into my ear. "Listen to me, child. This will not be pleasant." She pauses. "I'm sorry for putting you in this position." She is silent for a moment before I feel something against my chest. There is pressure for a second before the pain flares and I hear her shout. Somehow I don't think that this is going to be an easy task for her. I feel her touching me again only to be rewarded with another blast.

"I cannot extract it." Morta sounds quite put out. I hope I haven't hurt her too badly. She's been so nice to me. I wouldn't want her hurt on my account. "I cannot do it," she whispers raggedly. "I am sorry, child."

I don't want her to feel badly. It's not her fault.

"I've failed you."

I want to tell her she hasn't. She's helped me more than she could ever know.

I know it's impossible for me to tell her. So I start dissecting the problem as best as I can. *Come on, Ava! Use that big brain of yours!* I consider the problem. She probably can't do anything to me because I've manifested Dad's powers. So if she can't get into my chest then no other god can—except me.

"I'll...do it..." I barely hear my own words.

She leans closer and I repeat them. Shock and apprehension emanate from her. But I also feel resignation. She understands that I know what I'm getting myself into.

Someone leans in close again, so close that I almost feel the words against my cheek. "Ava." It's Mors. "You will survive. I swear it, by the River Styx." I feel the power of the oath swirl over us. It comforts me, and I'm wrapped in love.

Now I hear shuffling and barked orders.

"You, boy. Come here."

Mors wants Noah? What for?

"If anything...should happen... I will go against my nature. I will not take her. However, I will be compelled to. If I cannot resist, I will need you to stop me."

What? Is that even possible?

"Me? You want me to stop you? Why can't she do it? She's more powerful than I am." Noah's obviously talking about Morta.

"Morta must stay with Ava to collect the thread when it is successfully extracted." He sounds pretty sure that this is going to work.

Maybe there is some hope after all?

"You should be able to stave me off long enough. Have faith. With a little luck and love, we will prevail."

I hear a snort from Noah, but no argument. That's a good sign. I think. He sounds resigned, not argumentative. Though that snort is a little more scornful than necessary. Why am I even thinking about his snort? I have better things to worry about than dissecting the nuances of the sound Noah makes when he breathes through his nose.

At least I think I do. I'm starting to confuse myself now. Not that that's so hard to do right at this moment.

An icy hand closes over my forehead, leeching the heat and some of the pain from my head, making it easier to open my eyes. When I manage to lever them open, I'm looking up into Morta's face in all her scary glory.

"Ava, do as I tell you."

Do I have much of a choice? I give her a feeble nod.

She gives me what I'm pretty sure is supposed to be a reassuring smile. It scares me since I can see straight past it. Her fear is a cold, wet feeling. The fact that Morta is scared for me freaks me out more than anything. If I were strong enough I would run screaming just to get away from the sensation.

"Focus your energy on getting your hand through your chest."

Great, it's time to tear into my chest.

"Not tear. Reach into. There is a big difference. You have to concentrate on passing your hand through then extracting the thread."

Oh. Is that all? Piece of cake. I really wish I could snort right now, though it would be a colossal waste of energy.

"Concentrate!" She pushes my hand to my chest. "Do it now!"

For a while, my hand feels like a lead weight against my chest. I can't move it let alone will it through my skin. Do I really want to? It would be gross. Besides, the pain isn't getting that much worse. I can live like this.

Another flare of agony lances through my body, threatening to shred it from the inside out. I manage a low groan and that's enough to have all three of them jumping all over me.

"Ava?" Noah somehow beats Mors to me. "Come on! You've got to do this!"

They hover overhead like a weird kaleidoscope of worry. My head droops in a pathetic version of a nod, and they reluctantly take up their positions once again.

Happy that they're ready, I concentrate again, feeling my hand start to warm. Holding my breath, I go for it. Nothing to lose now, right?

Reaching into my chest is a weird feeling, but because I'm focused on finding the thread, my hand's not solid and passes through everything. I snag something with my fingertips and have to swipe around a few times before I get a grip on it. I'm not sure what it is, but I take the tingling shooting up my arm as a good sign and pull it out.

That in itself isn't so bad. The ache is about the same as I'm experiencing so far. No tearing sensation. No real trauma. I relax as much as my body allows. From the way they were talking, I was expecting to feel much worse.

I hold out the thread to Morta. The multitude of colors is amazing to witness shift and change. It's like watching a living rainbow pulsating in my hand. Morta reaches for it, but is repelled once again with a bright yellow flash. Not one to be deterred, she tries again, but is blasted across the room. She's annoyed. It's clearly written across those wrinkles, and if I could cringe and hide I would. Nothing is scarier than Morta in a bad mood. Well, except maybe Mors.

"You will have to separate them as well, it seems." She sniffs disdainfully as she makes her way back to my side. "Feel the two different energies and pull, once, very, very hard."

I get the feeling that this is an all-or-nothing type of situation. As in I get them apart or it's game over. I'll have to do it then, won't I? I've never failed anything yet and I'm not about to start now.

Lugging up my left arm to join the right one on my chest, I put both hands on the thread, trying my best to feel the energies that Morta was talking about. Of course, she's right. I feel the differences between the threads immediately. One is warm. The tingling pulse from it coincides with my heartbeat. It must be mine. The other is like touching a live wire. The zap is powerful, electric, amazing—Jupiter's.

I look at my friends and close my eyes. Centering all my energy, I wrench at the threads as hard and as fast as I can. I can't hold back the scream of pain that's torn from me. It's like everything about me is being ripped in two. The searing pain is too much for me and I feel myself losing consciousness. I hear Mors' anguished cry and Noah shouting at him, shouting at me. But the sounds quickly fade.

Just as the world starts going black and the pain reaches a crescendo, a booming voice fills my head.

"Thank you, my daughter."

I don't get a chance to contemplate what I've just heard, let alone who it came from. I feel like I'm being torn apart, ripped in two directions as the same time. There's a snap like a rubber band breaking and I suddenly feel light, airy. Detached. A definite improvement over what I've been feeling over the last little while. I feel good.

That is until I open my eyes and see myself lying on the bed, still and pale. The shock of it sends me floating back in recoil. *What the hell?*

My hands are transparent. As is the rest of my body. A spinning, floating check of myself confirms it. I think I'm in some serious trouble. I reach for my body but my hand passes straight through it. Yep. I'm in trouble.

Mors has to be able to help me. Turning, I find the god standing with Noah, who is clinging onto him, ready to hold him back. Mors did say he wasn't going to take me. He's fighting it. His hands are shaking, his face tense.

Noah seems to have noticed that I've fallen still and all color drops from his face. "Ava!"

He starts for me, but Mors holds him back. "Do not." Mors' voice is raspy, hollow. He looks at me, the floating me, and his face changes into the terrifying skeleton thing once more. He raises his emaciated hand and crooks a finger at me.

I feel a tug and I start floating toward him. I'm being drawn toward Mors. *No!* Arms windmilling, I try to hold back. But being without a physical body makes it a little harder to do. I only move steadily closer.

Noah finally gets what's going on and grabs Mors' hand, trying to stop him from pulling me closer. Too bad it doesn't work. Mors looks feral. As scary as a nearly skinless skeleton can get. He claws at Noah. Punches, kicks. His objective is clear. He's staring straight at me with those hollow eyes.

"Mors! Mors!" Noah's in the god's face now. "Stop it! You don't want to do this! It's Ava! *Ava!*" He shoves at Mors' chest, for all the good it does. "She means something to you! I know she does! I've seen how you look at her!" He shoves fruitlessly again. "You love her! Stop!"

Noah noticed that? Even in an incorporeal state I can feel my eyes widen. Love? He loves me? Enough for people to notice?

Amazingly, Mors stops pulling at me. His shriveled lips form my name. "Ava."

Is it possible for a non-heart to stop beating? Well, mine does, just before it starts to pound madly. I do believe I return the emotion. How about that?

His face returns to normal, but is grimaced in such pain that it breaks my heart. "Morta. Hurry."

There's a feminine grunt from the other side of the bed my body is on. Sitting on the floor is Morta, who looks like she's furiously trying to piece together my thread. Her fingers fly as she melds the multitude of strands together. She looks to be about halfway through with a million left. The way Mors is shaking, I don't think he'll be able to hold out that long.

His face is changing back again. His beautiful face shrivels away and the skull is staring at me once again.

The moment he changes, I start floating toward him again.

"No!" Mors shakes his head and turns away.

I stop moving. *Come on, Morta! Get a move on!*

At this rate, he's going to have me within arm's reach the next time he loses control. I really don't want that to happen. I can't keep my eyes off of Mors. He's glorious in this form. The power he's wielding is awesome. I can't help but be captivated. It's not like I can do anything else.

So I float, mesmerized, until he turns to me again.

This is it.

I hold my non-existent breath while he stands up, shaking off Noah. He does it so easily, Noah might as well have been a gnat. Mors, dark and beautiful, stands straight, his wings unfurling and gleaming. He steps forward, his right hand wielding a sword. The wicked glint of it stops my heart.

"Ava... I am...sorry." He lifts the sword.

Mors... No...

He cleaves the air, aiming straight for me. I start squeezing my eyes shut and await my fate when I see Noah leap in front of me.

There is a primal scream from Mors as he brings the sword down.

Then silence.

I open my eyes. I'm fine. A quick look at Noah tells me he's fine too. It's when my eyes reach Mors that my quasi heart stops and I scream. Nothing comes out of my transparent mouth, but I sure try.

Mors!

Mors' sword is protruding from his stomach, sunken to the hilt. There isn't any blood, thank goodness, but Mors doesn't look too good.

The God of Death withdraws the sword and looks at me. His beautiful face is back though it's paler. My heart wrenches at the way his eyes are already dimming.

Mors. What have you done?

He reaches his hand out to me, tracing my transparent cheek, his eyes searching mine. *"Aut viam inveniam aut faciam..."* Mors' lips curve into a small smile before he fades away.

What? I repeat the words to myself as pain lances through me. Wait. This isn't right. Aren't I beyond pain? I don't even have a body to hurt...

The pain shoots through me again. *What...?*

I fall back into my body, feeling like I just fell off a skyscraper. I struggle to sit up. My muscles are weak, as though I haven't used them in years. Muscles! I have a body! Which means I can scream.

"Mors! No!" It's more of a gurgle than a scream, but it's the best I can do right now. A cold hand grips my arm. It doesn't have to work hard to hold me back.

"Ava. Do not fret."

Do not fret? Is she crazy? Mors just reaped himself! I feel my heart rending. Shattering. That he would do something like this for me... I have to do something. There's got to be something we can do to get him back!

Morta releases me, reminding me that she's still here.

"There has to be something you can do!"

"Ava, child, this is the best way."

Her eyes bore into mine. Morta is in my head. She's trying to tell me something, but I refuse to pay any attention to it. How can this be the best way? How?

I feel as though there is a crushing weight on my chest as I struggle for breath. I need to get Mors back... I roll off the bed and fall onto my knees, fully prepared to crawl to find him if I must.

"Obstinate child." She picks me back up and tucks my resisting form into bed tenderly, as if I was a baby. "Is it so much to ask that you believe in us?" Morta presses her lips to my forehead and I feel a calm spread through me.

Then everything disappears behind a veil of black.

Chapter Eighteen
The End Is Where Something Else Begins

I open my eyes and stare at the ceiling, admiring the blank white. It's clean, clear. Not a single blemish. I wish I could feel like that. I wish I could just go back and wipe the slate clean, blank out everything that happened. I feel as though there's a huge chunk of me missing and what's left is shriveled up.

Dead.

I keep replaying the scene over and over in my head. How could a god give up his existence for me? What about his duties? Won't he leave a gaping hole in the pantheon? What about cosmic balance? Couldn't he have at least thought of that? Or the guilt I'd be feeling because of all this? Okay, so the last bit is purely selfish, but he could have at least cared about that.

I take a stuttering breath. I want to feel angry. I want to hate him. But how can I when he did this for me? I roll over and bury my face in my pillows, using them to muffle the sobs. At this rate I'm going to drive myself crazy.

Ava...

I swear I can still hear his voice.

Aut viam inveniam aut faciam...

I whip my head off the pillows. His parting words. They have to mean something. Why else would he say them?

I slide out of bed and make my wobbly legs carry me to my desk. Mercury's miracle search engine will know what it means.

There are a few messages blinking at me on Mercury's messenger, but I ignore them. I really don't feel like talking to anyone right now. Besides, I have better things to worry about.

I click on the icon and type the words in, or at least a reasonable facsimile, and hit enter. It comes back with a whole host of sites referencing famous Latin phrases. Apparently it translates as — we will either find a way or make one. A quote from Hannibal. I guess he made sure that his words would be easily recognizable. Thank goodness, because my Latin is beyond horrible.

We will either find a way or make one.

I smile, feeling hope bob in my chest. Perhaps this isn't the end after all...

"Good morning!"

My smile disappears. Hope evaporates. Annoyance rears its ugly head. "Go away." I wave my hand at the window, slamming it shut. The last person — being — *whatever* I want to see right now is that irritating dryad.

She presses her nose up against the window. "Hey, I'm just trying to be nice."

I look at her, incredulous at her claim. "You? Nice? Has Hades frozen over?"

"Ha, very funny. Will you open up?" She gives me the big puppy dog eyes.

"Fine. Just stay over there." I flick my hand and the window opens again.

"You're crabby this morning. You should be happy after being snatched from the jaws of death. Not only that, but you managed to save the world and destroy it all at the same time. A massive feat for a mortal. You'll be immortalized for sure. If people survive long enough to tell your story, that is."

"Thanks for that. You just know how to spread the sunshine, don't you?"

She rolls her eyes. "Still no word from Tall, Dark and Dreary?"

I glare at her. "He's not dreary. And it's none of your business."

"Touchy, touchy. I'll take that as a no."

I glare at her. The most serious and deadly glare I can muster right now. "Do you have a name?"

That gets her. She stops and looks at me. "Why?"

"So I can say, 'go away,' and add your name to it. It would make it much more satisfying for me."

"My name is Amice."

"Thanks. Go away, Amice."

She smirks. I think she believes I'm playing.

"Seriously, go away."

"If this is how you treat your friends, I'm amazed you have any at all."

"Amice, please. I just want to be alone."

Her smile is gentle. She actually looks like she truly cares. "I will just as soon as I give you this." She hands me a single white lily.

I'm touched. I really am. Completely charmed. "Thank you."

"Don't thank me. It's from Juno."

I yank my hand back as she releases it, but Amice catches the flower and tries to give it to me again.

I move farther away. "No thanks. Why is she giving me flowers?" I eye the beautiful bloom like it's going to blow up in my face.

"I doubt it will hurt you. She would hardly gift you her signature flower only to use it as a weapon. It's too obvious. It would be like putting a huge sign up over your house saying, 'Yeah, I did that!'"

"Very funny." Despite her attempts at humor, I still don't like it. It's just too weird.

When I make no move to take it from her, she shrugs. "Suit yourself. I'll just leave it on the windowsill."

"Thanks."

She does as she says then looks at me with pensive eyes. "Can I say something?"

There's nothing saying I have to follow her suggestion, so I nod. "Go ahead."

"It will be okay, you know. Things will work out in the end." With that said she steps out, pointedly closing the window behind her.

I stay staring at the spot long after she's gone. Does she mean it or is she just being nice? If I'm going to be honest, I know that when dealing with the gods nothing is concrete. There isn't anything that can't be changed. But what about something like this? Has anything like this ever happened? Can it be changed?

I sigh and stop myself before I start a searching frenzy on Google. What I need is some time to deal with this. Then maybe I can pull myself together enough to figure out what I can do about it.

First, I'm going to get rid of that flower, then I'm going to clean myself up and get out of this room.

I walk over and look at the lily. It's perfect and so beautiful. Of course it is. What did I expect from the Queen of the Gods? She sure wouldn't be sending me wilted dandelions. Should I touch it, though? So far she hasn't done anything against me...that I have any proof of. But if she was simply biding her time, waiting for me to fulfill my destiny, then this would be the time to start wreaking her revenge, right? You know, wait for the little girl to sort of save the world then — *wham!*

I'm heading toward the driving-myself-crazy train of thought again. She's not going to intimidate me or undermine my confidence. It's just a flower. Plain and simple.

I snatch it up and I feel a flare of power from it.

Crap.

Releasing it doesn't help since it seems attached to my hand. I try frantically to use my own powers to force it off, but it's no use. I'm no match for Juno. The moment I give up, I feel the familiar tug of teleportation.

In a blink, I'm standing in a very bright place surrounded by a ring of marble. I feel like I'm in a mini version of the Colosseum. Well, maybe not a mini version. It's pretty huge. And it's not empty either. The seats are filled with a dazzling array of toga-clad figures. I stare at them, dumbfounded. *What the hell is going on here?*

There are tugs on both arms as Fortuna and Flora appear.

Flora clings to me, eyes wide. "Ava! Why haven't you answered our messages?"

I know I look as confused as I feel. "I didn't exactly have the time. One second I was in bed and the next I'm here." I scan all the faces looking down at me. "What's going on?"

Fortuna peers around the room, a little fearfully. "We were trying to warn you. This whole mess with Mors… It's gotten…"

Juno strides toward us. "Goddesses, off to your seats." The two goddesses glare at her contemptuously, though they do as she orders. The Queen of the Gods slips her arm through mine as if she does it on a regular basis. Power radiates from her. It practically sparks and crackles against my skin. "Thank you for coming so promptly, my dear." She eyes my tank top and boxers and shakes her head. "But you needn't have come quite so hastily."

Should I point out that had she sent a normal invitation, I wouldn't have shown up in my underwear? Forget it. I concentrate my energy on turning what I have on into something suitable. Since everyone else is in a toga, and I've always wanted to wear one on an occasion that doesn't involve drunken frat guys, I change my clothes to match.

"Much better." Juno sniffs approvingly. "Now, if you'll go and stand over there, we can begin." She starts to steer me toward the center of the room but I resist a little.

"Start what? What's going on?"

"Do not worry. Everything will be fine."

Why are the hairs on the back of my neck standing on end?

I smooth my toga. As I stand, I clasp my hands and look at the crowd. I automatically scan it for familiar faces, Mors' included, even though I know he won't be there. After a fruitless search and a twinge of sadness, I see Fortuna, Flora and Venus clinging to each other next to Morta and Mercury in the front row. All the rest

315

seem to blur together in a sea of faces. What I do know is that they're all watching me with open curiosity.

Why? Am I that much of a freak?

"We are just curious." A goddess with gray eyes and gleaming armor leans forward to get a better look. The owl on her shoulder does the same. Must be Minerva, judging by the company she keeps. "How could you have fallen for a god such as Mors? And how could he have forsaken his own reason for being for you?"

"And what's wrong with me?" I'm offended. She makes it sound like he fell for pond scum or something.

Minerva smiles. "I did not mean to offend. It is just very out of character for Mors to do such a thing. I am curious at how things could have progressed to this."

No kidding.

"So you brought me here so you could all look at me? I've got to say, this freaks me out a little."

"No, Ava. That is not why you are here." That's a new voice. Or is it? It sounds familiar.

I look up at where the voice is coming from and see two thrones floating above the arena. One is occupied by Juno and the other could only be occupied by one other god—Jupiter. I can't tell for sure since I can't see through the dazzling glow. The power radiating from the both of them is dazzling. I wonder if they turn up the juice for these types of occasion, you know, to show off a little.

He's everything you would expect of the King of the Gods. He exudes authority just sitting there. I remember Mom's words about not really remembering what he looks like. I think it's the sheer force of him that blurs it. I stare a moment longer but still can't really make out his features. I do, however, sense his emotions.

Jupiter's feelings toward me are almost tender. Warm and a little fuzzy with equal parts of curiosity and pride. However, Juno's are practically giving me frostbite. Nothing new there, then.

His emotions quickly shift to something lukewarm, hesitant. He's apprehensive about something.

Wonderful. Whatever makes a god anxious can't be good news for me.

His voice is booming as he speaks. "We have convened to try to figure out what to do about the situation with Mors."

Hope buoys in my chest once again. "Can't you just bring him back? Don't you have that power?"

There's whispering now. Did I do something wrong? Jupiter seems unperturbed so I don't let it bother me.

"Unfortunately, we cannot. Mors and the Moirae operate on an entirely different level. Even the gods must bow to their will. What Mors has done to himself is…irreversible by me."

I feel the tears threatening to flow again. There goes that hope. "I thought…" I fight back a sob. I refuse to break down in front of all these gods and goddesses. I pull myself together enough to choke out, "I was hoping that you could fix what he did."

Jupiter shakes his head sadly.

"So what happens now?"

"There are several avenues we could explore, but there is one option that is most straightforward." Juno smiles, sending chills skittering down my spine. "We find a way of replacing him."

The chills hit the bottom of my spine and bounce, rippling upward again. Surely she's not suggesting…

"You agree that we must keep the balance. Without Mors things would become askew and chaos would ensue."

I hear snickering from the back and see Discordia looking very pleased with herself. The wheels in my head start turning. There was no way she could have planned this. Could she? There is no way. Mors wouldn't have played into her hands like this. I want to throw something at her, I really do, but I'm on my best behavior right now. It wouldn't do for the daughter of the king to throw a hissy fit, would it?

I won't let them win. Not Discordia. Not Juno.

I look up at the queen, wishing we were face to face so I could look her in the eye. "I think I know where you're going with this."

Jupiter glows brighter. He's impressed but still very uneasy. "Ava. Think about this seriously. It is not something you should enter into lightly. There is no reason for you to be the one to do it."

"But there is every reason, dear husband." Juno's glow is shining almost as brightly as Jupiter's now. "She is the reason Mors did what he did. She is the very reason we are on the verge of chaos. I think it would be very fitting for her to take the job." There's a pause. "Unless you do not believe that a daughter of yours should deign to take it."

Murmurs rumble through the crowd of gods. She's making it sound as if I'm too uppity for Mors' job. I know she's twisting things around, but I can't help but bristle. "I'd be honored to do what Mors did. He was a great friend. I know he probably wouldn't want to burden me with something like this, but after what he did for me, I would gladly do it for him."

Tough words for a girl who can barely stand up at the moment. I look up at Jupiter and feel how proud he is, at Juno who is stunned, and smile.

I address the pantheon as loudly as I can. "Please, let me help you."

The brilliant shine that is Jupiter seems to approve of my decision, though he seems a little saddened. But he agrees. "So be it."

There's a dead silence from the peanut gallery as they watch. I close my eyes and stand utterly still, awaiting my fate.

For a long moment nothing happens. Then a burning cold starts from the top of my head and slips ever so slowly downward, it encompasses my body. Rather than the awful sensation of being overtaken by Jupiter's powers, this is much milder. It seeps into my skin, my muscles, my bones until it is a part of me. For an instant, it's as though I'm coming out of myself. I can see everything—the past, present and future. I sense links to every living being. For a split second, I feel someone very familiar. I want to reach out to them but all at once the sensations stop.

I'm a bit dazed, but my heart is lighter knowing that Mors is still out there, somewhere. Even if it's a minute part of him. It will take me some time, but I will find him.

Mors' sword appears in my hand, weighing it down. I open my eyes as I curl my hand around the cool metal. My now black toga is reflected in the shiny metal. I suppose it suits the part. And on my back are two magnificent wings as black and glossy as a raven's. I spread them experimentally. *I. Have. Wings.* If I wasn't surrounded by a group of gawking gods, I know I'd be doing my happy dance.

For a breath, I simply stand and get used to being in my skin. I feel different, powerful, yet I am still myself. It's a weird feeling.

Shaking it off, I look up at my father and bow. I then turn to the rest of the deities and bow, simply because it feels right to show them respect. What I don't expect is that each and every one of them stands and bows to me. Even Discordia. She's scowling and it obviously displeases her, but she does.

My attention goes back to my father. His growing pride and his sadness at my decision wash over me. The King of the Gods watches me for a moment. He then stands and bows deeply. Juno reluctantly follows suit.

With one last look at them, I stretch out my wings and take to the air. I have important things to do.

I have someone to find.

About the Author

When she's not writing or sleeping, Kacie can be found discussing plot twists with her cat who usually seems to enjoy being a part of the process. On the days he's not she most often finds herself wishing there was a way to mainline coffee while she writes, deletes and tweaks until she sees something that makes her smile.

Kacie Ji loves to hear from readers. You can find her contact information, website details author profile page at http://www.finch-books.com.